THE GRAVEDIGGER

Rob Magnuson Smith

The Gravedigger
Smith, Rob Magnuson
Copyright © 2010 Rob Magnuson Smith
All rights reserved.
ISBN: 1-60801-010-4
ISBN 13: 978-1-60801-010-3
Library of Congress Control Number: 2009940207

University of New Orleans Publishing
Managing Editor, Bill Lavender

UNOPRESS

http://unopress.uno.edu

For My Wife

CHALK

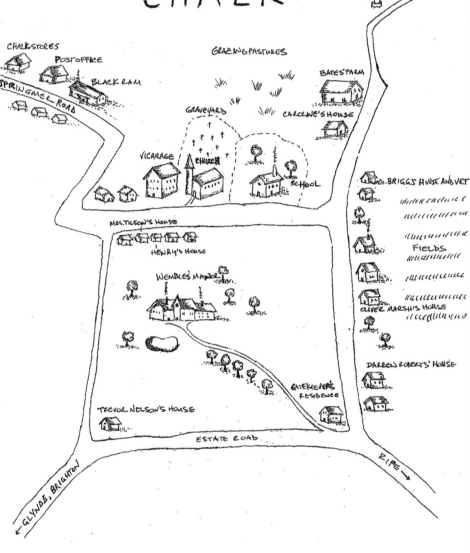

THE GRAVEDIGGER

O Death, where is thy sting?
O Grave, where is thy victory?
1 Corinthians 15:55

‡

People wish to be settled:
only as far as they are unsettled
is there any hope for them.
Ralph Waldo Emerson

ONE

Henry Bale stepped back from the open grave. He was tall, strong, and broad-shouldered. His overalls and boots were splattered with mud. Though forty-one, his appearance hadn't changed much since late adolescence. Dark hair covered his head and ears. His beard was poorly trimmed. His lumpish nose looked as if it had been punched and left to settle on its own. Women called him handsome, and he didn't know why.

Across the churchyard, Hetherington the undertaker inched his procession toward the grave. Water had started seeping into the bottom, but it wasn't bad. Henry dropped a bucket down. He dragged it by a rope down the length of the grave, catching what he could. There was no rush. Hetherington always took his time. Henry pulled the bucket clear and dumped it over a rosemary bush. Then, taking his wheelbarrow, he retreated to the boundary hedge.

Wind blew across the neighbouring sheep pasture. It was two in the afternoon, and the February frost sat fat and undaunted on the ground. Henry pointed his chin across the churchyard, still feeling in his bones the first turn of his spade. The frozen soil had wobbled his wrists like cement. His hands remained ungloved from the heat of the work.

The hearse finally came to a stop beside the path. The bearers opened their doors cautiously, shuddering in the wind. There were four of them. They wore black suits stained with bits of breakfast, and their cheeks were already colouring in the cold. Opening the back, they hoisted the coffin onto their shoulders and over to Henry's webbings—seatbelts from his father's old Vauxhall. The coffin was small, he noticed, glad for it. Though he always added his clearances, he dreaded the ornate caskets with great gold handles that locked in place, and made a mess of his grave walls.

"A nice young willow," Henry said under his breath, admiring the curving branches of the tree beside him. He spoke more often when he was alone.

"The Lord is full of compassion...slow to anger and of great goodness..."

Wind scattered the vicar's committal. Stray phrases whipped around monuments, as if searching for open ears. There wasn't anything for Henry to do at this point except keep out of the way. Yesterday he'd left a bit of his lunch in his pocket, a corner of a cheese sandwich that had kept him occupied. Above the grave, the bearers played out the webbings. They tracked mud across his mats, Henry noticed. It would mean some scrubbing this weekend, if the weather allowed.

The coffin sank evenly into the ground. The vicar blessed Hetherington's brass pot—a sign of the cross, a moment with his eyes closed.

"The days of man are but as grass..."

Hetherington knew his part well. He extracted a pinch of mole dirt and sprinkled it over the grave with an artful turn of the wrist. The wind blew most of it away. The vicar drifted past the mourners toward the church, his white robe flapping like a sail. He stopped to adjust his belt and the mourners caught up to him, milling and vulnerable. They snatched glances at the cross hanging from his neck, and the Bible in his hairy hand.

Hetherington raised his trousers above his ankles and made his way between the grave rows, grinning. "Hello, Henry!" he shouted. He took little mincing steps the closer he came, making a production out of his journey. At last he came to a stop at the handles of Henry's wheelbarrow.

"Hello, John," Henry said, rubbing his nose. Hetherington always smelled of cologne. His grin seldom left his face, even during a service.

Hetherington made a show of searching the ground. He squatted and peered around Henry's boots. "No Jack today?"

Henry glanced to his right where his dog would have been. "Something's the matter with him. I'm taking him round to Tracy's tomorrow afternoon."

"Nothing serious, I hope?"

Henry pictured his Jack Russell terrier, wheezing in the wicker cot. "I'm not sure."

Hetherington was still grinning. "Well. He *is* old, Henry."

The sound of an engine rumbled over the headstones. Hetherington whirled. "They'll be leaving me behind yet!" The vicar and the mourners had gone. The hearse pointed at the gate, and the driver smoked a cigarette from the open window.

"See you tomorrow at Burgess Green, then? Two o'clock?"

Hetherington held out a cheque, folded at the centre, tucked between his index and middle fingers. He always offered the payment like this—as if a gift from a godfather, or a bribe.

Henry pried the cheque from Hetherington's fingers and put it in the pocket of his overalls. The undertaker traipsed across the burial mounds toward the hearse. "Say John, can you ask your bearers not to track mud across—"

"Blast it!" Hetherington cried, turning round. "I just remembered it's a Catholic service tomorrow. Mary McGinty. Only a reopening, her husband Patrick's already in. Sorry, Henry—it'll have to be a *noon* burial. The Catholics like getting in the ground early." Grinning, he knocked on the passenger door to the hearse. "Think about it this way—you'll be home in time for lunch!"

* * *

Henry turned north off the motorway and into the fields surrounding Chalk. The sky was grey but didn't threaten rain.

Near the turn to the village, a sign above an iron gate read *Wembles Manor*. Behind the gate, a road lined with towering silver firs led to a manor house that tilted toward a nearby duck pond. It was a difficult time for royalty. Chalk had become a tax burden, and Samuel Wembles was starting to sell pieces of it off. Henry had heard the rumours—in the post office and at the shop, or walking past The Black Ram, where Chalk's parishioners hunched grumbling over their pints. The land grant to the first Lord Wembles would have been a poorly disguised insult, even in the sixteenth century. No river ran through Chalk. No hills surrounded it. It was a flat, degenerate parcel of grass, menaced by slate and deep deposits of chalk. The village was hidden. When found, it was forgettable. The nearest train station was a six-mile walk. An old bus passed through once a day, mostly out of charity.

As a young man Henry had been embarrassed, coming from Chalk. In East Sussex, a tourist county known for its seaside resorts and fertile downs, the village was a fossil. People thirty miles away didn't know it existed. He'd been tempted to flee to nearby Peacehaven, or even Brighton—places with names that inspired hope. But over time he realised, as his father and mother had, and their fathers and mothers before them, that Chalk suited him because of its shortcomings. His father Frank, now almost eighty and living out his days in a pensioners' home in Brighton, had been a gravedigger as well. Embarrassment slowly evolved into a sort of martyr's pride, a sense of doom that kept Henry's eyes lowered each afternoon as he returned home to his brick and mortar tenant cottage, wooden gate, and tiny front garden. Past the church, his house was the third on the left, its entryway so small it seemed built for a child. When Henry came inside, he had to duck.

In his wicker cot across the sitting room, Jack shivered under his blanket. His white bearded chin pointed at the fire, his eyes squeezed shut in a fight with pain. Henry had been studying Jack's chin for days now, as if to divine the dog's problem in it.

"Jack? Hello, Jack!"

The sitting room was brown. Along the ceiling, brown wood beams loomed just above Henry's head, causing him to stoop. There was a shaggy brown carpet, a brown leather armchair beside the front window, and a brown wooden coffee table. The yellow sofa against the wall practically glowed. Henry never sat on it. The sofa reminded him of his mother, and cancer had taken her when he was just a boy. His favourite memory—sitting beside her as she read from a book on trees—endowed the sofa with unreasonable significance, and he wanted it to remain a relic, frozen in time. He preferred the armchair by the window anyway, within arm's reach of the television.

"I wonder what you need, Jack," Henry said, leaning over the cot. As if for guidance he peered up at his parents' wedding photo on the mantle. They stared back at him mutely, clutching each other in the rain outside Chalk's church. The framed photo stood beside an antique clock and a pewter flask, never used—a Christmas gift from Mrs. Tilson, his neighbour. The phone rang.

It was Hetherington, wanting to make sure about tomorrow. He always gave his instructions twice. "Yes, John. A reopening at Burgess

Green." At the telephone table by the staircase, Henry watched the fire throw shadows on the walls. Others in the village had begun using mobiles, but he hadn't seen the need. People spoke too often as it was. "Yes, John, the grave will be ready by noon."

Jack might eat some chicken, Henry thought, hanging up. In the kitchen he tore a chunk of meat from the breastbone—leftovers from last night's supper. Back at the cot, Jack twitched his nostrils at the food. With effort he raised his head, then sunk his chin on the wicker. Henry drifted back to the kitchen. He made himself a plate of chicken and roast potatoes and ate standing up. He always ate his meals in the kitchen. A dining room held his father's dinner table and six oak chairs, but as long as he'd lived in the cottage—after moving from next door in a swap with Mrs. Tilson—he'd never sat in the dining room, not even once.

After eating he made a cup of tea and brought it to the armchair. It was five past six by the clock. "I almost forgot about the weather report!" Henry said, turning on the TV with excitement. "Early day tomorrow, Jack. Mustn't stay up late."

The black-and-white television took time to find its picture. Henry waited for the screen to settle, leaning forward in his chair. Slowly an image formed of a newscaster behind a desk, and the rest was static. Henry adjusted the aerial though he knew it was useless. The weather was for morning frost, the newscaster said, and cold temperatures throughout the day. No rain was expected.

Henry nodded as he listened. At one point in his life he might have cursed the draughty walls, along with whatever unseen forces had led him to this day, this year, this existence. Gradually he'd become a man in his father's chair, sipping tea and thumbing through a program guide. "John Wayne film tonight," he said, tapping the page. "Eight o'clock it starts." He glanced nervously at Jack in the cot.

* * *

Trevor Nelson couldn't get the bats out of his head. They flew at him from all directions, wings flapping. He pounded the kitchen table but it only made matters worse. Drunk, he'd thought it sensible to smash things, and as a result his great-grandmother's china lay in pieces on the linoleum. Dirty dishes sat piled in the sink. Sheets of plaster curled from the wall.

Trevor had mournful blue eyes, a delicate nose, and wispy blonde hair cut like a monk's. A troubled man, some said—an allegation Trevor cultivated as much as denied. Earlier tonight, the divorced brunette who'd followed him home from his favourite pub in Lewes had called him a playboy. It was just a jab, but it struck him as insulting, coming so quickly after they'd had sex. They'd been quietly having drinks in the kitchen, like a married couple.

"Playboy?" he'd yelled, slamming his glass of whiskey on the table. "You know me quite well, I suppose?"

The woman had thought his offense a joke. Then she wasn't so sure. She laughed nervously, and she closed her blouse to cover her bra. She noticed Trevor's lips quivering, and she took the comment back. But the damage had been done. Trevor had been wanting to let loose for some time, and he started smashing things. After she'd run from the house, he sat down and finished the whiskey. Then he found some gin—a full bottle under the sink, set aside for a night like this. It was a night that kept feeling early, a night of extremes.

Now the bats kept screeching, baring their teeth. Slumped over the table, he reached for the gin bottle, no longer bothering with the glass. The kitchen felt small and hot. He took a long drink, opened his mouth to get a little air, and kept going until the bottle was half gone.

When the gin took hold there was a roaring in his ears. Trevor loved this moment and dreaded the inevitability of its ending. He had a sudden impulse to run. He flung himself out the door and into the courtyard in his socks.

Trevor lived in the Caretaker's Residence on the edge of the Wembles Estate. His father had been Caretaker for over thirty years, and when he'd passed away the house had reverted to his son for as long as he occupied it, along with some grazing land overgrown with weeds. It didn't give Trevor any income, but he also didn't have the burden of rent. He ran out to the road and stood panting with his hands on his trousers. Here under the sky he could breathe easier.

Headlights swung around the bend. He waited for them with his arms outstretched. When the horn came he lost his nerve and jumped to the side of the road. When the driver berated him and drove off, leaving Trevor alone once more with nothing to do but return to the house.

The kitchen was still infested with imaginary bats. Trevor kicked over the table to get rid of them, and the bottle of gin smashed on the floor.

Trevor pulled out the cutlery drawer and heaved it across the room. Teaspoons scattered everywhere, jingling like bells. He wobbled on his feet as the sound died, his sobriety inching toward him from a distant smudge of darkness. He could see some gin slopping inside a broken saucer, like milk for a cat. He'd have to be careful approaching that saucer of gin. Any misstep, and it would tip over. He raised his arms in an arc above his head and rose on his tiptoes.

He placed his right foot on a section of linoleum and shifted his weight forward. The next two steps were clear—a space between a fork and spoon, and beside that, a clearing surrounded by broken glass. He moved expertly, as if he'd practised. Holding his breath, he reached the saucer and opened his mouth.

* * *

It didn't seem possible to Henry that the entire evening had disappeared. Had he watched any of that John Wayne film? The bedside clock said it was five in the morning. He must have been half-asleep when he'd come upstairs and changed into his pyjamas. He lay blinking at the dark, uneasily notching the passage of another night.

The bed ended at Henry's ankles and wasn't much wider than his shoulders. Against the wall, the radiator sputtered. Clothes lay in various piles on the carpet. A nightstand held a collection of magazines—*The Sussex Botanist, Geographic Society Monthly, Waterfowl.* Getting up, Henry drifted back and forth from the bedroom to the bathroom, muttering and blowing his nose. Finally, his thoughts more or less clear, he went downstairs.

"Come on, Jack! Time to go to work!" Under the blanket, the dog was motionless.

Henry placed a fresh log on the fire and blew on the embers until the wood caught. Jack's eyes stayed shut, encircled with crust.

"Let's go, Jack!"

Whimpering, the dog tried to stand. The sound of his paws

scrabbling in the cot made Henry wince. Just last month, Jack was chasing rabbits down The Beacon.

In the kitchen, Henry switched on the kettle for tea. "Jack needs his rest," he said. While waiting for the water he buttered two pieces of brown bread and put some chicken inside. He drank a cup of tea between bites of his sandwich, washed his face in the sink, and dried his beard on a tea towel. Then he poured some tea into a thermos and made a second sandwich for his coat pocket.

Jack had rested his chin on the edge of the cot again. His eyes were squeezed shut. "That's it, boy," Henry said, convincing himself the dog had followed his instructions. "Get some sleep." He turned out the lights and left.

The morning was quiet, the village black as coal. The neighbouring cottages sat dark and silent and shuttered against the cold. Henry paused in the road, gauging the sky. The only weather was the frigid wind, shifting the clouds to the north. He got in the van and warmed the engine, revving it as gently as he dared. He dreaded disturbing people with his odd hours. "Here we go, then," he whispered, putting the van in gear. His breath steamed up the windshield.

He brought the van between the hedgerows. As the road turned, his headlights picked up the pub sign—a faded black ram's head, swinging in the wind, followed by the post office and the shop. Just like that, he'd left Chalk. He continued west toward Springmer. Soon, lights glowed in distant barns. The road swelled under the beginnings of hills. Patches of grey appeared to the east.

Approaching Springmer, signs boasted business: *Tudor Bed and Breakfast, Organic Fruit Farm, Swiss Medical Clinic.* In the centre of the village a thatched cottage tilted beside a duck pond, a banner draped across the eaves advertising *Country Bygones.* The van's engine clattered. Henry put his hand on the dash, as if calming an animal. A few years ago he'd had a flat tyre in the centre of town, right in front of the chocolate shop. He thought he'd never survive the stares of Springmer's villagers.

The clatter disappeared. Henry rolled the van quietly through the village and out into grazing lands dotted with sheep, past the ploughed fields where sparrows circled, searching for worms. In the distance there approached a glorious abundance of trees. It was the wood surrounding Burgess Green.

"There's beech," Henry said, pointing. "Willows—lots of them.

An Irish yew there." Henry loved trees. He slowed as he approached them, craning his neck and gawking. "Maple, birch. And an old ash behind that barn, look at that."

The road sunk as it fronted the river bottom and rose gradually to a small stone church with stained-glass windows bulging out of their iron frames. Henry brought the van to the corner of the car park. He slipped on his overalls and changed into his work boots. He took down his wheelbarrow and placed his spade inside, along with a scraper and pitchfork.

Henry started down the footpath. His boots crunched in the frost.

"McGinty…McGinty…" The headstones tilted in various directions. Some pressed against each other, like lovers. The lettering on the newer graves stood out, while the older headstones, besieged by lichen, had become almost unreadable. Henry stopped where a wooden stick pointed at a grave. The stone was a good piece of marble. It was almost thirteen years old, and the letters looked as white as toothpaste.

In loving memory of Patrick William McGinty. Husband to Mary. Died 20th May 1994, Aged 68 Years. He who Believeth in Me, Though he Die, Yet shall he Live.

"Mary McGinty's coming," Henry said, parking his wheelbarrow. He liked saying the deceased's name before digging the grave. He walked over the mounds, where a tin sheet leaned against the church wall, and he carried the sheet back to the grave.

Stamping his feet, Henry sized up the memorial. He wedged the scraper under the stone, gave it a push, and walked it away by the corners.

His back tightened—dodgy work. This was moving heavy objects in the freezing cold. At the next plot he let the marble fall face down on the grass. Henry put his hands on his knees, his heart racing. Did hard labour reduce a man's life span?

*   *   *

The wet soil loosened easily. About eight wheelbarrow loads he'd need to haul away, starting at the head. He put his foot on the spade, tilted it back at an angle, and removed the dirt. The soil, dripping from last week's rain, felt heavier than he would have liked. He worked backward to remove the topsoil and stopped to catch his breath at the centre of the grave. When he finished the first layer—the spit—he celebrated by unfastening the top button of his overalls.

He took the dirt to the edge of the churchyard and dumped it over a pile of tree trimmings. After seven more trips, he unfastened another button. Then he moved the wheelbarrow aside and shovelled onto the tin sheet. This dirt was destined for the mound, and under that Mary would join her husband.

Henry had been digging twelve years in Burgess Green. The previous man was Charlie Cotton. Henry was surprised to receive the call—Hetherington it was, telling him Cotton was retiring. Henry had been reluctant. He already handled six parishes. He rarely had a day off. But Burgess Green was so near to Chalk he felt obliged. Though he'd never met Charlie, he became familiar with the man's style. Each grave was slightly bowed in the centre and deep— almost a full foot more than the six required. During reopenings Henry often found cigar butts in the soil, black and soggy with the chewed ends bearing the outline of Charlie's teeth. Judging by the size of his graves, Henry had pictured Charlie a giant. But during a reopening in Burgess Green, a man the size of a child appeared beside the grave. The bottoms of his jeans were rolled up around his ankles. He had large hands, and he smoked a black cigar. "That's my grave," the man said.

"Charlie Cotton?"

Henry hadn't known what else to say. He went back to digging while Charlie watched. The man stood there for over an hour, as still as a rooster. When Henry's spade hit the casket, Charlie grunted. "There's the husband," he said. "The spouse still goes right on top?"

Henry nodded. Charlie grunted again, as if satisfied that nothing had changed in the way of grave digging. Puffing his cigar, he made a few turns round the headstones and disappeared.

This McGinty grave would have been Charlie's as well. Henry pictured him smoking while he dug, flinging soil high over his head. "Slow down now," Henry told himself, planting the spade. He'd only been going an hour, and already his knees were underground. He'd finish too early at this pace. Water would trickle in, and he'd be busy bailing just to keep the grave dry. Hoisting himself out, he sat on the grass and dangled his legs inside the grave. The sun had almost broken through the clouds. A robin flew out of a nearby holly.

"Morning, Henry."

Henry scrambled to his feet. "Father Morris," he said, dropping his eyes. Being around clergy always made him ashamed. He could hardly call himself a believer.

The priest smoothed the sides of his robe and looked at the sky. His face was round, his hair reddish-brown. "Dry day at least."

"It is."

"Wet as a sponge last week. I expect it would have been very damp digging indeed."

Henry fumbled for something to say. "Last week *was* wet. Good weather for digging today, though." The words hung stupidly in the air. He'd done it again—expressed himself poorly, just to say anything at all. Was it ever a good time for someone to die?

The priest hadn't seemed to mind. "I don't suppose you knew Mary? I was hoping *somebody* would tell me a thing or two so I'd know what to say. Her children moved away, you see. She rarely came to mass." He looked into the grave and shook his head. "What a mess."

"Sorry?"

"The vegetation in this churchyard," Father Morris explained, waving his arm. "I don't know where to start. I have an idea, but... hello, where's Jack?"

"Sick. I'm taking him to Tracy's this afternoon."

"That bad, is it? Best of luck to him, the old boy."

Henry nodded. He thought he saw Father Morris start off for the church, so he hopped back into the grave, relieved to be back underground. Then, when he reached above ground for his spade, he almost grabbed the priest's shoes.

"I say, Henry," Father Morris said, leaning into the grave. "I'd like to ask you something. That is your *Sussex Botanist*, isn't it? The one on the dashboard of your van? Don't let me interrupt, I just need your opinion."

Reddening, Henry found his spade. When he put his boot on the edge, it slipped.

"People call my churchyard overgrown, and I suppose it is. Right now the flora do have the upper hand, but what about down the road? What happens when a new parasite takes over? That's why I've been reluctant to cut back on any of this—even though those Scotch pines are proliferating like weeds. And my blackthorns will only get wilder, I know. But...you're familiar with *Tineola biselliella*?"

Henry hacked at a tree root. "The maggot."

"No threat to plants, thank goodness. But it has companions. Take that nasty beetle *Aglossa cuprealis* wreaking havoc on our trees. You read November's issue?"

Henry had thought the article unconvincing. The beetle had been discovered in only the older oaks, and it might have been any number of larvae doing the real damage. But he hated arguing. Too often he lost control of his feelings and said things he barely believed just to make a point. "I must have missed it," Henry said.

Father Morris began summarising the article. Henry continued digging. Occasionally, he looked out of the grave and nodded, just to be polite.

❊   ❊   ❊

"Fifteen, sixteen, seventeen, eighteen…"

Henry counted out loud with the second hand of the dashboard clock, internalising its pace. The hand came full circle, and he looked away to count another minute in his head. When he checked the clock he was fast by four seconds. It had been a while since he'd counted a minute to the second. He'd been having lunch in the van, just like now, and he'd felt a little jump as he saw that he'd hit it dead on. Only three times he'd done it, in all the years he'd tried. It was a game his father taught him.

"Helps pass the time," Frank said during one of their first burials together. "Closing your eyes helps with your accuracy." But Henry, perhaps to be different, never did. He left them open, sometimes counting a headstone for each second, or tapping the steering wheel with his index finger. Not that his dad cared about his habits. Frank spent all day in bed at the pensioners' home in Brighton, his arthritic legs twisted like roots under the blankets.

It was still early, but Henry opened his lunch bag and ate an egg. He mixed the order of things now and then for variation. Sometimes he found a place outside for his lunch. But the weather had to be accommodating, and even then he was reluctant, knowing what he would have looked like—a gravedigger travelling the roads in muddy overalls, looking for somewhere to eat. The windshield steamed from the open tea thermos. In the glove box, Henry searched for his squeegee and came across a chewed pig ear. It was Jack's. He had to prepare himself—Tracy might recommend putting the dog down.

Over at the vicarage, a car started. Father Morris pulled out of his drive in a brown Mini.

Henry glanced at the magazine on his dashboard.

"What about the future of our trees?"

He went over the priest's argument—something about overzealous pruning and delicate plant life. Who could know what was best for the world? It was the kind of topic he never knew how to address—a topic for philosophers, not gravediggers.

"I could have told Father Morris that!"

Henry couldn't believe he'd become so agitated. His hands were clenched into fists. Truths, if they existed at all, were impossible to discover. Why did some people act as if they had a monopoly on knowledge?

"At least Gravediggers don't have a monopoly on knowledge!"

Henry glanced at the passenger seat. He half expected to see Jack there, gnawing on the pig ear. It was the kind of remark his dog would have appreciated. Jack appreciated every remark, for that matter.

Henry got out of the van and slammed the door. He didn't know what he'd do if he lost Jack. Standing in the windy car park, tears ran down his face. "Absurd," he said, wiping his eyes. "A dog, that's all."

The wind made him shiver. It was still too early to finish, so he shoveled at a slower pace. At least it would be warmer underground. Fortunately the hole was just as he left it—no water had seeped through the walls. He jumped in and grabbed his spade. After shaving level the walls he went up to the head to dig the next spit. As he bent over, a spasm shot across his back.

Unlike some gravediggers, who spent weeks in hospital with slipped discs, Henry had never missed a day of work. It was a record he felt proud of, if pride meant an ability to work like a mule for twenty years. But lately, after getting started in the mornings, pain struck. It came just above his hip, sharp and deep, as if he'd been stabbed. The pain tormented him—not the discomfort as much as the sinister way it took permanent residence in his mind. Sometimes he felt a twinge before he bent over, or as a disturbing thought entered his head. Each time, he pretended to ignore it. But the twinge lurked in his subconscious like an evil elf. Henry knew what pain represented. He was getting older, approaching death.

The spasm passed, and Henry worked backwards from the head of the grave. When he lifted out the soil he varied his placement of the dirt—packing a spadeful into the side of the mound, a chunk on top. He was good at what he did, and he knew it. He was meant to dig. When he reached the middle of the grave, he turned round, moving backward as he evened out the bottom. He left himself a little dirt platform in the centre of the spit and stood on one foot as he shaved down the walls. He might have been a boy playing in a sandbox.

His shoulders at ground level, he peered at the horizon. Something moved in the distance—legs in stockings and heels, walking across the churchyard about six rows down. Henry stepped off the platform and crouched. It was a woman in an overcoat, carrying a sprig of flowers toward a grave. She obviously hadn't seen him, and now he had to wait motionless until she'd gone. If he moved inside the grave, she might have a fright. It happened to him with more than enough frequency, inadvertently scaring people. Other gravediggers—Derrick Watkins, for instance—relished such moments.

Derrick covered a handful of parishes near Chalk. He was a drunk. Often Henry was obliged to drive thirty miles at the last minute because he hadn't shown up for a burial. "There was this lass," Derrick told Henry once, "praying as quietly as could be. She hadn't seen the wheelbarrow, you see, hadn't seen me below. She thought she was all alone. So I stood right up and moaned, and she scampered away, shrieking bloody murder!"

Henry kept his head down and waited. He watched over the lip of the grave as the woman crossed herself and started to sing.

"Keep me to thee, gentle and mild..."

Henry clutched the handle of his spade and stared at the soil. The woman's voice was clear and strong, and she knew the hymn as if she'd sung it a hundred times. She sounded almost business-like. Yet there was something about the melody—perhaps the words—that made him catch his breath. He thought he'd heard it somewhere before.

"...in great and peaceful majesty."

The woman placed her flowers on the headstone and left. Henry shovelled out the platform to start on the next spit. Water trickled down the walls. Patrick McGinty's coffin was close now—he could smell it. Pockets of released air rose like geysers. The water went from trickles to streams, shooting down the walls and filling the bottom. Henry dug until a stronger smell came from the bottom, rancid and sharp like mouldy cheese.

He leaned his head over the side for air. If Jack had been sitting by the mound, the dog might have twitched his ears.

*   *   *

The end of the half-term meant Chalk's awards presentations. Darren Roberts, the deputy headmaster, sat amongst the second form pupils in one of their child-sized chairs.

Beverly Smith had all the atention. She stood beside her desk in her green checked skirt. Even at eighty-one, with her silver hair, bright green eyes, and rounded back she was loved more than any teacher in the school. It didn't matter how carefully he corrected their grammar. It didn't matter how patiently he watched them play football with a benevolent smile. His dispositional timidity, along with his thinning hair, made him invisible to the children. The children always presented her with their watercolours and expectant faces and skinned knees.

Beverly called Gwen Simingtom up for the maths award. In her excitement, Gwen didn't notice her hat falling off.

"Beverly," Darren said, pointing at it. "Careful of Gwen's hat, there. I wouldn't want you to slip."

With surprising agility, Beverly scooped the hat off the floor and swept it onto Gwen's head.

"Landing on my bum would not be a pretty sight," she said.

"Hee bloody hee," Darren muttered, as the children giggled. He hated Chalk but was too lazy to leave. He'd even purchased a house.

Beverly held the next certificate high in the air, emblazoned with the school's silver seal. "This is a particularly impressive one, considering how far our winner has come this term. The second form reading award goes to Mr. Michael Hall."

As everyone clapped, a boy with pale cheeks rose from his chair in the front row. His tie was neat, his shirt clean. "Congratulations, Michael," Darren said. "I'm proud of you!" The boy didn't seem to have heard. He smoothed his hair though it was already perfectly combed, and he walked in measured steps to the front of the classroom.

"How many hours I've spent," Darren hissed, "helping that child spell?"

Beverly kept clapping, though everyone else had stopped. Since her husband Horace died, Darren noticed, a blank expression sometimes came over her face. Flattened and her mouth opened, as if she'd begun joining Horace for good. They'd been married over sixty years. Toward the end, they only seemed to grow closer. Everyday, Horace would come to school to walk her home. He would wait for her in the school office as early as noon, her purse in his lap like a life vest.

Beverly kept clapping, even after Michael Hall had taken his certificate and returned to his chair. A moment later she stood frozen in mid-motion, like a mime. Her smile turned crooked, and the stacks of certificates slipped from her arm. Then her knees wobbled, and she collapsed in a heap on the floor.

Darren bolted out of his chair. All around him pupils gasped with the beginnings of grief.

TWO

Henry patted his bailing bucket. The end and side boards neatly circled Mary McGinty's grave so the bearers wouldn't trip. The green covering mats looked clean enough for a picnic.

It wasn't pretty, a man losing his footing at a funeral. Once, a bearer had tumbled all the way into the open grave. The man had scowled at Henry as he'd pulled himself out. Easier to blame a gravedigger than account for clumsiness. "There's no winning with grave digging," his father always said, "only not losing."

Henry dragged the bucket along the bottom and dumped what water there was over the hedge. "Always prepare a dry grave," his father insisted, the words echoing in Henry's head each time he worked, "even if it means staying right at the hole until the last minute."

Now was the last minute. Any second now, the bearers would be coming out of the church. It was a trick, disappearing for the committal. Waiting in the van was an option, but in this churchyard Henry would have to slink past the mourners in his grubby overalls to do the filling in. It was obvious a grave needed a gravedigger, but nobody needed reminding. One day, to his horror, the mourners spent no time at all at the gravesite. They swarmed out to the car park as he stood there finishing his sandwich. Today the side of the church would be best, Henry decided. He used the bucket once more and placed the coffin's putlogs across the centre of the grave.

The door to the church opened. Father Morris emerged, followed by Hetherington, grinning in front of his black-robed bearers. They carried the casket on their shoulders, feet first. Henry pushed his wheelbarrow to the south wall of the church. He turned and faced the grave, his arms at his sides. He couldn't look away, but he couldn't stare either.

There were fourteen mourners. Those were Mary's children, Henry guessed, the men who might have been twins, shuffling forward with their wives and kids. A middle-aged woman looked like a younger unmarried sister. An elderly couple followed with flowers, and that was all. Everyone's eyes were watery, but it might have been from the wind.

Father Morris stopped at the foot of the grave. The bearers rested the coffin on the putlogs and backed away while the priest sprinkled water and said a prayer. Some of the mourners lowered their heads. Others searched the churchyard. Henry stifled a yawn. One of the McGinty grandchildren—a boy of six or seven—spotted him standing alone against the church. The boy yanked on his mother's coat and pointed.

His prayer finished, Father Morris made a sign of the cross. The bearers hastened to the grave. They hoisted the coffin so Hetherington could remove the putlogs, and then they played out the webbings. The McGinty sons hugged each other, then took turns hugging their sister. They were short, formal hugs, those of siblings who saw each other on the odd holiday. Father Morris lingered, making himself available for anyone in need of counsel. The boy who'd pointed picked up a handful of dirt. He took a full swing and threw it into the grave. His mother yanked him away.

"Hello, Henry!" Hetherington said, appearing at the handle of the wheelbarrow.

"Hello, John."

"Dry day, anyway."

"It was dry."

Hetherington winked. "Big coffin for a little lady. She wasn't more than five feet." He held out the cheque between his fingers, and Henry pried it out. "Nothing 'til Monday," Hetherington said, almost sadly. "Come to think of it, it's in Chalk."

Henry stared. "Chalk? I haven't heard of anyone dying."

"I think so, Henry. Don't hold me to it." He picked at his fingernails and sighed. "I just heard this morning on my way out the door."

"But…you don't remember the name?"

"I don't, mate. But I'll ring you with the specs. You shouldn't have far to drive!" Grinning, he headed back to the church.

Henry took his wheelbarrow to the grave. It was possible Hetherington had made a mistake. He folded up the mats, removed the planks and end boards, and began shovelling in the mound dirt. In twenty minutes he had the grave topped off. Damp soil always made a tidy mound. Standing the tin sheet on its side, he scraped it clean and took it back beside the church.

The flowers sat waiting on the grass. The largest arrangement was a wreath of frozen orchids with a message in blue plastic lettering. Rest in Peace, Your Loving Children. He draped it over the centre of the mound. The other arrangements were carnations mostly, wrapped in cellophane with announcement cards stuck in plastic forks.

"Oh, damn these bloody things." One of the arrangements kept tumbling off and onto the grass. Tearing back the cellophane, Henry held the flowers down and packed the stems with mud.

*　*　*

Something had changed in Chalk—Henry knew it as soon as he'd left the Springmer road. It was only two, and the car park at The Black Ram was jammed. The school children were already walking home. And at the Smith cottage there was David, Beverly's son, helping his kids out of the car. The last time David visited Chalk was for his father's funeral.

Henry pulled onto the shoulder of the road beside his house. His hands were shaking, and he sat on them to make them stop. Beverly had been his teacher. She'd taught everyone in Chalk. She'd smile almost apologetically, he recalled, while cutting a student to shreds. Not long ago, Beverly had sat on the churchyard bench and watched him prepare her husband's grave. She watched so intently he thought she might have been planning to grade him on it. At lunch, she'd even brought over a mince pie.

"Maybe it's a holiday," Henry said, as he left the van. That would explain children leaving school early, and The Black Ram filling up.

At his gate Henry kept his hand on the latch. He wanted to go into the vicarage and ask Reverend Pierce if anyone had died. He could always walk to the pub and sniff around. But Henry seldom talked to the vicar, and he hadn't been to the pub in almost ten

years. The situation brought all sorts of complications. If Beverly
Smith had passed away, Frank would want to attend the funeral.
Arrangements would have to be made with the pensioners' home
well in advance, and he'd have to schedule a trip down to Brighton
to collect him.

Henry headed up the road. The shop was the solution. If anyone
in Chalk had died, the customers would be discussing it. He needed
milk anyway. He hugged the wall as he set off and hoped he wouldn't
be seen. His hair, as usual, required a thorough combing.

At the Smith cottage, the door opened, and a man emerged.
It was David. He looked fit as usual, striding across his mother's
garden in a suit cut by a tailor. David was in London these days—in
computers, Henry tried to remember, or maybe it was finance. He
nodded hello but David only scowled.

The pavement ended, and Henry crossed the road to pick it up on
the other side. He could hear David following him. As he passed the
pub Henry peered through the open front door. The entire village, it
seemed, stood crammed together at the bar. He picked up his pace and
entered the stone cottage on the corner, where a sign below the roof
said, *Chalk Stores*. As he came inside Henry set in motion the brass bell
above the door.

The shop was the size of a sitting room. The walls were bowed,
and the ceiling low. Henry had to stoop. Boxes of produce stood
by the door—unripe pears, onions, bananas greener than grass.
Seeing Henry, Kevin Yapton leaned his elbows on the counter. His
hand drifted to his calculator.

"Hello, Henry!" he said, smiling. "Fine day." Mr. Yapton had close-
set eyes and cheeks so shiny it looked like he polished them. Henry
started to reply when the bell rang and David came in behind him,
still scowling. Henry moved against the wall beside the onions to
give him room.

Mr. Yapton's face took on a solemn expression. "David. I am sorry
to hear about your mother."

David came straight to the counter. "What can one do?" He
looked at Henry and frowned.

"That's right," Mr. Yapton said. Some cheer returned to his voice.
"That's it exactly. What can one do? A fine woman, your mum. A fine
woman indeed."

"Cheers, Kevin. She was that. I've come to place a notice."
He pulled a sheet of paper from his trouser pocket and left it on

the counter. "It's for the service Monday. Dad would have wanted everyone there. You understand."

"Of course! Not a bother at all." Mr. Yapton moved aside the newspapers and dusted the counter with a bit of cloth. "Now, I'll just put a little tape on the ends…" The notice placed in plain view, he looked at David and smiled. "There."

"Now I'll need some Digestives. And a pack of Pall Mall One-Hundreds, please."

"Digestives and Pall Mall One-Hundreds." Mr. Yapton located the cigarettes and scurried to the far wall. Passing the onions, he whispered, "I'll be right with you, Henry."

"No trouble," Henry said, reddening. David was staring at him again, and he didn't know why.

Back at his place behind the counter, Mr. Yapton took a deep breath, as if to prepare himself for the transaction. "Now. Three pounds ninety for the Pall Malls," he said, entering the amount on the calculator, "and sixty pence for the Digestives…comes to four pounds fifty."

"There's four," David said, dropping the coins into his hand. He fished in his pocket. "And there's fifty."

"Grand. Be sure and give my regrets to Linda. Your brother home yet?"

"Tonight. With Sarah and the kids. Ironic, really—the whole family together and mum not around." He started for the door. Henry had to lean over to give him room.

"Now!" Mr. Yapton said, just as the door closed. "How can I help you, Henry?"

"I've only come for a pint of milk," Henry said, making his way to the fridge.

"Right, Henry. You know where things are."

Henry brought the milk to the counter and placed it beside David's notice. He read it twice, shaking his head as if not believing the words.

MEMORIAL SERVICE. Beverly Smith, husband of Horace and schoolteacher of Chalk for over 62 years. Chalk Parish Church, 3:30 PM, Monday 7th February, 2007. All are welcome to attend.

"Terrible, isn't it?" Mr. Yapton said.

Henry nodded. It would be hard digging in that chalk. He'd need to use the pickaxe. Pain stabbed the small of his back, making him wince.

*   *   *

"What do you say, Jack?"

The dog kept his chin on the cot, his eyes pinched shut, his nose pointing at the fire. Henry let him sleep. He went into the kitchen, put the milk in the fridge, and stood motionless on the linoleum. Under his shirt, he felt a chill. He'd never heard the house so quiet.

He tried not to rush back into the sitting room and across to the cot. He lifted Jack in his hands. The head hung limp, the fur cold. "Jack," he said. "Jack." He wiggled his fingers under the dog's neck, searching for a pulse. There was nothing.

Henry rested the dog back in the cot. He started for the door, as if he had somewhere to go, then returned to the cot. He stroked Jack's head a while and pulled the blanket over the dog's shoulders.

"That's it, then," Henry said.

Luckily there were arrangements to make. He had to ring Tracy and cancel his appointment. He had to dig Jack's grave. And there was still the call to his father in Brighton, scheduling his day out on Monday. There would be work next week, and the week after that. Life didn't come to a standstill when a dog died.

In the meantime, the evening stood in front of him like a wall. Switching on the television, Henry found a human voice. When the screen settled a young man materialised, perched on a stool. The female host, standing in the audience with a microphone, slowly brought out the man's story. His girlfriend was pregnant, he said. He wanted to keep the baby, and she didn't. The camera cut to a young woman with pimples, waiting backstage.

Henry sat rigidly in the armchair, following the program as best he could. The story coursed over him, as meaningless as static. In his mind's eye he imagined kicking over the television and screaming. Instead he sat in the armchair until the program ended, then knelt by the cot. He turned Jack over and put his ear against the dog's chest. He used to take Jack for walks on Sunday mornings. What was he going to do with his Sundays now?

Later, when he checked the mantle clock, it was a quarter past nine. He'd been watching television for six hours and couldn't recall a single program he'd watched.

*   *   *

Behind his front wall, Henry ducked as a car approached. It would be the talk of the village if he were seen like this, past midnight in his garden with a spade and a dead dog. The headlights showed everything in a burst of light—the wicker cot, the empty grave, Jack's shrivelled nose poking out of his blanket.

It was because of the time they'd spent together. He was rattled, that's all. He kept putting his fingers to his own neck to find his pulse. He kept glancing across the road at the churchyard. After a while, living creatures became used to one another. He repeated the idea in his head, as if it might anchor him, or steady his feelings. He hadn't been fair to David Smith, begrudging him that scowl.

"The man's mother died, Jack!"

He gathered the dog in the blanket. The hole was ready, there was no getting around it. Jack had become alarmingly light—his legs felt like matchsticks. "You were a pup not long ago," Henry said, lowering him into the hole. Henry looked at the body in the dirt. He wanted to check Jack's pulse once more. His father's voice stopped him: *No point in worrying about things you can't change.*

There would be other dogs. It was easy enough to get one—every week, they were advertised in the papers. The idea made Henry feel better, even as he sensed it was wrong to think of it while burying Jack. He scooped up the first layer of dirt and looked away while tilting the spade.

*   *   *

The next morning Henry woke in shivers. It was so cold, the walls were damp. He'd forgotten to turn on the central heating, he realised, pulling the covers over his beard. Outside, the rain thudded on the windowsill.

Jack would be miserable downstairs. Henry sat up and reached for his clothes to go down and restart the fire. Then he stopped and remained halfway out of bed, his arm extended to the pile of clothes on the floor. As if watching from across the room, he saw himself in his nightshirt and pyjama bottoms. He pictured Jack's mound out in the garden, settling in the rain.

"Maybe it will be a mild afternoon," Henry said.

He did have things to do. He had a full schedule of digging

next week. And his mats needed cleaning again, didn't they? As he swung his legs out of bed, the phone rang. He pulled on his trousers and ran downstairs.

"Hello, Henry? Tracy here. Didn't we have an appointment yesterday?"

Henry looked at Jack's empty cot beside the fire. "I forgot to ring," he said. It took him a moment to say it. "Jack's dead."

"I am sorry," Tracy said.

Henry kept looking at the empty cot. He started to hang up.

"Henry? I hope you don't find it inconsiderate. My policy is to charge for missed appointments."

"I understand."

"I'll just post the invoice, then. Sorry about Jack."

* * *

"And what if it's my policy not to pay?" Henry said, as he scrubbed his mats. The conversation with the vet wouldn't leave his head. Hadn't he taken Jack to Tracy for almost fourteen years?

At least the rain had stopped. The mound over Jack's grave had turned to mud. Standing behind his front wall, Henry dunked his scrubbing brush into a bucket of soapy water. Now and then a villager passed by, and he kept his head down, pretending not to notice. Then a voice made him look up.

"Morning, Henry."

Henry took his scrubbing brush and joined Mrs. Tilson at the wall dividing their gardens. His neighbour was a widow. This morning she wore her usual white cardigan, green checked skirt over nylon stockings, and heavy brown shoes that had been her husband's. She was the finest woman in Chalk, Henry's father said. He said it as recently as a month ago.

Henry waited while Mrs. Tilson refilled her bird feeder. After his mother died, it was Mrs. Tilson who'd suggested they switch houses. Frank needed a change, she said, even if it was just next-door. She rested her bag of birdseed on the wall. "I have some lamb chops in the cooker. Must have made too many again—I'll never eat them all."

Henry smiled. Truth was, he was more a son to Mrs. Tilson than her own boys—grown men now, and moved away. They came back once a year for Christmas, if the weather wasn't bad. "It's kind of you," Henry said. "But I haven't much of an appetite—"

Across the road, the gate to the vicarage opened. Looking both ways, Reverend Pierce stepped onto the road. "My goodness," Henry said. "The vicar's coming."

Reverend Pierce was in his late sixties. He had a drinker's complexion—veins pushing the limits of his cheeks, a purplish nose ready to pop. He kept his hair dyed black with shoe polish and combed in neat rows across his head. When he wasn't in his churh robe, Reverend Pierce always wore a tobacco-stained brown pullover and brown corduroys. At Henry's gate, he cleared his throat. "Morning, Henry. Hello, Mrs. Tilson."

"Morning vicar," Mrs. Tilson said.

The vicar had evidently come to discuss Beverly's funeral. Mrs. Tilson started inside, but she didn't make it far. "Henry," she said, leaning over the wall. "Is that a grave?"

Henry glanced at the mud from the mound, creeping toward his boots. "That's Jack."

"Oh dear, Henry," Mrs. Tilson said. "Poor dear."

The vicar clasped his hands. "Not the best of weekends for Chalk, is it?"

Henry reddened under his beard. He'd been caught mourning over a dog while the rest of the village mourned Beverly Smith. "It's nothing," he said.

"It's not nothing, Henry," Mrs. Tilson said. She seemed almost angry with him. "Jack was a fine dog, and you shouldn't forget it. A fine dog."

"He was a good old boy. But I've no reason to call attention."

"Of course you do, Henry." Mrs. Tilson shook her finger at him. "It doesn't suit you to act as if you don't care." She went inside and closed the door.

Reverend Pierce cleared his throat again. He picked up one of Henry's mats and examined it. "Getting ready for Monday, are we?"

"I'll have things nice and tidy," Henry said, glad for the change of subject. "Hetherington still hasn't told me the time of Beverly's service."

"I shouldn't think we'll be at the grave later than half two, Henry. David's trying for a big turnout, you know. It's possible we'll have fifty in the congregation."

"Fifty!" Henry glanced across the road where the church stood separated from the school by the boundary hedge. He didn't see how they'd all fit.

"Won't be easy digging, will it? I don't suppose the weather will make a difference, one way or the other."

"No. Chalk's chalk."

The vicar nodded.

"I could use a dry afternoon to get these mats ready, though," Henry added, looking up at the sky. He'd never had a conversation of this length with the vicar.

Reverend Pierce looked up at the same time. "I should think you'll have it. Just dribs and drabs, this rain."

"I believe so," Henry said. The vicar was making sure Beverly was buried properly, that was all. There was little cause to be nervous in his company—after all, he'd known the man all his life.

"Frank coming down for the funeral?"

"I still have to ring the pensioners' home."

"Right, then," the vicar said. "Sounds as if you're well in hand, Henry. My sympathies about Jack."

"No need, Reverend, but thank you. No trouble."

The vicar continued up the road. On his way to the pub, Henry guessed. He hung his second mat over the wall to dry and dropped his brush in the bucket. Stepping over Jack's grave, he went inside to ring his dad.

* * *

Frank had seemed excited by the news of Beverly's death. It was an awful thought, but Henry couldn't deny it. As he sipped his tea in the kitchen he wondered what it was like for his father, surrounded by people waiting to die. He was probably happy for the excuse to leave. Henry arranged to collect him tomorrow night, a Sunday. He hadn't mentioned Jack.

Henry heard his gate rattling. He crept into the sitting room and parted the curtain. There in the garden stood David Smith, examining the grave mats drying on the front wall. Henry could see traces of Beverly in her son's appraising eyes. He had on a different suit from yesterday's—dark blue this time.

Henry didn't know what the man wanted. It grated him, the way David was loitered with one hand tucked in his trouser pocket, the other holding a cigarette. He kept studying the grave mats as if they were museum exhibits. Straightening his shirt, Henry opened his door. He wanted to be louder, but his voice came out barely audible, even to himself. "They'll be clean by Monday," he said.

David didn't respond. He may as well finish all his mats now, Henry thought, if the whole village was concerned. He plunged his hand into the bucket, found the brush, and started scrubbing. The last mat was almost clean by the time David spoke. "It's Henry, isn't it? Henry Bale?"

Henry looked up, as if just noticing David for the first time. He placed his brush on the mat and waited.

David took a last drag from his cigarette and tossed the butt into the road. "You'll be burying my mother on Monday."

Henry nodded. It sounded like an accusation. "The grave will be ready, as I say. Just this last mat to clean and dry."

"We're about the same age, you and I. But it bothers me that I don't remember you, growing up. Mum told me about you and your father, and your profession. She said she watched you dig dad's grave. Said it affected her, in fact. Do you know I think she expects me to…"

David put his hand on the wall to steady himself. "And I remember you that day. The day of dad's funeral, I mean. You were standing off to the side with a wheelbarrow and a little white dog, waiting to fill the hole."

Henry just nodded. It was part of being a gravedigger, his father said—how the deceased's friends and relatives often wanted to talk about their loved ones, how it was necessary just to listen. Last month, right when he'd started digging, the deceased's husband had appeared. He'd talked for over an hour about his wife—how they'd met, where they'd taken their holidays, how they'd tried for children and failed. The man had stayed beside the grave throughout a stiff rain.

David Smith was harder to read. He seemed to be confronting this moment, testing his grief. Henry only knew that Beverly had been lucky to have led a full life, and to have died at an old age. If he tried to say something meaningful to David it was bound to come up short. He stood silently with his head bent, waiting for the man to leave.

"I was wondering," David said, "if you'd join me for a pint."

Henry shook his head. "I haven't been to a pub in years."

"Just one? It might sound strange, but I feel I owe it to Mum. It meant something to her, watching you dig dad's grave. She sort of implied she wanted me to do the same."

"You're welcome to. The bench is there."

"That may be," David said, searching for his cigarettes. His hands were shaking. "But I'm not much for watching that sort of thing, you see."

Henry glanced up the road. He pictured himself inside the painted white pub with its thatched roof and hushed conversations and men sipping pints. The Black Ram would be crowded right now. People would stare, people would whisper. It would be awkward, visiting the pub for the first time in ten years with a Londoner, and the son of Beverly Smith at that. It was all very well for David—he could drive home and never set foot in Chalk again. Meanwhile, nobody here would forget. The gravedigger and the deceased's son sharing a pint, they'd say, how bloody quaint. And what on Earth would he wear?

Henry squeezed his scrubbing brush while David waited. There was nothing good about the proposition. David was feeling guilty about not visiting his mum more, guilty, perhaps, about not telling her before she'd died. He wanted to feel better somehow by having a drink with the man burying her. Henry started to say he couldn't make it. He started to shake his head, to speak, but he could only think of Beverly sitting quietly on the bench during her husband's burial and bringing him that mince pie. His father was right. There was never any winning with grave digging, only not losing.

"Tomorrow evening I have to go to Brighton," Henry said.

"Tonight, then. Around eight?"

"Okay." David smiled. It was the first time Henry had seen the man smile, and only then did he realise he'd said the right thing.

✳   ✳   ✳

Henry thought The Black Ram would be filled with strangers. He recognised almost everyone. After ten years, he might as well have been gone five minutes.

At first he'd tried on the blazer his father bought him for Christmas fifteen years ago. It still fit. But he was only going for a drink at the pub, so he replaced it with his anorak. His second pair of jeans were clean enough. In his closet he found a presentable long-sleeved shirt that wasn't too musty. It was pointless to brush his hair but he did anyway. By the time he reached the pub, the wind had obliterated his efforts.

Reverend Pierce, sitting at the near end of the bar, noticed him first. The vicar nodded briefly and returned to his crossword. To his left sat William Harvey, the bus driver who doubled as the church organist. Through a mess of blond curls that covered his eyes, he said, "Hello there, Henry."

Oliver Marsh occupied the far corner of the bar, both hands around a pint of Guinness. Oliver was a madman, or so people thought. Nobody had ever heard him speak. He had a pale, pockmarked face, and his long neck gleamed like a stripped elm.

Behind the bar, Sid Book rolled a cigarette. He was nearly bald, and his eyes sat deep in their sockets. "Evening, Henry," Sid said. "Pint of Cuckoo for you?"

"Not just yet," Henry said, amazed the man had remembered his former drink. He checked the snuggery. There were a few tables occupied, and a couple of dogs asleep on the floor. Armchairs faced the fire beside a stack of newspapers. A dartboard hung on the right wall, and on the left the front window looked onto the road. At one of the tables a middle-aged couple sat side-by-side, holding hands. Henry didn't recognise them. They were staring at the centre table, where Trevor Nelson sat beside his sidekick, Chris Crawley.

Chris was a mechanic. He was hairy and broad-shouldered, and he always wore red, oil-stained overalls. Three women sat facing them from the other side of the table. Henry knew one of them—Vickie Eckleton, the clerk at the post office. Along with her friends, Vickie looked absorbed with Trevor's every move. Chris, perhaps in protest, had turned his chair away. As he saw Henry, he stuck up his hand and waved hello.

Henry checked his wristwatch—it was five past eight. He took a chair under the dartboard and tried to appear relaxed. He knew how it looked, coming into the pub alone. The middle-aged couple against the wall appeared to be lost tourists.

"Imagine pissing away all that money!" Trevor held his hands out on the table, palms up. "Serves him right, ditching his mates like that."

Vickie nodded energetically. Henry remembered he'd met her friends a long time ago. Their names came to him as if no time had passed—Rosalyn and Claire. They leaned toward Trevor in their chairs, as if attending a particularly gripping play.

"I just don't understand," Trevor continued, his eyes widening. "Give me a man with heart!"

Rosalyn tried to sweep her hair behind her shoulders, but it stuck to her cheeks. "First of all," she said, "this is only a chat show you're talking about. Okay? People lie just to get attention. They're on TV! But let's be honest. If you won the lottery, wouldn't your priorities change?"

Vickie shook her head solemnly. "Not mine." Her blonde hair and blue eyes made her almost glamorous, at least in Chalk.

"It's a ridiculous question," Claire said, sighing impatiently. "Nobody knows how they'll behave until they're faced with the situation."

Exasperated, Rosalyn gripped Trevor's hands. "Winning the lottery wouldn't make you different."

Trevor stared at her intently. He put his elbows on the table, closed his eyes, and rested his forehead in the palms of her hands.

"I'll tell you what I'd do different," Chris said, as he rolled a cigarette. "Tell my friends to sod off."

Trevor sat up and burst into laughter. He clapped Chris on the back, his face instantly serious. "If I became a millionaire, I'd make my mates rich too. That was this bloke's problem—no heart. They needed him, and he turned his back! It was karma that made him lose it all. All we have in the world are friends."

"He's right you know," Claire said, turning to Vickie and Rosalyn. She looked drunk. "If I didn't have you two, if I couldn't leave the children with Mum and come out like this now and then—"

Vickie patted her arm. "Poor Claire," She said. "You've got more on your plate than any of us."

Trevor stood up and clapped his hands. "No more sadness!" He made a show of checking everyone's drinks. "Now sit tight, next round's on me."

Claire looked at her watch. Rosalyn searched the table as Trevor smiled benevolently. "What'll you have, Vick, another lager?"

She stood up. "No, I won't let you. There you are, poor dear, without a job and trying to buy a round of drinks."

Trevor took a half step from the table. "Now, Vick…"

Vickie shook her head. "I'm getting them, Trevor, and that's final." She marched off to the bar.

Chris Crawley rolled his eyes. "Christ almighty."

Trevor sat down and banged the table with his fists. "This girl once had a theory about me. She was one of those heady types—a real thinker. She said I acted like a lad because I couldn't accept that my life was going to end."

Rosalyn nodded. "What did you say to that?"

"I told her I still wanted to shag other girls!" He banged his fists on the table again, and Rosalyn and Claire jumped. "It's all about living!" he shouted, addressing everyone in the pub at once. "Beating death as long as you can!"

"Or in your case, staying on the dole," Sid shouted from behind the bar. The pub erupted in laughter. Reverend Pierce ordered a round for the regulars at the bar, including Oliver Marsh.

When Vickie returned, Trevor took his pint out of her hand. "That may be, Sid," he said, shouting back, "but I'll toast life just the same."

"Here, here," Chris Crawley said, raising his glass. "Here's to life!"

Each person in the pub—except the middle-aged couple and Henry—picked up their drinks. "To life!" Trevor yelled.

The door opened, and David Smith walked in. His eyes were ringed with red circles. The pub fell silent as he took off his coat.

Henry gripped the arms of his chair while David had two pints poured. "Sid said you drank Cuckoo," he said, as he joined Henry by the fire. Henry took his glass and nodded. David sat beside him, stretched out his legs, and started on his pint.

Henry had never had much of a taste for alcohol. When he was younger, he frequented pubs because there was nothing else to do. Each night he tried to socialise, ordering beer after beer though he would have preferred tea. He drank more than he needed and waited for something to happen. Nothing did. Nothing that mattered, anyway—a number of forgettable conversations, the odd encounter with a woman after bracing himself with drinks. It was against his nature to pretend, and after a while he stopped. Soon after he'd bought Jack, he started staying home.

David didn't speak after he sat down. He simply let his chin drop against his chest. Henry dropped his head too, offering this wordless sympathy as best he could. He sipped his beer, and it didn't taste as bad as he remembered. When David finished his pint, Henry went to order the next round.

The pub filled with the older regulars. They were all men, stubble-cheeked and cynical, each dressed in faded tweed jackets and ties. They hunched over their drinks, rolled cigarettes, and complained about the changing world. Times were better when they were young, they grumbled, yet they didn't seem to have enjoyed youth much, either. Two of them worked on the Wembles Estate—head butler Roger Lowry, an aging Scot with a lazy eye and hair sprouting from his ears, and Dick Miles the gatekeeper, who drank beside the door as if guarding it. The vicar finished the crossword and started another. William Harvey chatted with Sid about someone on his bus that morning. Oliver Marsh drank silently and fidgeted on his stool.

Henry paid Sid and weaved his way back to the fire. David started on his next drink straight away. Some color had returned to his cheeks. Across the room, the middle-aged couple were still holding hands with their drink glasses empty on their table. At the centre table Rosalyn had moved closer to Trevor. They weren't whispering in each other's ears, but they weren't exactly including the others. Chris Crawley stared at the wall. Claire gathered her belongings as if to leave.

"Claire!" Trevor said, reaching across the table to seize her hands. "What are you doing? You can't leave!"

"Mum's got the boys. I get up at half-five tomorrow, and I'm knackered."

"But what about me?" Trevor said.

Claire just stared. The question hung in the air for the whole pub to hear, absurd, unanswerable. Something in Trevor's manner—his deep, intangible neediness, perhaps—seemed to have an effect. Claire let go of her handbag strap. "One more, then."

Chris tapped his empty glass. "Another round for everyone?" Without waiting for an answer, he headed to the bar.

"I'm so happy," Trevor announced. "Every night, I want to go out. Every night I want to be with people. Is there anything wrong with that?"

Vickie shook her head. "I don't see anything wrong with it. People should do what makes them happy."

"That's what I say," Trevor said. "Why stay inside, moping and mourning? Aren't we social creatures, after all?" He stood up. "I need to use the toilet."

"He's right, you know," Rosalyn said, to the table after he'd gone.

Vickie nodded. "Trevor's always right. You need a man in your life, Claire."

Claire's mouth dropped. "It's all very well for you two, shagging every bloke you meet. Just where do you think that will lead?" She seized her coat and purse, and she stormed out.

"I've never seen her so vicious," Rosalyn said.

Vickie stood up. "She didn't mean it. C'mon, let's catch her." Rosalyn collected her purse. Dick Miles opened the door for them, and they were gone.

Henry had been listening the whole time, partly queasy, partly thrilled. Memories came back to him—fragments of so many drunken conversations, meaningless as wind. He couldn't even be sure his memories were real. David Smith kept staring at his shoes, his pint glass tilting. It was strange he'd wanted to go out at all—they'd only exchanged a few words.

Chris Crawley returned, his huge hands bracketing five pints of beer. He stared at the empty table as Trevor came back from the toilet.

"Where'd they go?" Trevor asked.

Chris shrugged. "Their things are gone."

"They couldn't have left. Not without telling us." Trevor glared at the tourists against the wall, as if holding them responsible.

"Maybe they'll be back," Chris said, putting the pints on the table. He sat down and started on one. "Then again, maybe they won't."

"How can you be so calm about it?" Seizing a beer, Trevor circled the snuggery. He almost ran into the dogs asleep by the fire. "Who can I chat with now?"

For the first time Henry felt grateful for David's company—even Trevor would respect a man mourning his mother's death. But before he could react, Trevor stood in front of them.

"David," he said, "I want to say how sorry I am. About your mum, I mean." He gulped some beer. "She was a teacher—a teacher for the whole village. And a fine lady to all who knew her. I was lucky enough to know her, as a matter of fact. You might say we respected each other from afar. And...well, she'll be missed."

"Thanks," David said. "It's a difficult time, all right."

"That's as it should be." Trevor took a chair from an empty table, swung it around, and sat in front of them. "I don't mean to intrude. It must be hard for you. But we should grieve for those who deserve it."

"You're right," David said. He looked up and nodded slowly, as if Trevor had revealed a mysterious insights. "My mum—she wanted me to help Henry dig her grave. Or at least watch. She hinted as much. But I just can't. Anyway," David went on, looking at Trevor the whole time, "that's why I invited Henry for a drink."

Henry sat up in his chair. He felt pushed over, somehow. Why was David talking to Trevor and not him? "Here now," he said, "I told you that you're welcome to sit on the bench Monday morning."

Trevor tried to pat Henry's shoulder, but Henry pulled away. "That was a wonderful gesture," Trevor said, his lips trembling. "Excuse me, perhaps it's the drink, but…" Standing up, he wiped his eyes. "My sympathies again, David. And best of luck on Monday."

David seemed moved. "Cheers, Trevor. Thanks very much."

Trevor stumbled to the centre table. He finished his pint, picked up another and drank it straight down. Then he reached for a third.

"Sit down, for heaven's sake," Chris said. "You're making a scene."

"Well, why not?" Trevor said, raising his voice. "We've no women left—they've turned out without even a goodbye! Poor David over there has lost his mother…"

Chris shook his head violently. "Shh!"

"No, thank you!" Trevor shouted. One of the dogs sat up and barked. "If I want to say something I'll say it. I'm sick of people holding things in."

"I think I'll be moving on," Henry said. David didn't move. He kept looking at the carpet.

Chris grasped Trevor's wrists. "Come along, Trevor. Sit down."

"No!" Trevor screamed. He pulled his hands free and pointed at the couple against the wall. "What about you two? Who are you, anyway? What is it you're after, parading around in Chalk like lovesick newlyweds?"

Chris stood up. "Trevor. Stop this right now before I—"

"It's all right," the man said. "I'm Paul, and this is my wife Maureen. Beverly's little sister."

David sat up. "Uncle Paul? Aunt Maureen? You came all the way down from Scotland?"

Her lips pressed together, Maureen rose from her chair. "Haven't seen you since you were a lad," she said. She crossed to the fire as David stood up to greet her. "Silly," she said, "how families drift apart. If it weren't for this young man's speech, I might never have had the courage to say hello."

THREE

Early Sunday morning, the doorbell rang. Mrs. Tilson stood in Henry's garden with a basket on her arm. She fished in her purse. "I know it might be a bit soon, but here are some dog advertisements. We both know you'll never find another Jack. But there's no shame in looking, Henry. And you're picking up your father this afternoon—don't forget."

"How did you know?"

"He rings every Sunday. To catch up on the village, I suppose."

Henry stood up too quickly and banged his head on the beam. His father might have rung his own son once in a while. "You didn't happen to mention Jack, did you? Dad was very attached to him."

"I certainly didn't, Henry." She straightened the basket on her arm. "But I don't have time to chat. I'm going up to Bates Farm to get a roast in. Dinner's at seven for the two of you, don't be late."

"Dinner…tonight?"

"Your father is most eager," Mrs. Tilson said over her shoulder, already walking away. "I don't imagine the food in that pensioners' home is very nice."

Henry closed the door. He sunk into his armchair and stared at the mantle holding the pewter flask, the wedding photo, the ticking clock. There were too many changes all at once. Jack dying, going to the pub with David Smith, dinner at Mrs. Tilson's—it was more tiring than digging graves. He dreaded driving into Brighton today.

Henry hated cities. Just thinking of Brighton made him nervous. In his mind he went over the turns he'd need to make, the time he'd need to allow to arrive properly. It had been six weeks since he'd last been. His father had needed collecting for Mrs. Tilson's Christmas dinner.

Henry had arrived at the pensioners' home a full hour ahead of schedule. His father was still taking a bath, the nurse told him, so Henry had waited outside in his van. It would have been normal—healthy, Mrs. Tilson would have said—to walk round the shops, visit some museum. But there were too many people in the city, too much clamour. Henry felt a guilty pleasure by sitting in the car park while everyone else went scrambling about, spending money and wasting time.

That was one good thing about Chalk—he never had to pretend. He started to say as much to Jack, but the cot stood empty. "A pathetic human being, I am," Henry said, unfolding Mrs. Tilson's newspaper cutting.

The dog advertisements were organised by breed. There were two listings for Jack Russells.

Four pedigree pups, £250 each, Humphrey Lodge, Berwick.

Two pups from litter of eight, females, £300, Mrs. McIntyre, Glynde.

Henry sat up and slapped his knees. Fourteen years, it was, since he'd found Jack. What had changed from then until today? There was a good chance he was wearing the same clothes.

Henry had never owned pets, growing up. "We've no need for animals," his father had said, as if referring to weeds. Frank's position on the matter had been relatively firm, but it became inflexible after Henry's mother died. After his father moved out, Henry had started to scan the listings. He'd seen photos of Jack Russells and liked them. The first puppy he saw, he paid for on the spot, and he'd named him after the breed.

Jack, as it turned out, was everything Henry had wanted in a dog. He took him on walks up to The Beacon and even to work. Jack would run after moles and rabbits, but he'd never cause a disturbance. Mostly the dog sat patiently, watching him dig. During the service he was almost respectful the way he waited beside the wheelbarrow with his chin on his paws. Henry had never seen Frank show affection to animals, but he'd spend hours with Jack, bending his head over the dog's face and whispering words nobody could hear.

"It's too soon," Henry said. He left the advertisements on the coffee table.

A few minutes later he was at the phone, making appointments. Both of the litters were at farmhouses toward Brighton, and he told himself that these stops were practically on the way. Before he could change his mind he fetched his car keys and set off.

Off the A-27, just before Glynde, a small white sign said Somerset Turkey Farm. Henry could smell the turkeys as he left the van. The smell didn't sit right with him, and though he walked up to the house, rang the doorbell and came inside, he knew he wouldn't be buying one of the farm's dogs. The puppies might have been perfectly fine, he realised, after it was all over and he'd said goodbye, but he couldn't remember anything about them.

The next farmhouse was a few miles down. Mrs. McIntyre, the manager of the bed-and-breakfast attached to the farm, met him at the door. "Only two remaining out of a litter of eight," she said, eyeing him significantly. She was a sturdy woman in an apron, with bare arms and a bun of black hair. She drew Henry inside her house like a wayward child.

They came through the sitting room and into the kitchen. In a basket against the wall, an elderly Jack Russell bitch lay panting on a blanket. The last two pups slept beside her. Mrs. McIntyre leaned into the basket. "Up we go," she said, raising them by the scruffs.

Henry stood back and tried not to stare. It was like looking into the sun. The dogs were blinking and yelping, and their little white legs kicked the air. One of them mewed like a cat. It had a black patch on its hind leg. Henry felt something inside of him shift. "No," he said, moving to the door, "I'm really looking for a male."

Mrs. McIntyre frowned. "The ad said female pups." She held out the one he'd liked and blocked his way. He was forced to encounter the animal once again—the white ball of fur, the pair of sad-looking eyes—and he turned to get away. Mrs. McIntyre quickly stepped in front of him, the puppy extended. "There, there," she said. "She's a good girl. Just needs the right home."

Averting his eyes, Henry managed to slip by. He hurried through the sitting room and opened the door, mumbling apologies. It wasn't until he reached his van that he felt safe.

"No need to rush things," he said, as he left the drive. As he idled at the entrance to the A-27, waiting for a break in traffic, he half expected Mrs. McIntyre to come running after him, the puppy in her hand.

Each time an opening presented itself, Henry's foot remained on the brake pedal. The little Jack Russell was right in front of him, it seemed, mewing, kicking its paws. At last he raced onto the motorway, and the signposts for Brighton forced him to pay attention.

* * *

The lobby of the West Brighton Old-Age Pensioners' Home held a square Formica table with plastic chairs. A plastic fern stood in the corner. Henry sat against the wall, facing the room. While waiting he thumbed through a gardening magazine.

"You're Frankie Bale's boy?" the counter nurse asked. She spoke to Henry while putting makeup on her nose. "You're lucky, having him for a dad. Frankie keeps us quite entertained."

Henry looked at her over the top of his magazine. He wondered if she'd confused his father with someone else. He'd never heard anyone refer to him as Frankie, nor had anyone found him the least bit entertaining. Mrs. Tilson said he rang every Sunday morning "to chat." Was it possible his father, at seventy-nine, had changed?

The double doors opened, and a nurse entered the lobby, pushing Frank in a wheelchair. His hair was still wet from his bath, and he wore a jacket and tie. Once sturdy, almost menacing, Frank had lost a great deal of weight. His blue eyes bulged like a frog's, and his hands looked enormous on his narrow wrists. "Hello, Dad," Henry said, standing. "When did you start needing a wheelchair?"

"A month now. Not much feeling left in my legs, I'm afraid."

Henry held the door for the nurse and ran ahead across the car park. They hoisted his father onto the passenger seat. The nurse collapsed the wheelchair, and Henry put it in the back of the van beside his tools. "Bye, Frankie," the nurse said, kissing his cheek through the open window. "Enjoy yourself at home now, dear."

All the way to Chalk, Frank just stared out the window. His dad saved his conversations for women and dogs, Henry gathered. As he drove, he remembered how it had been after his mother died, how the silence in the house had made him fearful to come home from school. He turned off the A-27 and down into the flatlands surrounding Chalk. "Jack died Friday," Henry said. "Went in his sleep."

Frank's ears moved back along his scalp. He kept looking out the window.

"The old boy wasn't moving much, toward the end. Wasn't eating either. He'd lost weight. Wasn't the same dog. I had an appointment scheduled with Tracy, but..." Henry waited. It was like talking to a wall. "I know how much you liked him."

Henry came into the village and parked outside his house. He wasn't looking forward to the evening of silence. "Sit tight," Henry said. "I'll just bring the wheelchair round." As he left the van he heard the passenger door open. "Dad?"

Frank had already made it through the gate. He thrusted himself along in short, lurching steps. Henry ran up behind him. "What is this, Dad? You've got feeling in your legs after all?"

Frank stood in the garden, studying Jack's grave. His shoulders, broad and bony, poked sideways inside his suit jacket. "Tell me, Henry. Are you content?"

"Pranks like that aren't very polite," Henry said, fumbling for the door key. "You can't pretend to be wheelchair-bound and have people running after you."

"Answer me," Frank said, taking his wrist. "Are you content?"

Henry pulled away. "I am...as I am." He unlocked the door and pushed it open. "What are you on about, anyway?"

Frank seemed ready to stand outside all night. "A stone is as it is. You're a human being, last I checked."

✳   ✳   ✳

Her roast sliced and served, Mrs. Tilson passed round the mashed potatoes and gravy. Next came the Brussels sprouts. Henry tried taking the server, but Frank held on. "You still haven't answered me," he said. "And you're not getting Brussels sprouts until you do."

Mrs. Tilson's house had exactly the same dimensions as Henry's. There, the similarity ended. Her walls were freshly painted, her curtains brushed. Flowers decorated on the mantle, the end table beside the settee, and the dining room table. The mantle was lined with photographs of her two boys and their families.

At the head of the table, Frank repeated the question. "Well, Henry? Are you content?"

Mrs. Tilson pulled at the ends of her shirtsleeves. She sat directly across from Henry. "Now, Frank," she said. "What's going on here?"

"You've prepared a lovely meal," Frank said. "Now be patient while I wait for my son to answer."

"Good God," Henry said, letting go of the server. "You can eat them all."

Mrs. Tilson pretended not to hear. "I almost forgot," she said, getting up. She went into the kitchen, returned with a bowl of horseradish, and placed it beside Frank's plate. "There you are, dear."

Frank served himself some sprouts and passed them back to Mrs. Tilson. "He doesn't get any," Frank said.

Mrs. Tilson sighed. "I'd very much like to know what this is all about."

"I asked Henry if he was content."

Mrs. Tilson leaned over and spooned some Brussels sprouts onto Henry's plate. "Shouldn't you mind you own business? People are content some of the time, and other times not. Henry's no different than anyone else." She frowned. "Well, no different than I am, anyway—I wouldn't presume to know about other people. Fancy you bringing up such a thing after Jack has died. You're having a hard time, that's all, because of the service tomorrow. Goodness knows the whole village is doing their best to cope."

"I'm not having any difficulty," Frank said. "Beverly Smith was eighty-four years old. And old Jack lasted longer than most dogs. There's no sense in mourning what needn't be mourned."

Henry tried his beef. He wondered what did warrant mourning, in his dad's opinion. He kept chewing, but he couldn't seem to get the beef to go down.

"Just because you've decided to try and enjoy yourself," Mrs. Tilson said, "doesn't mean others move at the same pace. Flirting with nurses doesn't automatically make you content, does it?"

"It does for me."

"Well, not everyone moves so quickly, do they?"

"I'm almost eighty. Henry's not moving with any pace at all!"

"That's enough, Frank," Mrs. Tilson snapped. "Now eat, both of you, before your food gets cold."

Henry looked at his plate. Mrs. Tilson had prepared a meal like this after his mother died. He'd turned seven that day, and after dinner she'd brought a birthday cake out with candles on it. Before they were allowed to eat, his father said he had an announcement to make. Even with Evelyn gone he was going to keep working, he'd said, keep working without fail, and he expected Henry to do the same at school. His son's seventh birthday, he said, would be the day everyone stopped mourning and returned to normal. Then Frank had started to say something else, but his mouth just stayed open, and soon he was crying into his hands. To this day Henry hated birthdays and celebrations of any kind.

Now, as he looked at his father's hands, Henry realised Frank had done what he'd pledged. He'd kept working. He'd dug and pushed and shovelled until he couldn't feel the wheelbarrow any longer. He'd worked as a way to forget. His fingers were proof—curled and knobbed, as if still wrapped around his spade. Henry knew his own hands were heading in the same direction, and he didn't have an excuse.

*   *   *

The sermon would have to be bright and hard, like a diamond. Why else climb the pulpit? Sitting in his pyjamas in his kitchen—the only place he ever felt clear-headed enough to write—Reverend Pierce pulled at his hair until it stood stiff on his scalp.

Penny brought down from his library the books he'd asked for— Berkeley's *Confessions*, Freud's *The Future of an Illusion*, Kierkegaard's *The Sickness Unto Death*. She stood there in her slippers and bathrobe as he stacked the books around his notepad. He leaned the Church of England's *Suggested Funeral Service Sermons* against the teapot as a reminder of the outmoded style he wanted to avoid.

The funeral presented an opportunity to place God permanently into the villagers' minds. These days it was too much to ask for, he knew, but if he understood his job, he'd been charged with this task the day he'd been ordained.

Penny stirred milk into his tea, kissed his head where the rows of hair had separated, and traipsed upstairs to bed. By the time she'd turned out the hallway light the vicar had given up trying to move the whole village. If he could get one, that would still be something. Over fifty of them would be crammed into the church, shivering, restless, barely listening, and he had to find a way to get at them— one of them, anyway, he'd settle for that.

The vicar read his favourite passages from Berkeley. They

provided moral sustenance, reminders of what he wanted most to believe. He savoured the confident, high-minded prose and let it transport him to a nobler time. Berkeley gave him courage. He'd need that for the Freud. He opened that next, with hesitation and dread, like a football manager opening the playbook of his opponent.

Reverend Pierce found a page at random and scoffed. Religion, a sublimation? God, an elaborate fantasy manufactured by subconscious impulses? Freudians wanted the world to sink into the mire. But the more the vicar read, the more he found himself in a sort of troubled awe. The arguments came neatly wrapped. The logic was scientifically precise, the language imbued with humour and insight and philosophical flair. Were the ideals he took for granted— such as salvation and grace—only replies to a fear of death?

Hunched over the square folding table under the lamplight, Reverend Pierce kept reading as the kitchen grew cold, the tea bitter. He reached for his Bible and thumbed through its pages in a frenzy, searching for a rebuttal. Too many of the verses read like stories now, fairy tales for children. He skimmed book after book, his favourites Mark and Corinthians and then the delightfully obscure Numbers. He got up from his chair and read standing up. He read as he paced the floor. He wasn't reading as much as simply turning pages, search for signs, his chin lowered like a charging bull's. Soon he'd banged his forehead on the cabinet.

"Damn!" He sat back on his chair, his ears ringing. The phrase "subconscious impulses" kept turning in his mind.

"Is everything all right?"

Penny stood at the bottom of the staircase in a mud mask and nightgown. "Yes," he said. "Go back to bed."

"I heard a noise."

"I'm fine." He did his best to smile.

She waited a while, her silence its own scepticism. "Why haven't you finished your tea?"

"I don't know."

"Wasn't it good?"

"I'm having difficulty with this bloody sermon, that's all. I'm fine."

She nodded. "Do you want to read me what you've got so far? That helps you sometimes, you know. Gives you further ideas."

"No thanks."

"You haven't written anything yet, have you? Don't worry," Penny said, as she went back up to bed. "You'll find something to say. You always do."

The vicar sat motionless in the cold. Then he seized the Kierkegaard, like a child unwrapping a Christmas gift. Yes, man despaired, and feared death, but his very despair gave birth to belief. It wasn't knowledge that mattered—it was faith. The humble proclamation of our ignorance only saved us if we were courageous enough to admit it.

The vicar folded his hands and said the Lord's Prayer. His notepad remained horribly blank. He opened the Kierkegaard again and considered summarising the main points. He could pay tribute to Beverly with a provocative sermon on faith. For his opening remarks he copied his favourite passage:

The real reason men are offended by Christianity is that it is too high, because its goal is not man's goal. Christianity wants to make man into something so extraordinary that he almost cannot grasp the thought.

The vicar balled up his paper. Words like these weren't appropriate for a funeral service. The villagers would think he'd gone mad. Exhausted, more confused than ever, he still had no idea what to write. The little booklet, *Suggested Funeral Service Sermons,* leaned against the teapot. It was the text his elders had prepared for exactly this predicament. Reverend Pierce opened it, and the first passage struck him as surprisingly fine. It seemed, in fact, a consolation of the very ideas he'd been struggling with, a declaration of fact in simple, powerful prose.

In the midst of life, we are in death.

* * *

At dawn Henry dressed quickly and rubbed his knees to get warm. The night had been a difficult one. He'd woken a number of times shivering and cursing his stupidity for forgetting to turn on the heat. He'd given his father the only duvet in the house, which left only a thin blanket for himself.

In the bathroom he studied his reflection in the mirror. Did everyone in Chalk think he was discontent? He heard Frank stirring in the guest room and wondered if all retired gravediggers kept rising at dawn out of habit.

It was even colder downstairs. Henry hurried into the kitchen, where he made a plate of eggs and toast. He ate quickly and fixed a second plate for his father. Upstairs, footsteps scraped toward the landing. "I'm going out now, Dad," Henry called. He heard Frank grunt as he worked his way down.

The evening's frost had whitened the grass. It would to be a clear day if the morning stars were bright enough to see by. His pick was buried in the back of the van, and Henry had to crawl inside to fetch it. "Christ!" he cried, doubling over and clutching his hip. The sharp, stabbing pain had found him again. Climbing gingerly out, he tossed his tools into the wheelbarrow and made his way across the road to St. Margaret's.

Chalk's church was the oldest structure in the village. There was a chancel, a nave, and a steeple with missing shingles, as if the parish had run out of money during construction. The church stood surrounded by an increasing number of headstones, as if under attack. The limestone walls dripped with moisture, even on a sunny day.

Henry pushed his wheelbarrow up the path that led from the gate to the front door. An enclosed entryway held a notice board where news was posted, when there was any. Other churches advertised art exhibitions, food drives, book clubs. St. Margaret's notice board held only a yellowed copy of The Church of England Table of Parochial Fees:

Wedding Service – £44. Funeral Service - £68. Burial in churchyard following on from service in church - £123. Burial in churchyard without service in church - £148.

The door was made of heavy oak, as if designed to keep people out. A black iron ring served as a handle. The church remained unlocked day and night, but few exercised the privilege. Reverend Pierce normally presided over a congregation of six, including the organist. A strong smell of mildew lingered inside—Henry heard it came from rotting choir robes, unused for decades, locked away in a forgotten wardrobe. He continued around the side of the church, past the stained glass windows faded to variations of grey. The last time Henry attended church—another funeral—the wind had whistled through cracks in the window frames. Above the nave, two circular chandeliers hung from chains. Shadows danced on the pulpit, which loomed at a frightening height, just below the eaves. Even the congregation stalls seemed designed for intimidation. Built of the hardest oak and outfitted with latching doors, the stalls felt like medieval stockades.

Henry brought the wheelbarrow to the graveyard at the back. Grassy mounds rose here and there. Chalk deposits ran beneath the topsoil. There was one door at the back of the church, and it led to the cellar. Henry stopped and jiggled the handle. He hoped one day to find it unlocked, but as far as he could tell the cellar hadn't been used in centuries. Next to the door, a window the size of a handkerchief looked into the Wembles' private chapel. Inside, alabaster effigies of the first Lord and Lady Wembles, George and Anne, lay recumbent against the wall, their stone hands folded over their chests. Henry headed toward the Smith grave, up and over the mounds. The churchyard might have been a burial ground for elephants.

There were four trees—a Scotch pine, a willow, and two ancient yews, bending toward the neighbouring pastures. A three-foot shrub separated the churchyard from the school playground. A wooden bench sat beside a footpath, dividing the grounds into two sections. On the north side, newer headstones formed neat, upright rows. Some were currently decorated with flowers. On the southern side the headstones were mostly unreadable.

Hetherington had removed Horace Smith's memorial—at David's request, Henry guessed, to get the letter cutter started. To Horace's left a granite stone read, *In Loving Memory of Madge Constance Lewis, of Chalk, Who Died 20th May 1991, Aged 86 Years. He who Believeth in Me, Though he Die, Yet Shall He Live.* Henry would have dug this grave, but he couldn't remember anything about Madge. To the right, an older headstone was faintly legible, *Sacred to the Memory of Lucy, Beloved Wife of James Ellis, of this Parish, who Departed this life March 10, 1895, aged 39 Years. Also of their Son, Belton James, Who died April 25, 1884, aged six weeks. I Know that my Redeemer Liveth.*

"Here we go, then, Beverly."

Henry paced off the coffin's measurements. Using the edge of his spade, he carved an outline in the frosty turf. Then he broke the plot into smaller sections and lifted out the turf with a pitchfork. Soon, he was digging through the topsoil. His joints loosened. His blood warmed. Veins of chalk surfaced, jamming his spade like cement. Henry used the pick to break it apart, swinging patiently, conserving energy until it crumbled before him into white powder.

The sun slipped above the horizon. It brought no tangible warmth. By the end of the hour Henry had carted four loads away. After his final load he left the wheelbarrow near the path and crossed to the willow in the corner of the churchyard. Under the tree a small granite headstone stuck out of the grass. The sides were streaked with lime, but the lettering was clear: *Evelyn Bale, 4th June, 1939 – 12 December, 1970. Rest in Peace.* Space had been left at the bottom of the stone for Frank.

Henry wished he'd had more memories of his mother. She had been tall with gentle eyes. His favourite memory of her was in the old Vauxhall. She'd been sitting next to Frank and pointing across a field of grass. Henry didn't know why, but he always made sure to think of this beside her grave. The other memories were hospital visits mostly, leaving school to drive down to the cancer ward in Brighton. He remembered how she'd been bald as an egg as she gripped the end of her blanket. Not long after that, his father had been out here, digging under the tree.

It would have been difficult digging, with all the tree roots and the chalk. Henry stamped his feet to keep warm. Soon he'd be digging at this spot himself. His dad, after all, was getting on. Henry returned to the Smith plot and shovelled straight onto the tin sheet. As the mound formed, he sunk slowly into the earth.

FOUR

Play time!"

Caroline Ford expected a rush to the door, but Beverly's pupils, eight and nine years old, remained defiantly in their seats. They were testing her. Their teacher's death offered an advantage.

Caroline had been waiting for a village like this. At twenty-seven she already felt too old for Brighton. When her employment agency told her a supply teacher was needed in a place called Chalk, the village sounded appealing. She'd become tired of nightclubs, and evenings that flew by quickly by without anything left behind. Her eyes had two shades, one a deeper green than the other. Her black hair curled, it seemed, in every direction. Her friends called her a gypsy.

The pupils kept to their seats as if by agreement, waiting for Caroline to betray discomfort. She decided to slip outdoors by herself. The class followed. From the top step overlooking the playground, Headmaster Briggs studied her as she brought the class outside. Briggs kept a tidy helmet of white hair and carefully cultivated eyebrows that turned up at the ends.

The pupils ran for the swings, began games of jacks, formed sides for football. Caroline drifted to the edge of the playground. On the other side of the boundry hedge, the churchyard seemed of a darker, colder age. The walls of the church deflected daylight. The lonely trees stood draped with frost. Nearby, a gravedigger was working. Dirt flew over his shoulder as if from a machine.

That was Beverly Smith's grave, Caroline realised. A hand grasped her elbow and she jumped.

A man in an olive green suit smiled at her. "You're the supply teacher?" The man's hair was thinning, but his eyes looked somewhat intelligent. "I'm Darren Roberts."

"A pleasure," she said. He was openly staring. Wind gusted across the playground, giving her the opportunity to turn away. "You're Deputy Head."

"I am."

"You've a lovely school here. A nice village."

He laughed. "Chalk?"

"I think it is."

"You haven't been here long. Are you from Sussex?"

"Not originally."

"Where, then?"

Here it came, Caroline thought—the flurry of questions, the requisite dissection of her background. Caroline considered such facts irrelevant. To keep things interesting, she sometimes lied. "Nottinghamshire," she said, telling the truth this time for safety's sake. "In a perfectly benign village called Pevingly. But I've been in Brighton the past nine years."

Darren nodded. "You went to university there. Me too. And Chalk, you think, is preferable to Brighton?" He cocked his head, exaggerating his surprise.

"They're obviously very different, aren't they? I mean, do you like taking a drive into the country or gorging yourself on Indian takeaway? They're both enjoyable."

"And what about—"

"My boyfriend? He's on the way out."

Darren turned pale. "I wasn't asking about that."

She pretended not to have heard. She'd almost completely turned her back to Darren. Something about the gravedigger—the movement of the man's shoulders, perhaps—distracted her. "My sympathies," she said. "I understand Beverly was everything to this village."

"Most people thought so. She—sorry, am I bothering you?"

"Not at all," she said, facing him once more. "I have a bad habit of daydreaming."

Darren peered over the hedge. "Look at that chap dig. The builders on my house aren't working like that. It's taking them months to add a blasted wing."

"People ignore you when you're alive." Darren kept staring. "Don't pay attention to anything that comes out of my mouth,"

Caroline said.

An elderly man in a suit lurched up the churchyard path.

"That's our chap's father, there," Darren said. "He used to do the gravedigging in this churchyard."

"Amazing how everyone knows each other. Have you lived in Chalk long?"

"Six years," Darren said. "Six, long, tiresome years. I worked previously in Hailsham. Never heard of it? A metropolis, compared to Chalk. A relative urban empire. Six years here and it seems like my entire life. It's bloody rare, I may as well tell you candidly, to meet someone like you. I mean, someone who—"

There was a loud, high-pitched wail. A girl came running across the playground, face red, pigtails bouncing. Caroline held out her arms, but the girl pointed to a paper aeroplane, sailing high over the hedge toward Beverly's grave.

*　*　*

Henry had made good progress through the dirt and chalk—over three feet. As he hoisted himself out of the grave, he gasped. His father's head sat propped on the neighbouring headstone.

Frank stood up with a grin. He was already in his suit, dressed for the service. "Surprised you, didn't I?"

"Not really." His dad's pranks were getting on his nerves. "I was just stopping for lunch."

"You've been motoring!" Frank said, coming over to the grave. "You're almost at Horace's coffin, and it's just gone ten!"

Henry wiped his forehead with his sleeve. He was breathing heavily, and dripping wet. "Yes, I suppose…"

"Look at you sweat! You ought to slow down, boy. If you get hurt, the vicar will have to finish. I'm certainly not getting pressed into service." Frank laughed.

Henry stared at the ground. He hadn't heard his father laugh in years. He took his spade and circled the grave, flicking in stray pieces of dirt.

"That's it, get that grass spotless. And don't forget the area around the mound."

"I won't." Henry unbuttoned his overalls. He couldn't stop

sweating, even out in the cold.

"It's bloody freezing out here," Frank said, catching his breath. "And you look like you've been for a swim!"

"A man works, a man sweats," Henry said.

Frank stopped laughing and pointed at the mound. "What's that?"

Henry leaned over, his hands on his knees. There was a paper aeroplane, perfectly folded, resting on top of the soil. "Must have come from the school."

Over at the hedge, someone shouted. "Wonderful," Henry said. A small crowd had formed. One of the pupils—a red-faced girl with pigtails—was pointing at him.

"Better take it back over to them, boy."

"I know, Dad." Henry wiped his hands on his overalls. He took the aeroplane by the nose and made his way over to the hedge.

*　*　*

Only after he'd returned to the grave, and his father started asking about his boots—how long ago he'd bought them, how much longer he thought they'd last—did Henry digest what had happened. "It was last September I picked them up," he said absently, glancing back at the school. The supply teacher had liked him. She'd started staring as soon as he'd reached the hedge. Her eyes had been green. "Three months they've got, maybe more."

He'd felt it more than seen it. She'd locked onto him with those eyes, too beautiful for Chalk. The girl with the pigtails had snatched the aeroplane out of his hand without even a thank you, and then the boy's questioning had begun.

"You're digging Mrs. Smith's grave, aren't you?"

Henry nodded. It wasn't the first time a child had spoken to him. The teacher's eyes were still on him then. The Deputy Head, Darren Roberts was his name, started herding the pupils away.

"So it's true she's dead, then?"

Henry located him—an older boy, smirking, his arms folded. Some pupils stood on their tiptoes, craning their necks over the hedge. The girl with the pigtails started wailing even though she had her aeroplane back.

"Did Mrs. Smith die?" one of the younger boys asked. He sat

on the ground.

"All of us will," the older boy said. "And this man will dig our graves. Unless he dies first, of course."

"That's enough, Sam," Darren said. "Come inside."

"Is it, Mr. Roberts?" the boy kept on. "Is it enough now, or after I ask my next question? I want to ask this gravedigger," he said, his voice getting louder, "where Mrs. Smith is, right this moment. Is she lying on a table? I want to know—"

Darren took the boy forcibly toward the school. Only then, Henry remembered, did the teacher stop staring. It gave him an opportunity to take a good look—the bare arms exposed by the rolled-up sleeves, the full mouth, the hair black and wild like gorse. She'd scooped up the little boy on the ground and carted him off to the school. Henry had stayed at the hedge, eyes darting, until the sound of his own voice startled him. "Must be Beverly Smith's replacement." Even after he'd returned to the grave her image wouldn't leave his mind.

"Still a couple of months on those boots?"

Frank wrung his hands.

"I'd go through mine faster. And that was back when they made them properly, Henry. When the stitches held. It wasn't the stitches that broke, mind you—it was the damn soles."

"I know."

"Sometimes I wish I were still digging."

"I know, Dad." With effort, Frank leaned over and picked up the shovel. He held it out with both hands, like an infant.

Henry went over the woman again in his mind's eye. She'd been wearing a dark blue skirt. How long had it been since he'd noticed a woman's skirt? She wasn't even thirty. She was beyond his reach even if she did stay in Chalk, which she wouldn't if she had any sense. There was no point in thinking about it, but he did anyway, down the churchyard path and all the way back to the house for lunch, ahead of his father so the old man could walk alone and unexamined.

The teacher would be at the church service. Henry paced in his kitchen, trying in vain to stop thinking of her. He needed to press his suit. He needed to trim his beard and the hairs in his nose. The kettle was ready for his tea but he ignored the whistle. As he walked back and forth in the kitchen it was his father who took it off the hob, regarding him suspiciously as he poured the water into the pot.

✳ ✳ ✳

It was the gravedigger's innocence that attracted Caroline the most. The students were reading and finally calm. Her hands folded on Beverly Smith's desk, Caroline went over everything about him—how his voice rumbled as if from the ground, how he'd lingered at the hedge, blushing like a boy. A pupil in the third row raised her hand.

"Miss Ford?"

Caroline hurried to the girl's desk and helped with a vocabulary word. Then she returned to Beverly's chair and gazed out the window. The gravedigger was about forty, she guessed, and he had the demeanour of an adolescent. She imagined taking him on a picnic to make him confess what it was that attracted him to her. Then she'd make her own confession. It was the honesty of his gaze, she'd say, the strength in his shoulders, the way his hair covered his ears.

"You looked like a gentle savage, holding that aeroplane," she'd say, watching his reaction. None of her friends in Brighton would find her in Chalk, going about with a country gravedigger. The man was a throwback, like Chalk itself. He was silent, unassuming, odd. Who did she know that embodied an entire village?

Pevingly had been something like Chalk. Growing up, Caroline had felt her neighbours constantly whispering, forming judgements. She couldn't choose her friends in peace. Brighton gave her the freedom she wanted. It also offered men like Trent.

They'd been seeing each other steadily for months. She went to clubs to watch him play drums in his rock band. She drank with him, listened to his friends. It seemed at first he had an expansive mind. But over time she realised the opposite was true. Trent never really cared about anything other than his own views. He was just as provincial as the men of Pevingly, and he deemed himself profound. Trent belonged to an urbane, self-anointed Brighton set of artists who held opinions as dogmatically as the people they rejected. One night she told him his failings—this habit was her own failing—and ever since, they'd started arguing. Their future was plain enough. He'd grow steadily morose. She'd become disillusioned with him and pretend she wasn't. One day, he'd take a position in sales, and they'd split up.

Fantasising about the gravedigger gave her much more pleasure. Caroline clunked her knees together, thinking about him. They hadn't even had a conversation! But she was a believer in first impressions. You could tell a great deal about a man by the way he stood at a hedge and spoke to children. The gravedigger had a kind of patient intelligence—it was obvious from his expression. He seemed unhindered by ambition, uncorrupted by guile.

What if she could stay in Chalk for the whole school year? It had been a long time since she'd felt attached to a landscape, a community. Fancy desiring a gravedigger! He'd be at Beverly's funeral service, most likely. Reaching under the desk, Caroline grasped her knees and held them still.

* * *

Henry waited in the shadows near the door of the church. After finishing the grave, he'd rushed home to wash and change into his suit. Now as his eyes adjusted he realised there were shapes beside him, shuffling, blowing their hands in the cold. Here and there, above the organ, sneezes and coughs rose from the stalls.

A stream of light shot down the nave, illuminating the empty trestle. At the organ, William Harvey's blond hair shone. In one of the stalls, Frank's overlarge head loomed beside a hat that looked like Mrs. Tilson's. There were whispers and the scraping shoes. Out of the shadows the teacher appeared. Henry shrunk back and right away she turned, sensing his movement. Her eyes took him hungrily. The pupils followed her into the church. Headmaster Briggs and Darren Roberts pulled up the rear, herding the children forward until they formed a single line along the left wall. The door creaked shut. The church darkened.

Henry couldn't stop smiling, even after the bearers had brought in Beverly's coffin and rested it on the trestle. Disrespectful as it was, there was nothing he could do about it—the corners of his mouth just wouldn't come down. It was too dark for anyone to see. He kept thinking of her flickering green eyes, and he barely noticed Reverend Pierce up in the chancel. The vicar's hands trembled with what looked like nerves. He stepped forward in his white robe, flanking the coffin and William Harvey stopped playing the organ.

"The eternal God is thy refuge," the vicar said, reading from his Bible. "I know that my Redeemer liveth. The Lord redeemeth the soul of his servants, and none that trusteth in Him shall be desolate." He made a motion toward the cross. William Harvey played a chord, and Reverend Pierce sang alone.

"You Christ are the King of glory:
The eternal Son of the Father..."

Henry's mind opened like a trap door. Voices flew at him, arguing all sides. *She's only here a few days. You never know—maybe she'll stay longer. She won't, not if she's normal. Regardless, talk to her as soon as possible.*

"When you became man to set us free:
You did not abhor the Virgin's womb..."

At the grave, after the service. Sounds rash. What are you going to do, hope she watches the filling-in and then talk to her as you're shovelling dirt? It doesn't matter. Why not? Because I'll never have a chance with her anyway.

"You overcame the sting of death:
And opened the kingdom of heaven to all believers."

William Harvey stopped playing. Reverend Pierce moved to the podium below the pulpit, opened his Bible, straightened his reading glasses. "From the fourteenth chapter of the Book of John. 'Let not your hearts be troubled; believe in God, believe also in me. In my Father's house are many rooms; if it were not so, would I have told you that I go to prepare a place...'"

You need to act now, you fool, and talk to her. What's the point? The point is she's from another world, a miracle.

The vicar closed the Bible. "Words alone will not quell our pain. But if there are words, the word of our Lord should be our starting point. As it is written in Corinthians, 'My beloved brethren, be steadfast, immovable...'"

I'm happy on my own. Then? Then what? Then that's all you'll ever be, alone, partner to a series of dogs.

"Beverly Smith was respected, and she was loved. The proof is here before us—in her family and friends, her current and former students, gathered to pay respects. Beverly was Chalk's truest teacher."

You have to talk to her. A funeral's hardly the time. With you there's never a good time. Oh, leave me alone. I won't—you saw the way she looked at you, you shouldn't forfeit this possibility and let her think you incapable.

"Is there ever reason to despair when the Lord is our redeemer? Today, Beverly joins her husband Horace forever. God-fearing, she discovers the kingdom of heaven. 'I will not leave you desolate,' the Lord has told us. 'I will come to you.'"

The congregants rose in their stalls. The bearers, like a gang of murderers, slinked toward the coffin on the trestle. Someone started sobbing. The bearers surrounded Beverly and hoisted her onto their shoulders. Reverend Pierce led the procession out.

Henry lowered his head as the stalls emptied. The teacher would pass by soon. How long had it been since he'd looked straight at a woman, with his feelings on display? Not since his pub days, and even then it was never like this, never a juncture that felt urgent. The footsteps disappeared. The church fell silent.

* * *

Reverend Pierce was still reading by the time Henry joined the crowd in the churchyard. The wind had dropped, and the sun fought through the clouds. Beverly's relatives gathered at the open grave, and around them the entire village had assembled. People filled the length of the path. They bunched together in burial plots. They inched forward and back, jostling for a view of the coffin.

Henry stayed at a distance. He'd see the coffin soon enough. Reverend Pierce spoke at the head of the grave with Penny just behind. To their right, in black woollen coats, stood Samuel and Georgina Wembles. Lord Wembles resembled a tall cardboard crane. Georgina looked bloated, as if cotton balls had been placed in both her cheeks. Kevin Yapton appeared beside them, panting and flustered from moving his family toward the spot near the royalty. His young daughters wore identical tweed coats and kept pulling at each other's hair. Kevin's wife Belinda, thin and bird-like, swallowed the air in little gasps.

Henry searched for David Smith and found him barely standing. His wife had her arms round his waist. Their children—a girl and two younger boys—shot nervous glances at the coffin. David's two brothers looked well-dressed and athletic. Each had wives with tinted blond hair, and each of the wives looked after their own children. David's aunt and uncle from Scotland stood nearby, holding hands.

Frank occupied the foot of the grave. The might have been reading right to him, but he appeared more interested in the placement of Henry's end boards. Mrs. Tilson stood at his side, her hand in the crook of his arm. Henry scanned the remaining faces— William Harvey, Sid Book, Vickie Eckleton, Roger the butler and his wife Pat, the Wembles' gatekeeper Dick Miles and his wife Bea, Trevor Nelson, Chris Crawley, Mr. and Mrs. Bates, who owned the dairy farm at the bottom of The Beacon. Even Oliver Marsh had made it. He stood alone under the Scotch pine.

Reverend Pierce finished his reading and started another. Henry edged closer. John Hetherington, grinning as usual, waited with his brass pot. Some schoolchildren stood behind the burial mound, Headmaster Briggs on one end, Darren Roberts on the other.

Suddenly, the vicar raised his voice. His final words thundered across the churchyard, and everyone looked up. "If you remember nothing else today, remember these words of the Lord: 'In the midst of life, we are in death!'"

Henry looked up, too. He'd heard the phrase before—the epitaph marked hundreds of headstones—but hearing it now, searching for the teacher in a state of near desperation, made him think of its meaning for the first time. His entire life collected to a single point, and that point represented nothing. "In the midst of life, we are in death," he whispered. Others were whispering it as well.

Hetherington sprinkled mole dirt on the coffin. Henry was near tears. It didn't make sense for her to be gone. She'd been at the church. Where in the world could she have found to hide? Finally, a figure shifted behind Beverly's burial mound, and the teacher came into view. She stepped out into an open area of grass, leading a girl by the hand. Time seemed to move again, to offer hope. Henry started toward her while rehearsing his hello.

It seemed everyone examined the replacement teacher. The bearers ogled at her as they lowered the coffin. Women pointed. John Hetherington gawked at her from behind. Henry kept coming until Trevor Nelson bounded over the burial mounds. Darren Roberts tried to block his way, but it was no use. The woman had turned the men of Chalk into jackals.

"Get back! You'll scare the children." Darren held out his arms like fence posts.

Trevor flipped Darren's tie into his face. "Move out of my way."

"Sorry," Darren said, still holding out his arms. Behind him, the replacement teacher watched. "You're drunk," he said, "and I won't let you past in your condition."

"I'll give you one more chance to get out of my way," Trevor said.

The teacher led the little girl toward the school. Trevor started after her, and Henry did too. She'd stared at him, after all—not at any of the others. Someone clutched his arm. "Just the filling in, then?"

It was David Smith. Henry peered over David's shoulder.

"I'm ready now," David said, his voice wobbling. "Ready to help with the filling in." His wife blinked at them, her eyes smudged with mascara. "Go on, dear," he told her. "Take the kids back to the house. Henry and I are going to finish Mum's grave."

FIVE

Down the motorway, as he took Frank back to Brighton, Henry welcomed the silence. He didn't feel like scrutinising himself, and he certainly didn't want his father filling in the gaps. But as he turned off the A-27 into the outskirts of Brighton, Frank's bulging blue eyes bore down on him.

"No missing that supply teacher."

Henry rolled down his window to create the illusion of distance. He sped up, pushed through the traffic lights. The old man's presence had become stifling. Even after Beverly's funeral, as David sat doubled over and helpless on the churchyard bench, Frank lingered by the grave, surveying the placement of the soil.

"Could be she becomes permanent," Frank added.

Henry tried to roll down the window some more, but it was all the way down. "What are you getting at, Dad?"

"I'm not blind. I saw you clamouring along with everyone else."

"I wasn't clamouring, I just—oh, it doesn't matter. A woman like that won't stay in Chalk."

Frank pointed at a pub. "Pull in here."

"I don't feel like it, Dad. I'm done in."

"One drink."

"No."

"It's what I miss the most. A nice pint in a pub. They don't let me have beer in that damn place."

Henry pulled in. It was just like his father to use guilt like a weapon. Inside, he bought two pints and brought them to the back where Frank had already found an open table. It was a newer pub, or one that had been made to look new—there were pachinko machines, neon beer signs, televisions lining the walls.

Frank loosened his tie and gulped down his beer. "I don't know what to make of you," he said. "Maybe if you'd done better at school, things would have been different. But you never really tried, did you? You never cared about advancing yourself."

"A nice conversation starter, you are." Henry took a sip of beer. "You can't have it both ways, you know—you can't criticise me and be a concerned father at the same time."

"I'm trying to help you, boy." Frank waggled his finger. "You hear me? You don't have to keep digging. You don't have to stay in Chalk. You're still young, damn you."

Henry watched the spittle fly from of his father's mouth. It was like looking into the future, except worse. At least his father had something to show for his life—he'd married, he'd fathered a child. As he looked into his beer Henry tried to recall when he'd decided to dig. It wasn't a decision as much as an avoidance of one. "You're just thinking about yourself, Dad," he muttered. "Wondering what you could have done differently. This has nothing to do with me."

"It's been years since you've had a shag. Years. You used to at least do that."

"I can manage my own life."

"But you aren't managing it, Henry. You act like you've already finished it."

"I'm not the one being dropped off at a pensioners' home."

He'd let the old man chew on that one, Henry thought. They drank in silence like strangers. When Frank finished his pint he lurched out of the pub. He was out in the car park at the van when Henry reached him. "You all right, Dad?"

Frank gripped the door handle. Sweat dripped from his temples. "Open it," he said.

"Let me help you in." Henry took his father's arm, but Frank swatted his hand away. Henry held the door and the old man swung himself inside. They drove the rest of the way without a word. Then, as they pulled into the pensioners' home, Frank jumped out of the van before they'd stopped.

"Hold on, you fool!"

Henry slammed on the brake. His dad had killed himself, he was sure of it. He got out of the van in a panic.

Somehow Frank had landed on his feet. He stood in the car park scowling at the sky, as if angry with God for letting him live.

✳   ✳   ✳

The day after Beverly's funeral, Headmaster Briggs offered Caroline a permanent position. She accepted immediately because she didn't want to change her mind. She'd always wanted to teach in a country village, she told him. It was the opportunity, she added, of a lifetime.

After leaving his office Caroline wandered the village. This took about twenty minutes. Exploring took around twenty minutes. What had she done? She tried to convince herself that Chalk *was* an opportunity of a lifetime. She expected the terrace houses squeezed together, the dark and depressing pub, the tiny shop with its dated goods. But at four in the afternoon, how could everyone already be indoors? The village seemed not there—or if it was there, sent down as a test from God. She went into the pub for a cup of tea, beset by dread.

Darkness, like a living force, dominated The Black Ram's bar. It crept into the snuggery and blanketed the windows. It brought a heaviness to the air, a leaden feeling of fatigue and misery that had been compounded over the centuries. Caroline stood by the door, her eyes adjusting to the darkness, and she realised she wasn't alone. A man stood behind the bar watching her. He was bald and pale, the colour drained out of him after years of standing exactly where he was now, surrounded by packages of crisps.

"Afternoon," he said, nodding to her.

"Hello," she said. "What's your name?"

"It's been a long time since anyone's asked me that." He smiled. "I'm Sid. Sid Book."

"A pleasure to meet you. I'm Caroline Ford. I've just agreed to replace Beverly Smith."

"Chalk will never be the same."

"May I have a cup of tea here?"

"Of course you can."

She sat at the bar. To her left, two men resumed the conversation that had been suspended by her arrival. Evidently one of the men worked for Lord Wembles. "I'm going to cut the melon early tomorrow," he announced. He was an elderly Scot with a lazy eye. "I don't care what Wembles says about the ends browning."

The other man shot his friend a malicious smile. He was younger, but not by much. "Of course you care what Wembles thinks."

"I don't."

"Yes you do. You'll cut the melon just as he asks. You'll cut it right before you serve it tomorrow, even if it means you running round at the last minute like a chicken with its head cut off. You'd cut it with a cricket bat if he asked you to. That's why he's lord, and you're the butler."

The Scot grunted on his stool. From the back of the pub, Sid brought out Caroline's tea. He took her money and gave her change from a cigar box. In her pocket, Caroline felt her mobile vibrate. It was a text from Trent. Rather than read it, she turned the phone off. Then she found a notebook in her handbag and started a letter.

Dear Trent,

I needed a change. It was fun with us, but it would have been stupid to keep on pretending. You'll probably think I'm searching for myself. That may be. I don't think that's such a bad thing. Here we are fighting and it's only in my letter. Anyway, I've decided to take a job in the country. Right now I need the sort of place I don't feel lost in. I don't expect you to understand, but I thought I owed you at least an explanation.

All the best,

Caroline

"Sid," Caroline said, "do you ever have music here at the pub? You know, where the locals bring in fiddles and accordions?"

"No, nothing like that."

"I noticed you don't have a billiards table."

"No."

"But you've a dart board, I see. Does Chalk have a team in a league?"

"Haven't seen anyone play darts here," Sid said, wiping the bar with his rag.

"What about a karaoke machine?"

"Sorry. About all you'll get round here is conversation."

Caroline looked at the Scot. He seemed to have been waiting for an opportunity to speak. He pushed his pint glass across the mat. "One more, please, Sid," he said.

✳　✳　✳

After posting her letter to Trent, Caroline headed for the bus stop to wait for the afternoon service to Brighton. A farmhouse at the edge of the villiage had a small bungalow beside it with a weathered Bed and Breakfast sign tilting over the road. A woman in a nightgown and hair net opened the door. She leaned over a newspaper on the step. Seeing Caroline, she jumped.

"Sorry to bother you," Caroline said.

"I'm just getting out of the bath," the woman said.

"I won't keep you. I noticed your bungalow. If it's available on a monthly basis, I'm prepared to move in straight away."

The woman steadied herself in the doorframe.

"I'm Karen. Karen Bates. And that's my husband Glen."

She pointed at the near pasture, where a man walked rigidly toward a barn, a bucket in each hand. Caroline came partway up the drive. "My name is Caroline. I'm the new teacher at the school."

"Come along," Mrs. Bates said, taking Caroline by the hand. Still in her nightgown, she led her across the grass and up to the front door of the bungalow. It was unlocked. "You might change your mind after you see it."

"How lovely," Caroline said, as they came inside. She meant it—there was plenty of room and lots of light. The kitchen opened into a dining room and even had a view of The Beacon. The bedroom had the same view.

"There's a small patio," Mrs. Bates said, opening the back door. A settee and two chairs looked across the open field.

"It's ideal," Caroline said. "And so close to the school. I won't change my mind after all."

"Glen won't believe it. Neither will my friend Penny. Think of it—you staying with us! Now you'll be quite safe here," Mrs. Bates said, showing her how the lock on the door worked. "It's an important thing to keep in mind. Considering all the men you'll be contending with."

"I'm sorry?"

Mrs. Bates patted her hair net. "Gaping at you, they were, during Beverly's funeral."

Caroline laughed. "They just haven't gotten to know me yet."

"Do you have a boyfriend?"

"Not any more. As of today, as a matter of fact."

"Oh, dear. You'll be kept busy at first. It won't do to appear completely unreceptive. Not in Chalk."

"I think this is all very silly," Caroline said, moving to the kitchen window.

"Take my word for it," Mrs. Bates said, following her. "There's a shortage of available women in the village. Now, if you want my advice—"

They turned. Darren Roberts stood in the open doorway, ringing the bell. "I thought I spotted you in here, Caroline."

Mrs. Bates shot Caroline a knowing glance. "She's moving in!"

"Come for supper to celebrate. I'm on my way home right now—how about you join me?"

"I was on my way to Brighton," Caroline said. "As you can see I haven't been able to move all my things over in the past five minutes." Mrs. Bates raised her eyebrows at her, and Caroline produced a smile. "But I suppose I could manage tomorrow night."

✳ ✳ ✳

Mrs. McIntyre stayed squarely in the doorway, her hands on her hips. "Just looking again, are you? Or have you come to buy?"

"I'm quite sure," Henry said, holding up his billfold.

"Put your money away, dear, no need to rush. Come inside."

She led him through to the kitchen. In the wicker basket there was only one puppy left.

Mrs. McIntyre lifted the pup out. "Just the little one now."

Henry searched for the black patch on her hind leg. It was there. The dog squirmed out of Mrs. McIntyre's hands and into Henry's arms.

"She's getting that beard wet," Mrs. McIntyre said, trying to take the pup back.

Henry held on. "I've got her. I am buying her, after all."

"You're sure, then?"

"Quite sure." Henry started to leave and realised he hadn't yet paid. "Sorry—hold onto her, please, while I get your money."

"There, there," Mrs. McIntyre said, cradling the dog like a baby. "I almost hate to see her go. What are you going to name her?"

"I haven't thought of it." Henry didn't want to go over the possibilities in Mrs. McIntyre's kitchen. He left the money on her table and waited.

Mrs. McIntyre scratched the pup behind its ears. "Let's see. What I've been calling her is—"

"My last dog was Jack," Henry said quickly, taking her back. "So I'll name this one Jackie."

∗   ∗   ∗

Henry's first stop was the vet's. Tracy Briggs shared the house with his twin brother Robert Briggs, the school Headmaster. The boys had never left home. They were rumoured to have shared a bedroom until their mother died two years ago. Henry had dug the grave. Apart from Tracy and Robert, there hadn't been anybody at the service. It made Henry wonder who might come to his own funeral. Everyone he knew would probably be dead.

He rang the bell and heard the buzz that unlocked the front door from the surgery. He came through a sitting room cluttered with books and empty cages. In the surgery, an elderly woman sat holding a guinea pig. Tracy's nurse Peggy swept a pile of reddish hair into a corner. "Henry," she said, smiling sadly, "I am sorry about Jack."

Peggy put her broom down and squeezed his wrist. Henry looked at her hand on his skin—the first time in ages someone had touched him—and right away it was gone. Tracy wheeled a cart loaded with instruments toward the operating table. He switched on the light over the green rubber sheet. Tracy looked like his brother, except he stooped. He had eyebrows that turned up at the ends and a habit of pointing his chin at people when he spoke.

"You'll have to wait a minute, Mrs. Jenison," Tracy said. "I want to get this pup out of the way ."

The woman with the guinea pig nodded. "I don't think she's gone into labour."

Tracy took Jackie out of Henry's hands and placed her on the operating table. "I'll need a distemper shot," he said.

Peggy sterilized her hands in a sink and opened a box of vaccinations. Henry sat beside Mrs. Jenison on the bench and waited.

Jackie whined and nipped at Tracy's wrists.

"You've got a little fighter, Henry."

Henry sat up on the bench, half proud, half embarrassed. "Sorry about that," he said.

"There, there, Jackie," Tracy said, tilting his head so that it covered the pup's body. "Calm down." Jackie stopped biting. Peggy handed Tracy the needle, and she held the dog's paws while he rubbed the flesh over the shoulder and sunk the needle in.

"That's it," Tracy said, dropping the used needle on the cart. "Come back next week for the second shot. Now then, Mrs. Jenison, let's look at that guinea pig."

*   *   *

"The best I could do with Mr. Yapton's produce," Darren said, serving the pasta he'd prepared.

Caroline poured the wine. She liked that he cooked, that he'd worn a jacket and tie. But why would a man stay in place he hated?

They ate in a formal dining room, which looked on to the sitting room where drop cloths covered the furniture. Buckets of paint waited in the corner and sheetrock lay stacked against the walls.

"How long have you been renovating?" Caroline asked.

"A year," Darren said. He finished his plate and Caroline did the same with her wine.

"Darren," she said, "do you mind if I ask why you decided to renovate if you don't like Chalk?"

"These walls made me claustrophobic," Darren said, wiping his mouth. "Eventually I'll move to a bigger school. Maybe in London, in administration."

"That sounds nice," she said.

"In the early stages, you shouldn't keep moving round. It makes you look unreliable."

That jab was for her, Caroline thought.

"What about you?" he asked, leaning across the table. "What would you like to be doing in five years?"

She started on the pasta and redirected her hands to the wine. She didn't like to discuss herself. "I'm chronically unable," she said, "to plan in advance."

"Why?"

"Because I don't exactly live for the sake of reliability." Caroline looked up. Darren had grown pale.

"The way I approach life is tedious?"

"Don't get defensive," she said. "Let's keep our conversation theoretical."

"Okay." He pushed his plate to the side. "I'll ask you a theoretical question, then. Why would an attractive, single woman move from Brighton to a place like Chalk?"

She shrugged. "To try something new?"

"My guess is you'll want to try something else new soon."

"I thought we were speaking theoretically," she said.

Darren leaned back in his chair, and a smirk travelled across his mouth. "Chalk has a way of dismantling ideals. I once heard the vicar say this village holds a mirror to the soul."

"A mirror to the soul?" Caroline poured more wine. She felt like getting really drunk and saying exactly what she thought. "One of the reasons I like Chalk is because nobody would believe I'm here."

"Hang on—I thought you came here because you saw it as the opportunity of lifetime? That's what you told Briggs, right"

"I'll choose my words more carefully next time."

"Or maybe you came to the country because of a relationship that didn't work out?"

She felt his eyes pass over her. "That would assume that I'm running away." She had an impulse to walk across the room, pick up a roller, and paint the length of Darren's face. "I prefer to think of it as running toward. Listen, I've just signed a contract to teach for the remainder of the term. I'll do my job, you don't have to worry about that."

"And then?"

"Who knows? I don't know if the pupils—or Briggs—will like me. One thing I do know. We have to work together, you and I. Don't we?"

Darren sat up straight. For a moment he resembled a pupil being scolded. "Maybe you really are the next Beverly Smith," he said.

*　*　*

Every afternoon for a week Henry found an excuse to walk up the road to the shop. He was obliged each time to buy something he didn't need—a head of cabbage, a lemon, a packet of crisps. Once he stopped by the post office on the pretence of buying stamps, but Vickie Eckleton didn't volunteer any information. He couldn't just ask about the status of Beverly Smith's replacement—his enquiry would have been noted and reported across the village by day's end. He spent his evenings with Jackie. Facing the window and watching the road, he taught her to sit, fetch, and bark on command.

His first morning without a burial Henry ventured into the churchyard for a look over the hedge. He timed his visit with ten o'clock playtime. It was raining, and the doors to the school were closed. That night, his curiosity at the breaking point, he caved and headed up to the pub.

Having been to The Black Ram the week before made it easier to go again. Nothing could have prepared him for what he saw—the replacement teacher sitting by the fire with Trevor Nelson. With her cream turtleneck, her leather handbag and heels, she looked like a visiting dignitary.

His first instinct was to leave. He didn't want to sit anywhere near them. Without anywhere else to sit, he took a stool at the bar. Oliver Marsh occupied his usual post at the end, gripping his Guinness with both hands.

"Here you are, Henry," Sid said, pushing over his Cuckoo.

Henry tried to appear calm as he reached for it. The teacher, when she saw him, would think he was lonely. She'd think he was a man with nothing better to do with his evenings than drink at a pub.

It was true—he didn't have anything better to do. If they met, shouldn't she see him for who he was? Henry drank quietly and stared at the bottles along the wall. He didn't want to leave too quickly, and he didn't want to stay any longer. Before long, Trevor appeared at the bar. Making sure everyone heard, he shouted, "Was that a merlot you were having, Caroline?"

Henry kept his head down as Trevor paid for the drinks. The man knew very well what she'd been drinking. It was silly to be jealous of Trevor, but the jealousy was out there in the open, as naked as his hands. When Henry looked up, Sid leaned toward him. "Why she chose Chalk I can't imagine," he whispered.

"She's taken the job?"

"She has, Henry." Sid glanced over to the snuggery as he wiped the counter. "I've always liked the name Caroline.

"Have you heard where's she from?"

"Brighton, most recently. Before that it's anyone's guess. It's bloody odd. Do you know I get the feeling she likes it here?"

"Likes Chalk?"

"She was in the other day, asking about a billiards table. A karaoke machine."

"There's never been billiards or karaoke."

"Exactly. As she was asking, Henry, she looked happy the pub had nothing to offer."

"Why would she be happy about that?"

"I haven't the foggiest idea." Sid grinned. "But you've got to hand it to old Trevor. Not even a week, and she's firmly in his grasp."

Henry grunted. Down deep, he wasn't worried. If the teacher had any taste, she wouldn't suffer Trevor long. He finished his pint and got up to leave. At the door he couldn't resist looking over his shoulder. Caroline was staring at him, just like before.

*   *   *

At dawn, Caroline woke and looked through her bedroom window at The Beacon. Chalk's ancient radio tower stood on a small grey hill, and under that stretched the stubbly grazing pastures attached to Bates Farm. Chalk might never make it onto a picture postcard. But she liked this view better than the car park below her Brighton flat.

In her nightgown, Caroline went into the sitting room to open the last of her packing boxes. She was still getting used to the silence. As she carried her cups and saucers into the kitchen, her footsteps on the linoleum sounded alarmingly loud. Last night she'd gone up for a drink, to see what the pub was like in the evenings, and she'd ended up staying until closing. Trevor Nelson had cornered her in the snuggery. It could hardly have been called a conversation. Mostly she'd just listened.

"However bad you think I am," he'd said, "I'm worse! Worse than anyone you can imagine. The things I've done in this village."

A smile formed on his lips and disappeared. "Terrible," he said, shaking his head, "how I've made the women of Chalk suffer. I can't begin to tell you the gruesome details. Well, the post office, for instance. Have you been in yet? Yes? The clerk…"

"You mean Vickie? The woman at the counter?"

He leaned in and whispered. "A pretty thing, isn't she?"

"She sold me some stamps."

Trevor raised his eyebrows. "She's one of many! The poor men of this village. Not even husbands are safe!" He put his hand to his mouth. "You don't think I'm really bad? You don't think I'm boasting, I hope?"

"Maybe you are," Caroline said, laughing. "I really don't know you, Trevor."

"You'd be a good influence on me," he said, though he hadn't yet asked her a single question. "You'd encourage me to make something of myself. Do you know my dad was once the caretaker of the Wembles Estate? By the time he died, he'd arranged lifetime tenancy for me. I really don't need to work."

"Free tenancy?"

Trevor winked. "I know what you're thinking—that I'm a lucky man, that I'm not such a bad person to get to know." He fingered a lock of her hair and withdrew his hand before she could protest. "You've only just arrived, but I feel this connection…"

"You're getting carried away," she said. "And you're drunk."

"We have to be careful, Caroline. People can be ruthless. They'll try to ruin our romance, begrudge us our pleasures. You'll see. People will be discussing this all over the village tomorrow—you and I, here by the fire."

"We're not doing anything."

"But they'll talk about it. You'll see!"

"Oh, for God's sake." She stood up to go. But Trevor begged her not to, and somehow she'd been obliged to pay for two more drinks. After the last round, Trevor began to cry. He said she was the answer to his sinful nature. She was the woman he'd been waiting for, he said, the woman to put a stop to his philandering. In the end, she had to tear herself away from him to walk home.

At least Chalk had the gravedigger. Caroline held him in her mind's eye as she sipped her tea in the brightening kitchen. The birds broke the silence, and the sun turned her white walls amber. Everything about the gravedigger appealed to her—his poorly concealed anger at seeing her with Trevor, his untamed hair and square hands. The barman said his name was Henry.

✳ ✳ ✳

As Henry came home from digging he found Jackie in the corner of the sitting room, wagging her tail. The leg of the armchair lay in shreds. Bits of leather and wood littered the carpet. When Henry took off his boots, she ran over and gnawed at the laces. "Bad dog!"

He started cleaning up what she'd done. She scampered over and snatched a scrap of leather out of his hand. He swatted her.

Yelping, she bolted across the room. She crouched behind the arm of the sofa and gnawed at it.

"Stop it, Jackie! Bad girl!"

Jackie pressed her ears against her head and watched him approach. Just as he reached the sofa, she sprang into the kitchen.

Henry knew he should have wrapped the furniture in towels and tape for the first few weeks. It's what he'd done with Jack. He came into the kitchen and found Jackie squatting in front of the fridge, a puddle spreading across the floor. When she was done, she just watched him and waited.

Henry closed his eyes and counted to ten. Then he searched for his keys and went out to the van. In the glove compartment he retrieved Jack's pig ears. Then he called Jackie outside and held a pig ear for her in the front garden. The next time she squatted, he gave her the pig ear and praised her.

The weather was warming, and rain clouds hung on the horizon. Maybe a walk up The Beacon was what the dog needed. Henry hurried back upstairs to wash up. His reflection in the mirror startled him. His hair hadn't been trimmed in months, and neither had his beard. As Jackie watched from the bathroom door, he found a pair of scissors and went to work.

* * *

Caroline turned at the top of The Beacon, taking the wind against her face. After teaching all day it felt good to go traipsing along the sheep trails.

It was warm for February. There would be rain soon, she could smell it. She circled the mesh fence surrounding the control tower and started back down. Below, the village was a speck. It grew bigger as she came down, but not by much.

A man came up the trail toward her. Caroline could tell right away it was the gravedigger. He moved in long, measured strides. His dog slipped away and ran up the trail until it stopped at her feet and rolled on its back. It was just a puppy.

Caroline bent down for the dog's lead and when she stood up the gravedigger was already there. He was even taller than she expected. He wore a tattered green jumper that was too small for him.

He took the lead from her and slowly wrapped it in great loops around his wrist. "She has a great deal of strength for a pup," he said. He spoke quietly, as if he were talking to himself.

"What's her name?"

"Jackie."

"He raised his eyes and lowered them quickly. "I had another Jack Russell, you see. Jack. A lovely dog, but—well, he died."

"I'm sorry."

"Last week, it was." He took a deep breath. "I know it's too soon for another."

"I'm not sure if there are any rules about that," Caroline said. She could tell the man had trimmed his beard today, and made a mess of it. One side of his face was clumpy, the other cut to the skin.

"Maybe you're right about the absence of rules." He smiled. It was the first time she'd seen him smile. There was another person, it seemed, behind the beard. The wind picked up, and Caroline zipped her jacket up to her neck. It took some time because the zipper kept catching.

"I'm Caroline," she said finally.

"My name's Henry."

"I know." She laughed. "I asked Sid at the pub. You're the gravedigger."

"It's a small village." His dog strained at the lead, and he tugged her back. "Heel, Jackie."

"I saw you my first day in Chalk," Caroline said. "You were digging Beverly Smith's grave."

He frowned. "I'm the teacher replacing her," she said. "I was in the playground when that girl's paper aeroplane...do you remember?" He didn't reply, and soon she became self-conscious. "Maybe you don't. It was a busy day."

"I remember," Henry said, looking across the pasture.

He sounded disappointed, as if they'd had a secret understanding that she'd spoiled. Of course they recognised each other. It had been silly, she thought, to pretend. She wondered if his attraction to her was all in her mind.

Jackie tugged at the lead again, and the gravedigger allowed the pup to drag him all the way to the fence. The wind died. Caroline took a step down the hill. The man's shoulders, under his jumper, formed a thick block of muscle.

"Henry? Are you going all the way up?"

He didn't move. "You there, Henry?"

Suddenly he wheeled. "Of course I'm here! You've seen right through me since you arrived."

The tone of his voice frightened her. "You're right. I mean, I should have realised…"

He watched her fight for words. He had a hungry stare, like an animal's. Without knowing why, she started to run.

She kept going, all the way down the hill. She didn't stop until she reached the road. Panting, her hands on her knees, she turned and searched the empty trail.

The Beacon's lights flashed green and red in front of the setting sun. "My God," she said. "What a disaster." She didn't understand how she'd become so frightened. She rushed into her bungalow and locked the door. The whole village felt like a lunatic asylum.

Drifting into her kitchen she stood with her hands on the sink, too rattled to move. She poured a glass of wine and left it standing on the counter. Then from the window she saw him—a dark smudge against the horizon, moving along the crest of the hill. She watched him, until the sun went down, and then he faded into the dusk.

*   *   *

"So this is how things are," Henry grumbled as he dragged Jackie down the trail. He had to be careful of his footing in the dark. He was evidently far removed from the process of courtship if a woman disappeared—ran away, more like it—as soon as he stopped to think.

The pup whimpered, tired at last. He talked to her as he stepped over the rocks and brambles, getting out his frustrations, reassuring her that they'd soon be home. "I'll never let myself get drawn in again, Jackie—even if that teacher stares across the pub at me a hundred times."

Henry's neck itched from shaving. His face burned and he felt like a fool. At the bottom of the hill he spilled off the trail and onto the road.

"She knew my name!" he whispered. "Asked after me at the pub!" He couldn't help smiling, despite it all. There was no getting past a woman like that, no matter how hard he tried. The teacher had found her way into his head. She didn't seem put off by his profession the way some women were.

"I only wanted to speak my mind," he said. "How can I be blamed for that, Jackie?"

A light went on inside the Bates' bungalow. Henry stopped. He'd never seen a light on in there, ever since it was built. "Heel, Jackie. Wait a minute."

Through a part in the curtain, Caroline passed. She was carrying a packing box. She was wearing a tee shirt, and that was all. A mist descended. Jackie whimpered, and Henry kept walking.

Caroline had taken residence at Gates Farm? What kind of woman moved to Chalk? She'd probably responded to a government initiative. Extra holidays amd pay bonuses for teaching where nobody important lived. He'd read about programs like that.

"What difference does it make, Jackie? She's beyond my reach!"

He didn't get any arguments from Jackie. It was the kind of companionship a man could get used to.

SIX

The next morning Henry heard a knock at his door. When he parted the sitting room curtains there was the teacher in his garden wearing an anorak in the rain.

"Jackie. Sit up in that cot," he said. "Look cute, God damn you."

The pup sat up. Henry combed his hair with his fingers. He checked his socks for holes.

"Good morning," Caroline said, as he opened the door. "I was hoping you'd be home."

The rain collected in the downspout and gurgled onto the grass.

"No graves today," Henry said. "A good thing, with this weather."

They stared at each other a moment. "I wanted to explain why I ran away yesterday," Caroline said. "Something came over me. It happens from time to time and I'm not exactly apologising. I just needed to be alone."

Jackie ran between them, wagging her tail. "I should have responded in a more timely manner," Henry said. "I was only thinking. Sometimes I think too long about what to say. It's because I don't like saying the wrong thing. Still, I could have been more polite, especially—" Henry realised he was babbling and shut up.

Caroline looked up and down the road. "Quiet morning," she said.

He nodded. "They're all like that."

"Would you like to go on a walk?"

"You mean now?"

"It's a Saturday," she said, "and I suddenly feel I'm on Mars. If I don't do something with myself, I'll go batty."

* * *

She probably had no idea, Henry thought as he put on his boots, of the silences he put up with—the endless, empty days with nothing but his thoughts to keep him company. Maybe she'd known about silences like these and forgotten. Growing up, he'd endured weeks of silence at a time. His father had seen to that, scolding unnecessary speech, forbidding even a radio.

Henry put Jackie on the lead. Then he discovered that with Caroline, it was as if all his years of silence might never have been. In the pouring rain they slogged up the road and onto the muddy trail. She asked him questions and listened to him describe beliefs and feelings he'd only partly known. It was as if he'd been cured of amnesia. At one point she took Jackie's lead without asking, allowing him to walk unencumbered. He swung his arms and painted a picture of his work as best he could.

There were three types of graves to dig, he explained—new singles for people who died single, new doubles for the first member of a couple to pass, and reopenings for the partner to follow. No, he told her, England's churchyards were simply too small for any machinery, and yes, gravedigging would probably remain the same for hundreds of years to come.

There were the vicars of each parish to describe—some invited him in for tea, others barely knew his name. One time a vicar neglected to place the burial marker, and he hadn't known where to dig. When he'd knocked on the rectory door the vicar said that Henry had to ring the undertaker for the location of the grave, that he couldn't be expected to interact with gravediggers. Henry asked to use the telephone, and the vicar refused him even that.

"The nerve of some people," Caroline said. It was only the polite response, but in Chalk you couldn't always count on manners. The way she listened made him feel vindicated.

As they crossed into the neighbouring hills Henry let himself think out loud. He discovered views on politics and art and the news he'd unconsciously catalogued, as if in preparation for this moment. When he stopped talking she pressed him further. Finally, when she seemed satisfied he'd finished, she offered her thoughts on the same topics.

He paid attention as a matter of caution. He didn't want to ask stupid questions. But gradually he linked the points of her life with his own. She was an only child as well, and wasn't close to her parents. There was nothing particularly wrong with them, she said, she'd just never felt much of a connection. As a teenager she'd left home searching for the ideal destination, and she was still looking.

"How will you know you've found it?" he asked.

"I don't know the answer to that," she said, laughing. "But I need somewhere that forces me to grow."

They circled back across the wet pastures. Then they turned at the top of The Beacon and headed down the trail. Slowly they came back onto the road and approached her bungalow at Bates Farm, where their parting would leave him alone once more. Henry dreaded the rest of his afternoon, his evening by the telly before heading up to bed like a zombie.

"My house," she said, "is perfect for cooking meals. Would you like to come for supper tonight?"

Henry's mouth opened and closed. At first he was too surprised to speak, and when he recovered she hadn't run away this time.

"Tonight shouldn't be a problem," he said.

*   *   *

Trevor inched into the post office. "Good morning, Vick!" He shut the door behind him and squinted under the fluorescent lights. He'd just woken up.

Vickie sat up behind the counter. "Trevor, you loon, it's not morning."

He started to look at his watch and realised he didn't have one. "What time is it?"

"Two in the afternoon."

The way she studied his reaction made Trevor nervous. "How are you, then, Vick?"

"Fine. You just leaving my house now?"

"Mmm."

"Helped yourself to breakfast, I hope. The little French pastries I left you. The grapefruit."

He nodded. The attention she gave him always made him guilty, because he never returned the favour. He'd eaten the pastries and grapefruit anyway. Vickie leaned her head through the glass partition. "What are you doing all the way over there, then? Why don't you come up and pretend you want to post a letter? Where are you off to?"

"Nowhere in particular. Stretching my legs."

"You could have lied, you know. Said you were popping in to see me."

Vickie slumped back on her chair. She swept her length of blonde hair behind her head. He thought of the way she'd looked last night, desperately clutching his shoulders as they'd had sex.

He drifted toward the carousel of post cards in the corner. "Listen, Vick, don't think I'm a brute, all right? But I need to tell you something. It's better if I say it straight away to avoid any confusion."

"Go on, then."

"I just can't be bothered with commitment right now."

Vickie picked up a packet of envelopes and straightened it on the counter. "I know that," she said.

"It's just not a good time."

She gave him a crooked smile. She wanted a better explanation, it was clear, especially after he'd turned up at her door last night saying he loved her. It had been a month since their last time. I love you too, she'd said, and I always will. They had both been drunk but Vickie hadn't believed that made a difference.

"It's the same with Rosalyn," Trevor went on, glancing at his shoes. "Last time, I got this horrid weight on my shoulders. I couldn't get anything done!"

Up at the counter, Vickie stayed quiet. It made him feel guilty all over again. He spun the carousel of postcards angrily. "I just don't want there to be any expectations. Okay?"

"I know not to have any." She sighed. "So. Who's next then?"

"Jesus," he said, throwing up his arms. The post office had become uncomfortably hot. He went to the door and reached for the handle. "I knew you'd get this way."

"Trevor, you're just leaving my house, for God's sake. You probably planned this little speech as you were eating the breakfast I laid out for you. Don't you care about my feelings?" She made a little noise, as if something were stuck in her throat.

His hand stayed on the doorknob. He couldn't leave her like this. "I do care."

"Like hell." Vickie pulled at her fingers nervously. "I heard you were in the pub the other night with that teacher. It's her you're onto next, isn't it?"

"I don't know what you mean."

"She's taken Beverly's job, as I'm sure you've heard. You'll be seeing a great deal of each other."

Trevor shrugged. As far as he was concerned, it was only a matter of time before he and Caroline were together. "Maybe so," he said.

"You're a pig." She started to cry again.

"C'mon, Vick. Stop it, now."

He kept his hand on the door. "Isn't it better that I'm honest? I mean, we've never had anything regular, you and I. And nothing's official or anything between me and Caroline. I just wanted to tell you, before—"

"Before what? Before I see it with my own eyes? You're a pig, Trevor. Go on, now, before someone comes. I don't want anyone to see me blubbering." She slid the glass partition shut and reached in her purse for a handkerchief.

Trevor lingered a little out of politeness, then bolted straight for the pub. Watching Vickie cry like that always put him in a bad mood.

Inside the pub, Trevor didn't have to think about it. There was Sid and the beer taps and a wonderful quiet darkness. It took some time for his head to settle, for the remnants of his guilt to dissipate. Then, not long after he'd started on his first pint, he became himself once more.

* * *

Perhaps Caroline had been destined for Chalk. Perhaps she'd been destined for him. The thought jolted Henry as he paced the room, compulsively checking the mantle clock. In four minutes it would be six o'clock and time to ring Caroline as he'd promised, just to let her know he was on his way over. He'd wait until a couple of minutes past the hour, he decided, so as not to appear overanxious.

The next minute passed slower than any minute he'd remembered.

"I can't wait any longer, Jackie." Henry went to the table and picked up the phone. Then he put it back down and made himself sit in the armchair. He stared at the clock on the mantle until he thought it might break apart under his gaze.

"I must have caught you at a bad time," he said, when she

answered. She sounded out of breath.

"No, you haven't," she said. "I literally just walked in the door."

"Well, I was just ringing as we'd planned. I understand if you've changed your mind, but you said to—"

"Does this mean you're still coming? You haven't changed your mind?"

"Me? No." He reached for the bottle of wine on the telephone table that he'd bought at the supermarket four hours ago. He'd driven up the A-27 for it. He'd collected dessert as well, but he couldn't understand why he'd chosen the rhubarb pie until he remembered it was his father's favourite.

Henry hung up and walked in a kind of waking dream to Bates Farm. He made it through the evening by being unswervingly polite. Primarily he didn't want to make an ass out of himself. Throughout the meal he kept looking at the clock until ten o'clock came, when he'd decided ahead of time to leave without a second's delay. He couldn't presume Caroline wanted anything more than friendship. Then, just before ten, she took off her jumper. He kept looking at her bare arms, and it was everything he could do not to grab them in a mad frenzy and kiss her. It was still a few minutes early, and they hadn't had the rhubarb pie yet, but he got up from the table without a word and walked to the door.

"You're not leaving?" she said, following him.

She leaned toward him as he turned, and against his better intentions he started to kiss her. "I don't want to," he said, and he left without saying goodbye. Only by the time he'd returned home did he realise what he'd done. The telephone was ringing as he opened the door. It was Caroline.

"You're back already," she said.

"I'm not in my right mind tonight," he said. He felt relieved to be away from her gaze, back in the security of his own house.

"What are you talking about?"

"I didn't thank you for supper. I had such a nice day and evening. And I didn't say goodbye, either."

"Oh, don't worry about that. I was only ringing to say how much I enjoyed your company. It might not be proper for the woman to be asking and everything, but I wanted to know if you'd like to do it again."

Henry gripped the telephone table. He tried to keep his voice low and level. "All right. When?"

"I don't know, my calendar is so full. How about tomorrow night?"

Getting through the following day proved as equally torturous as the previous evening. He didn't have any graves to dig. Henry spent the day pacing except for a drive to Springmer for flowers. At six he arrived at Caroline's bungalow, and as soon as he walked in she gave him little chores while she cooked. She had him taste the meal as she prepared it. She had him boil water and chop garlic and all the while she made him talk about his preferences. It was fun, she explained, to investigate the relationships of different flavours. He didn't have to lie when they sat down—the meal was delicious. After all this time, how had he never once tried eggplant Parmesan?

After eating, they went outside to the patio. Caroline lit some candles, and they sat overlooking the fields. They finished a bottle of wine. Henry wondered what was happening to the appearances of things. Somehow The Beacon appeared almost beautiful. He started to tell her how happy she made him when she put her hand on his arm and said, "Stay here. I'll get dessert."

The wind gusted across the fields. He jumped up to stop the candles from blowing out, and as he stood there, shielding the wind with his chest, he glanced at the kitchen window and caught her, equally determined, placing strawberries in exact circles around dishes of vanilla ice cream. It was then—only then—that he suspected he really had a chance with her. She came out with the tray and sat beside him.

They didn't talk. They left their desserts on the table and listened to the wind. Henry fought his desire a while, then let it win. He turned and took Caroline's face in his hands, and he kissed her. Her mouth still parted, she asked him to do it again. He looked at her and kissed her until her face became just as solemn as his.

"Why me," he said. He kept his voice low, so she couldn't hear. It didn't matter—and she crushed what was left of his restraint.

* * *

"It's true!" Karen Bates whispered She gripped the handle of her basket with both hands. "What else would they be doing together after walking The Beacon? And she doesn't always come home,

Penny. Because I'd see the light, wouldn't I?"

The vicar's wife glanced at the counter. Kevin Yapton turned quickly away from them, his elbows on a stack of newspapers. Penny moved Karen over to the box of onions in the corner. "It's not possible," she whispered. "Henry Bale has never once had a girlfriend."

Karen leaned in further. Their noses were almost touching. "Four times, I've seen them now, taking walks in the afternoons. And that's only when I've been watching—I can't look out the window every day, can I?" Mr. Yapton left the counter. He picked up a scrap of paper from the floor and neared the onion box. Karen tightened her scarf, as if shielding herself from the wind.

"I've always thought he was handsome," Penny confessed. "But I just can't see that girl taking up with him. He's hardly her kind. Then again, nobody is."

"What do you mean?"

"The vicar says she's got the look of a girl from Paris."

Karen's eyes widened. "You mean she's a prostitute?"

"Of course not. She's worldly. Not made for Chalk. You know."

Karen nodded. "Mrs. Tilson knows what's going on, I'm sure. She's the nearest to Henry. If only she weren't so holier than thou, then we'd know what was happening, once and for all."

Penny pulled her friend by the arm as the bell jangled. Mrs. Tilson came inside. "Morning, Mrs. Tilson," Mr. Yapton called. "Can I help you find anything?"

"A box of Weetabix, please."

"Of course." He carried a footstool to the opposite wall. "A box of Weetabix," he repeated. Climbing up, he located one and dusted it off.

Mrs. Tilson placed her purse on the counter. "Warming up, isn't it?" she said, nodding to the women by the door.

"The vicar says we're in for a rainy March," Penny said.

Karen, still clutching her handbag, looked vaguely about the shop. "We were just saying we haven't seen Henry about. Not since Beverly's funeral, in fact."

Mrs. Tilson frowned. "Henry? He keeps to himself, you know."

"Here we are," Mr. Yapton said, placing the box of Weetabix on the counter. "Will there be anything else?"

"Still," Penny said, "we might see him up at the shop now and then. Wouldn't we, Karen?"

Karen nodded. "Mind you, I was just saying to Penny…I'm sure I saw him with our new teacher. Walking The Beacon."

Mrs. Tilson paid for the cereal and put it in her basket. "Sounds as if you've seen him recently after all. It's Henry's business where he walks, I should think. Goodbye."

The bell jangled, and she was gone. "Keeps to himself," Karen said, glaring out the window. "I'll say he does. Especially with Caroline Ford."

✳   ✳   ✳

Trevor set off on foot for Bates Farm, swigging gin. It didn't seem right that Caroline kept hanging up each time he rang. It didn't seem decent. Not after he'd made room for her, so to speak, with Vickie. All over the village, it would be, how he'd made a serious play only to come up empty handed. Couldn't she appreciate that?

Once more, the bats threatened. Trevor could see them swooping near his head as he reached the midway point of the gin bottle. It was too tidy in his kitchen to sit around by himself. He'd cleaned his house for her, after all, and he'd stayed sober yesterday to do it. He picked up his pace. She'd cut him off yesterday night, right after he'd rang, and tonight was one time too many. When he reached Caroline's bungalow, he stopped in the road.

He could understand the gin in his left hand. But why did he have flowers in his right? That was it, he remembered—he was going to tell Caroline she wasn't a stupid cow. Every woman's a stupid cow, his father used to say. He said it to everyone, especially his mother, as often as he said good morning. But Caroline was different, and he wanted her to know it.

Trevor left the bottle under an oak tree. He crossed the road, climbed her little cement steps and rang her bell. Over at the Bates' farm house, a light went on upstairs. He could hear a dog barking inside the bungalow and he tried to recall if Caroline mentioned one. Caroline opened the door. Behind her, Henry Bale stood holding back a little Jack Russell pup.

"You look nice, Caroline," Trevor said. "Beautiful tight jumper. Listen, I'm on my way to the pub and thought you might like to join me." He held out the four roses, wrapped in cellophane.

Caroline tried pushing the flowers away, but he succeeded in leaving them in her hands. "I thought I told you on the phone," she said. "Last night, and the night before. I'm not interested."

"I had something important to tell you." He looked up at the sky. "But now I seem to have forgotten."

The gravedigger came partway toward them, still holding back the barking dog by the collar. "Is everything okay out there?"

"Perfectly fine," Trevor said. He started to come inside, but Caroline blocked his way. She put her finger right in his face. "Trevor, we want to be alone. The two of us."

"You don't want to sneak out for a pint? I dressed up. It's not for every girl I put on a blazer. You're not a stupid cow—that was it! That's why I brought you the roses!"

She tried to hand them back. He put his hands behind his back and shook his head.

"Go away, please," Caroline said. Before he knew it, she'd closed the door.

Trevor jiggled the handle. He stepped back onto the road, and for a long time he waited under the oak across from the bungalow, drinking. It started to rain.

"It's wet out here!" he cried, returning to the door. The same lights went back on over at the farm house. Trevor pounded until Caroline opened up. In the kitchen, Henry stood chopping something with a knife.

"Hello again," Trevor said. The dog barked and ran at him. "New dog?" He bent down, and it jumped at his trousers. Caroline pulled it back by the collar. "Energetic puppy," Trevor said, the rain dripping down his face. "Still cooking in there?"

"Go away, Trevor," Caroline said. "I'm serious."

She was the type of woman that might test him, and he liked that. He squeezed her arm. "We could have fun tonight, you and I. I've got some gin left under the tree!"

Caroline started to close the door again, but he blocked it with his foot. Over her shoulder, a bottle of wine stood on the table along with place settings. Henry came toward him. The gravedigger couldn't be here on a date, Trevor thought as the man lifted him off his feet. He didn't bother struggling—it was like being in the arms of a polar bear. Henry carried him all the way to the tree and flung him to the ground.

Then Trevor felt a hand around his neck. The gravedigger started to squeeze.

"Stop! Help!"

"What I should do," Henry said, "is kill you, right under this oak."
He gasped for air.

Things started to turn black when the gravedigger stood up. He
loomed over Trevor with his head under the branches. "Go home
now," Henry said. "By the time I get inside, you'd better be gone."

He kicked the gin bottle toward Trevor and strode across the
road.

Trevor jumped to his feet. He felt faint—too faint to move, let
alone walk—but as he heard Caroline's door open, he managed to
run.

* * *

Inside his van, overlooking Cuckfield's churchyard, Henry watched a
paper bag float across the headstones, borne by the wind. All week,
each time he opened his eyes, surprises appeared.

He opened his tea thermos, and the windows steamed. He'd
dug the better part of a new single without a break, and it hadn't
even winded him. He wiped down the windows with his squeegee.
On his way to work today, he'd noticed a boy under an umbrella,
holding a cat. Surely there had been boys with cats under umbrellas
before? In the village, people seemed to be treating him with more
respect, waving as he approached instead of turning away.

It had been made for a tense evening last night, handling Trevor
the way he had. But it had been thrilling, too. Henry had acted calm
as he came back inside, but his heart raced as he'd looked out the
window to make sure Trevor was gone.

Over supper he'd told Caroline the bits and pieces he'd heard
over the years. He'd told about Trevor's father, the violent drunk
and bully who'd somehow kept his job as Estate Manager until
collapsing from drink on his way home from The Black Ram. It had
taken the police a week to find him, under a hedge and stiff with
frost. Lord Wembles had taken pity and let the family stay on as long
as they needed. Trevor's mother, unable to cope, had moved up to
her sister's in Crawley. Since the age of fourteen, Trevor had lived
alone in that house, more of a stable than a residence, from the tales
he'd heard. Henry almost felt sorry for the man.

"It's still no excuse," Caroline had said, shaking her head, "to behave like he does."

"I didn't say it did. It explains a few things, that's all." They'd had a bit of a disagreement over it. But as he'd argued his point she'd put her arm around his neck and not long after, they were making love. Never before had Henry felt such satisfaction in simply being alive.

He used the squeegee once more on the windscreen. The rain picked up. Out in the churchyard the grave would be filling with water. Even as he pictured it—the wet and clammy hole, the bailing he'd have to do—he realised how little it mattered, compared to his excitement.

Henry studied the dashboard clock. Looking up at the headstones, he counted a minute in his head. He was slow by a full fifteen seconds. He couldn't remember when he'd been that far off before. He tried again. Once more he was behind, underestimating a minute by a full nine seconds.

"A fluke, that's all."

Taking a deep breath, Henry gripped the steering wheel. Time was objectively measured. It passed with the same regularity, no matter what a man did or didn't feel. But try as he might, he couldn't help thinking he'd been manipulated by some evil force. Time flies when you're having fun, people said. He'd never believed it until now.

He got out of the van and ran to the grave. Jumping in with a splash, he started bailing at a furious pace. If time was moving faster, he would beat it at its own game.

✳   ✳   ✳

The mattress bulged in its plastic wrapper as Henry wrestled it from the back of his van. It was bright pink and king-sized and an obscenity on any village road. Luckily there was nobody about. Henry muscled the mattress through his gate and leaned it against his house. He stood panting in his garden, sizing up the front door.

A month ago, he never would have considered such an extravagance. Things were different now—he had new opportunities, new priorities. His bed was too small for two. When Caroline stayed over the other night, they'd struggled in vain to get comfortable before walking to Bates Farm at two in the morning to sleep in her bed.

He unlocked the front door and called off his barking dog. The mattress had to get out of sight before the whole village gathered. Henry intended to surprise Caroline with it this evening.

He picked up the mattress and tried to ram it inside. He tilted it at various angles, but it kept hitting the frame. "Damn it!" He tried shoving, bending, even leaping on the top, but it was no use. The doorway was too narrow.

Mrs. Tilson emerged from next door, holding her reading glasses. "Is everything all right, Henry?"

"I'm fine," Henry said. He wiped his forehead with his shirtsleeve.

She came over to the wall. "What a pretty bed."

"This? It's nothing, really."

"It's huge! And such a nice pink."

"It was time for a new one. They had a special price on the colour." He looked up and down the road. With a grunt, he tried the end through the door again. Pain shot up his back.

"You'll never get it in that way, Henry. Bobby had the same problem. That very door it was, right after we were married. A smaller bed than that, too."

Henry blinked at the ground and waited for the pain to pass. He cursed himself for not planning this properly. "What did Bobby do eventually? I mean, to get the bed inside?"

"He went round the back and brought it through the kitchen."

Henry just stared. "The kitchen?" He'd never even opened that door. He'd forgotten it existed.

"I'm afraid so, Henry. And you'll have to take the whole door off its hinges."

"I should never have bought this thing. There's the box spring and frame to think of, too!" It wasn't the work he minded—it was keeping the mattress out in the open. He'd have to cart it all the way round to the first terrace house in the row, where a common gate gave access to all the back gardens.

"It looks like a very nice mattress," Mrs. Tilson said. "Heavy to lift, I'm sure. I'm sorry I can't be of any help in that regard."

"I'll manage," Henry said, though his arms were getting wobbly. He wanted the whole thing over with, and he hadn't even begun the hard part. Hoisting the mattress once more, he started back through the gate.

Reverend Pierce appeared in the road. "Hello, Henry," he said. "You're not carrying that all by yourself, are you?"

"No trouble, vicar," Henry said. Sweat trickled down his nose.

The vicar lifted the other end. "My, this is a big bed."

"I thought it would be good for my back," Henry said.

They carried the mattress down the road. Mrs. Tilson followed. They had almost reached the last house when a van approached. "Watch out!" Mrs. Tilson said. "Oh, we're in luck—it's Chris Crawley. And he's got Trevor with him, too." Waving her arms, she flagged them down.

The vicar let down his end. "Wait," Henry said to Mrs. Tilson, "it's not necessary…"

Chris had already pulled his van to the side of the road. "What's all this, then?" he said, getting out. He came lumbering toward them in his overalls, as if ready to carry the mattress all by himself.

"These boys are having a devil of a time," Mrs. Tilson explained.

"I hate to be a bother," Henry said, his voice barely audible. He wanted to disappear. Trevor got out of the van and stood beside Chris.

"This thing's a monster!" Chris said.

Trevor snorted. "Henry's got business in the bedroom."

Chris picked up the vicar's end with one hand. "I've got this bit," he said. "Now get round that wall, Trevor. Open the gate."

"Very kind of you lads," Reverend Pierce said, dabbing his forehead. He fell in beside Mrs. Tilson at the rear of the prosession.

"Mind that pipe," Chris said, driving Trevor forward.

"Hurry up with that gate and get out of the way." They crossed the neighbouring gardens and stopped at Henry's kitchen door.

Chris took a screwdriver from his pocket and went straight to work on the hinges. "The frame and box spring are in the van, Henry? Go help him with it, Trevor, while I get this door down."

Trevor swatted the air with his hand. "I don't see why I—"

"Don't be a prat. Go."

Reverend Pierce followed Henry and Trevor back across the gardens and onto the road. He took a half step in the direction of the pub.

"Please, Reverend," Henry said, "you've done enough already."

"You're well in hand as usual, Henry," the vicar said, starting off.

"Of all the bitter ends," Trevor muttered, sliding the metal bed frame out of Henry's van. "Here I am, helping you haul a trampoline into your house so you can shag Caroline more comfortably."

Henry pretended not to hear. Together they carried the box spring and frame back through the gardens. Chris had already removed the door and taken the mattress upstairs by himself. By the time they made it upstairs, Chris ducked inside Henry's bedroom, together with Mrs. Tilson.

"Right," Chris said, leaning over the old bed in the corner of the room. The tiny mattress lay sunken and misshapen, the sheets crumpled into a pile. "What are you going to do with this, then?"

Henry hung back in the crowded room. Jackie ran around sniffing at everyone's feet. "I don't know," he said. "Toss it, I suppose."

"My niece is looking for a bed," Chris said.

"It's yours," Henry said. "It's the least I can do."

"That bed was John's," Mrs. Tilson said. "My oldest." She stepped forward a little, her hands clasped together. "I gave it to your mother, Henry, right after you were born."

Trevor shook his head. "What? Henry's been sleeping on that damn thing since he was an infant?"

Henry nodded. "I suppose I have."

"There's justice for you," Trevor said. "Caroline's gone for a grown child."

The words hung in the air and couldn't be refuted. "He's well on his way to adulthood now," Chris said. "Which is more than we can say for you. Now grab that end, Trevor. Let's get this down to the van and join the vicar for a pint."

* * *

Darren Roberts stared as Caroline ran across the playground with the second formers. Her shirt billowed in the wind, and from where he stood by the hedge he had a good view. Up on the top step Briggs was staring too. What nonsense, Darren thought—this so called obstacle stopping co-workers from dating. Did she really believe it, or was it just an excuse?

He moved closer, trying not to gawk. He put his hands in his pockets to block what might stick out. She was in his sights now, every last bit of her. He shuffled his feet as if performing a dance. "Caroline!" he called.

"Not just now," she said, barely glancing at him. God, she could be a right bitch. He was the Assistant Head! "Caroline!" he called out again. "Join me for a chat. When you get a chance, of course. School business."

He shuffled over to the hedge and waited.

Eventually she came over, adopting a casual tone. "What's up?"

"Nothing much. Would you like to come for supper tonight?"

She frowned. "School business?"

"Does this constitute harassment?"

"I'm not an extremist. There's no crime in asking someone out." She kicked at a piece of gravel. "But I can't."

Darren squeezed his hands into fists inside his pockets. "Other plans, have you?"

"I'm still getting organised, to tell you the truth."

He nodded. "When people insist they're telling the truth, they often aren't."

"Think what you like, Darren," she snapped.

"Sorry," he said. "I didn't mean to be rude."

She smiled sympathetically. It looked like a smile reserved for all the men she wanted to turn down but not offend. "Darren. We're working together. Remember?"

He knew he was doomed. Still, he couldn't help but press on. "If you don't like me, fine. I understand. But don't say it's because—"

"Play time's over!" Briggs called from the top step. "Back in!"

Caroline patted Darren's shoulder and hurried off. Darren wanted to strangle someone, or scream. Instead he limped toward the school, his ears burning with shame. All the children in the playground knew he'd been rejected, he could have sworn it.

✳   ✳   ✳

"I thought it would give us flexibility," Henry said as he led Caroline upstairs. His words bubbled over. Don't think I'm getting overly serious just because I bought it. Of course, it doesn't necessarily mean I'm not serious—"

Caroline seized his wrists. "I've never broken in a new mattress."

She pulled him to the bed and they rolled around on it, hitting the edges and returning to the centre. They lay beside each other on their backs. "It's a treat to finally stretch out," Henry said. "I should have bought one of these a long time ago."

"Especially with that back of yours." She turned him sideways, reached under his shirt, and massaged his shoulders.

His eyes rolled back in his head. He loved the way she touched him. He turned and started to undress her and she squirmed away. "I have to go home and collect a few things. I came straight here from school."

"I'll come with you." He searched her eyes desperately. "I mean, can I?"

"Of course." She kissed him hard on the mouth in the way that she did when she meant business.

They went downstairs and outside. Down the road, Oliver Marsh came creeping along the wall toward them.

Oliver kept his eyes straight ahead. His skin was bone white under his black clothes. Caroline took Henry's hand and leaned closer as Oliver passed. They were still holding hands when Darren Roberts appeared. Caroline stopped to greet him.

"You're working late, Darren," she said.

They waited, giving him time to respond. He stood speechless in his suit. They left him by the school, and by the time they'd turned up the road to The Beacon, Caroline had gone pale. "I didn't think there was any point in telling you. Darren asked me to supper once, and I went."

Henry felt the blood drain from his face. "Do you like him?"

"He's a colleague."

They were still holding hands, but there wasn't any feeling left in it. She and Darren saw each other at school every day.

"You have the eye of every man in Chalk," Henry said.

"No, only one man. You."

It was silly to be angry, but he was anyway. "I wonder if one man will be enough." He stopped in the road.

"I'm not responding to that," she said. "It's the remark of a fool."

"I'm sure people think I'm the village idiot. How do I know you won't get bored and leave in a few weeks? I bought a new bed. I—"

"Henry." She took his shoulders and turned him round. She was rough about it. She clutched his arms right on the Estate Road, her eyes flashing. "You don't know what's going to happen. I don't know, either. What we do know, right now, is that this is good. Really good. And we also know that before the sun sets we're going to be up in that new bed of yours, fucking like rabbits. All right?"

He nodded. Of all the things to argue about in the world, this wasn't one of them. "All right."

SEVEN

The first Friday of March meant quiz night at The Red Lion. Trevor arrived a little after ten. He preferred coming late—after hours of questions on rivers and dead kings, the women were typically restless. He bought a pint and leaned against the wall to survey his options. The pub was packed. It had been hell, driving twenty miles to Kington through a steady rain, but if all went well he wouldn't have to drive home until tomorrow. His shagging record at The Red Lion was four out of five.

"Number forty-nine!" the barman called. He was in his early twenties, with freckles and an aggressive smile. "Who was Glasgow Rangers' leading scorer in 1979, 1980, and 1981?" The teams huddled together. Trevor spotted a potential target—a brunette in a striped pullover, tapping her pencil against a pint glass. She looked a bit like Caroline, but her mouth was too big.

"Number fifty! When your team's done, turn in your answer sheets at the bar. Right. What is the largest of the lakes in the Lake District?"

Trevor moved to the rear of the pub. A couple of women bounced past him on their way to the bar, and one shot him a glance. She was ready and willing, but that was the only charitable phrase he could find. Her eyes might have been painted on. Still, it was too late to be choosy. He tugged her elbow, and as she turned, something stuck in his throat.

His failure with the teacher still haunted him. In Chalk he couldn't go out in public without enduring the embarrassment of it. Trevor retreated into the shadows of the pub, and he kept searching the tables.

"An impressive score tonight. Forty-seven out of fifty correct! The winning team is just one man, believe it or not. Kington's very own Derrick Watkins!"

Everyone clapped as a bandy-legged drunk made his way to the bar, his mouth hanging open. This was the winner?

Trevor repeated the man's name in his head. There was something familiar about him. Then Trevor remembered his uncle's funeral here in Kington, how it had been Derrick digging the grave. Grabbing his cigarettes, he followed the man to the bar.

* * *

Trevor plied Derrick with a round of drinks and pulled him to a table at the back of the pub. The man's stubbly face was streaked with tobacco spittle. He might have been a drunk, but somehow he still had his wits about him. "Why would I want to do something like that?" he kept asking. "Why?"

"For fun." Trevor winked, like he did with women.

Derrick smiled shyly. "I've done some slippery things in my time. But Henry Bale's been a good mate over the years. He's covered for me on many an occasion. I'm not keen on doing something nasty to him."

"He'd never know it was you. Surely this happens naturally from time to time."

"Once in a while. But—"

"Especially in this weather."

Derrick squinted. "True. But it wouldn't be nature. It would be me."

Trevor rolled a cigarette and leaned back in his chair. "He's hardly your mate, Derrick. He gets paid to cover for you. Well, I'm offering to pay you as well." He paused, letting the words sink in. "Good money, too."

"You must be cheesed off with him for some reason. What did he do?"

"I told you. It's just a good-natured prank. Let's say I've got a diabolical streak."

"I'll have to think about it," Derrick said. He peered at his empty glass.

"Sit tight." Trevor rushed to the bar and brought back a couple of pints. Derrick had almost fallen asleep by the time Trevor returned. He sat up and opened his eyes at the sight of the drinks.

"Have you been thinking about it?" Trevor asked.

Derrick took his beer in both hands and shook his head.

"Just one grave, Derrick. Dig it a few feet wide. That's all. Then when the next one in the row's needed, fall ill. Henry will cover for you like always, and—"

"It'll be a bloody mess for him. A great big wall caving in like that."

"That's the point!"

"Where are your ethics, boy?"

"Ethics," Trevor said, sneering. He felt himself turn pale, as if some greater force had overheard. "Listen, Derrick. I'm not a bad person. Sometimes there just needs to be justice in the world. A balancing of the scales, if you like."

"This doesn't make much sense to me, I have to say." He gulped down half his beer. "All right. I'm digging at the parish church on Wednesday. A new double for this bloke Dick Simmons who died. Most likely his wife will order a chipboard coffin for him—which in this weather will rot like tissue paper. I'll go two feet into the next plot. No more. But that should…"

Trevor shuddered, half delighted, half repulsed. "Yes?"

"That should create the effect you're after. When Henry digs the next grave in the row, let's just say he'll have company."

"And how long do you think it will be before the next one?"

"There's another one gone every three weeks or so in Kington. I'll ring you. As you say, I'll be doing it for fun. But I'll want that three hundred quid up front."

*　*　*

Day after day, the rain came down in solid sheets. Roads flooded. Shoes, forgotten in the school playground, floated away. Chalk seemed singled out by God. The parishioners grumbled proudly about this, like mountain climbers with sore feet.

For one afternoon, the rain paused. Caroline had been washing dishes in her kitchen, and the sudden silence made her look up. A shaft of light broke through the clouds. The sun came streaming down and spreading out, as if accompanied by trumpets, and the entire horizon became bathed in a warm glow.

Seizing her anorak, Caroline rushed outside. She sloshed through the fields and past the farm's outbuildings, and she stopped at the base of the hill where The Beacon loomed darkly above her. She took off her anorak and sat on it. Closing her eyes, she turned her face to the sun and let her thoughts drift.

Chalk was a mirror to the soul, Trevor had said. A village this small made people so restless, they had nowhere to look but inside. Did she even have a soul? What, if anything, did she believe?

How was it possible for a normal, thinking person to live without any beliefs at all? She was falling in love—that much was clear. Wasn't that enough? If so, why did she feel self-conscious about it, like right now when she opened her eyes and looked up at the sky? Rain, once more, began to fall.

Caroline put on her jacket and started home. In the distance Mr. Bates came out of the barn, with a piece of machinery in his arms. Seeing her out in the fields, he stopped and stared. Caroline kept traipsing across the field. Someone was waving from the downstairs window of the farmhouse. At first she pretended not to notice, but as she came closer, she had no choice but to wave back.

Karen Bates pushed up the window and leaned over the sill. "Everything all right, luv?"

"Oh yes," Caroline said, stopping by the window. "I was just enjoying that bit of sun we had."

"But you were just sitting in that wet field! For the longest time, it was! You're sure everything's all right?"

Caroline gave a little laugh. "Sometimes I like to sit and think, that's all."

Karen frowned. "Sometimes I worry about you all alone in that little house. All alone! You have everything you need, do you?"

"Of course, Karen. I'm quite content."

The rain picked up. Caroline put her hood over her head and started to go. "You're finding friends in Chalk?" Karen asked.

"I am. Everyone has been quite friendly." Caroline took another step toward her bungalow.

"Henry Bale's a nice man, isn't he?"

Caroline nodded. Karen had finally come to what she wanted—gossip. "He certainly is."

"I don't mean to be nosy." Karen turned up the bottom of the curtain and examined it as if for the first time. "I'd be bored too, I should think, coming here from Brighton. But I suppose people from the cities sometimes fancy strange things."

The rain was pouring now, but Caroline wasn't about to let the comment pass. "What do you mean, Karen? You think it's strange I fancy Henry?"

"No! Henry's normal…I mean, a rare catch." Karen turned white. "What I mean is, sometimes people from the cities notice things we might take for granted. There. That's what I'm trying to say."

"I see."

Karen sighed, exasperated. "Now don't take offence, dear. If my husband and I went away to Brighton for the weekend, we might notice things you wouldn't. The buildings, for instance. That's my point."

"I suppose you might. But I'm not exactly here on holiday. If you went to Brighton for more than just a weekend, you might notice more than just buildings. You might discover new ideas about the world as a whole. That's the point of life, isn't it?"

"My goodness that rain's coming down," Karen said. "Better get inside now, dear. You'll catch a cold standing there."

Karen closed the window, and Caroline stood seething in the rain. She felt the village itself close down around her. She understood now Darren Roberts' decision to build his wing, simply for the sake of pushing back.

* * *

"This brings back memories," Mrs. Tilson said, peering over Caroline's shoulder at Henry in the van. "My Bobby was just as excited as Henry, the first time we went away together."

Caroline turned round. "He'd look ten years younger with that beard gone." She took Jackie off lead, and the dog ran inside Mrs. Tilson's. "Thank you for taking care of her. Now you should get out of the rain. You've only got a cardigan on."

Mrs. Tilson rested a hand on Caroline's arm. "Henry is so very dear to me. He's been waiting a long time to be generous with his feelings."

"I have as well," Caroline said. "Don't worry—we're just happy together!" She ran across the road to the van. Mrs. Tilson waved as they set off.

They headed west to Wales. In a few hours, signposts appeared with unpronounceable writing. They left the motorway and came through villages smaller than Chalk, where old men sat smoking pipes under the canopies of petrol stations. They took detours by whim. Hills rose around them, blanketed with maple trees. Toward evening they stopped at a sign for a bed-and-breakfast.

After they'd checked in and were alone in their room, Henry sat silently on the edge of the bed, his eyes on the wall. Caroline had become accustomed to his bouts of nerves. Sometimes he just shut down, and there was nothing she could do about it. This time she put her hand on the chair, balancing herself as she took off her shoes and socks, her trousers, her jumper. She unclasped her bra and pulled her hair across the back of her shoulders. She came across the room toward him, forcing him to look at her, but he kept his hands folded in his lap. She unpeeled his clothes, brought him into bed.

"I don't know what's happening to me," he said. He turned his face to the wall. She waited for him to explain, but the only sound was the rain on the windowsill.

"Henry. Talk to me—what is it?"

"I love you, Caroline."

She wrapped her arms around his shoulders. She turned him round and kissed him. "I love you, too. Since I saw you. I love you, too, Henry."

Caroline held him close, so he couldn't see that she was crying. She hadn't known the extent of her emptiness. She only knew it was emptiness now because of how Henry made her feel.

He sat up and held her out like a child. She felt more naked than ever before. "Caroline," he said, smearing her tears with his fingers. "We said we loved each other."

"Yes."

Caroline was tired of holding it in, tired of stopping her love from finding its way out. "I get so lonely when you're not around. Do you understand?"

He wrapped the sheet around her shivering body.

"I worry that you'll get bored with me," she said.

"No chance of that."

"How do I know?"

"I've more reasons to be worried."

Caroline laughed. "Listen to us worrying about our love! But it's

better than being silent all the time, and lonely inside your head."
She pulled the hair that curled around his ears. "Let's relax. Let's not
think about what all of this means."

As he looked at her she heard what sounded like a hammer
against a wall. She put her palm against his bare chest. "My God,"
she said, "your heart is simply pounding."

*   *   *

Henry woke in the middle of the night with his neck drenched with
sweat. In his dream he'd been stretched out on the green rubber of
Tracy's operating table. Peggy rolled a monitor toward him.

"There's the problem," Tracy said, pointing at the screen with a
pencil. "Look here, Henry, it's easy enough to see."

A heart appeared on the monitor. Henry could see it all—the
quivering muscles, the red fleshy chambers. Peggy lowered the
operating light. An alarm sounded.

"Stop it!" Tracy shouted. He tilted the operating light at Henry's
face. "Stop being so anxious, Henry! Don't you see what it is you're
doing?"

"It hardly matters," Peggy said calmly. "Can't you see he's just
old?"

The alarm grew louder and warned of death. Henry's heart beat
even faster. Henry felt like his lungs were being squeezed. He tried
counting. He tried taking deep breaths. "Stop panicking," Tracy said.
"Don't you know that all this worrying will kill you?"

Henry squeezed his hands into fists. The aorta on the screen
swelled like a balloon. "I'm trying not to think about it!"

"He's gone," Tracy said, switching off the light. The screen went
blank, and Henry had woken up.

Being awake didn't change matters much—the tightness in his
chest remained. Henry sat up and took deep breaths, but he still felt
short of air. Beside him, Caroline slept quietly on her side, her back
turned. She might have acted insecure last night, but he had double
her concerns.

He couldn't hear her breathing. It was the same silence that
pervaded his house when Jack died. People sometimes went like
this, he knew—in their sleep, without warning, seemingly in perfect

health. He leaned over her in the dark. Her lips appeared bluish and frozen. He leaned closer until his nose touched her hair. Why couldn't he hear anything? As gently as he dared, he nudged her shoulder.

Caroline's skin was warm, at least. He kept pushing until she made a noise that meant she was alive. Then she turned on her other side, facing him with her head on her pillow. He put his face beside hers to feel her breath. Gradually the tightness in his chest loosened, and he returned to sleep.

*　*　*

The next morning as Henry watched Caroline get dressed, his heart thudded louder than he would have liked. She slid up her jeans, her hairclip between her teeth, and he didn't know how he'd make it from one moment to the next. There was no use denying it any longer. He was terrified of everything ending.

He could hardly have been called a coward. He moved granite monuments, encountered corpses that surfaced in heavy rains. Many men wouldn't have the stomach for his job. But every time Caroline left the room, even for a moment, he felt as desperate as a child. Death waited in the corner, threatening to destroy them just when they'd found happiness.

Henry left the bed. Outside, through the curtains, there was sunlight. "We've got a break in the rain," he said. "Let's have a picnic." Pamphlets on the table told them where they were—outside of Abergavenny, at the foot of the Black Mountains.

They dressed and hurried out to the van. They drove to the nearest shop for bread and wine, and they continued up toward the clouds. The hills were dense with blackthorn. In the valleys below, the fields appeared bright green in the sunlight.

They followed signs to the Beacons of Brecon. The first beacon revolved in the darkness, like a lighthouse on a pier. Rain came in bursts. They dropped into a valley and up again, and the second beacon shone down from a dizzying height. Henry pulled into a car park. They took the food and started up the footpath, and right away a hare jumped out of a briar patch. Without knowing why, Henry ran after it. Never would he have visited Wales, he thought as he ran, never would he have imagined chasing a hare in his forties, if it weren't for Caroline.

At the top they found a bench. They uncorked the wine and spread out the food. The wind blew the rain sideways. They couldn't see more than a few feet. The cheese and bread tasted better because they were cold. They drank the wine straight from the bottle.

Caroline zipped up her jacket and put her hood over her head. He started to tell her about the dream he'd had and changed his mind. "One day you'll find a man with more life in him," he said. The sentence flew from his mouth before he could stop it.

"How romantic," she said, making light of it.

Henry laughed. But it wasn't his laugh—it was his father's. A part of him had already started to sink. Since it would all sink anyway, one day, he felt like speeding the process up. "You're young," he said, "and impulsive."

She studied him a while. When she saw that he was serious she drank more wine and slowly seemed to retreat before him. "You're a spiteful man, Henry Bale."

He didn't say anything. "But maybe you're right," Caroline went on. "Nothing in life is certain. You can doom this before it gets going. Or, you can have faith."

"Faith," he muttered, sullen now, full of an almost pleasant self-pity. "I've never known the meaning of that one."

"Me neither. But if you want to know, you often inspire it. I'm not sorry that I love you."

He wanted to ask what she meant by that. They sat silently beside each other on the bench, but it wasn't long before Henry was kissing her like an adolescent again, and staring straight into her eyes like he hadn't just tried to sink things moments earlier. He felt dwarfed by her. He couldn't help being mesmerised.

"Do you know what I'd like to do?" She seized the bottom of his beard and yanked it with both hands. "Shave this off. Completely."

"Well…why?"

"To see you! When's the last time you took it all off?"

"I don't know." Her eyes kept searching him, dismantling his defenses.

Caroline laughed. "Stop. You must know."

He stood up and circled the bench. He didn't want to shave. He didn't know why, he just didn't. "I really can't remember, Caroline."

"Okay. Why do you wear that beard, then?"

"I can't be bothered with shaving. That's all there is to it."

He began packing their things. Didn't she just say she loved him as he was? She stood up beside him, her arms round his waist. Her hood had fallen down, and her hair blew across her face. "It was only an idea," she said. "Keep your silly beard for all I care."

He was trapped. She did care, or she wouldn't have said anything. Her arms stayed tight around his waist, and she was waiting. It was his turn to sound as if it didn't matter. "I suppose I can always get rid of the damn thing."

"Are you sure? You'd really do it?"

"I'll shave it off." He didn't know who he was any longer.

Caroline kissed him. Then she broke away and started running down the hill. Henry tried to let her go all the way down without him. It took everything he had. What if something happened—what if she slipped and fell? Unable to watch, he ran after her. When he finally caught up, he picked her up and carried her in his arms. Laughing and kicking her legs, she begged to be let go.

"Hang on," he said. "I've got you." It wasn't easy to carry her down a muddy trail. He half expected to fall over and kill them both. By a miracle, it seemed, he made it to the road without so much as scratching her skin.

EIGHT

In England, the average life expectancy for men was seventy-three. Give or take, Henry had 11,365 days to live. An average was only an average—people often died young or old—but he couldn't stop dwelling on this number, now that he had it in mind. The more he thought of it, the smaller it seemed.

In his bathroom Henry trimmed the rest of his beard to the skin. He put the scissors down and checked his reflection. For the first time in almost twenty years, he could see the outline of his face.

It was late March now, and two weeks since his promise in Wales. He'd been postponing this day, knowing it would only make him more vulnerable, more humiliated when she left him. If things didn't work out between them, the act of shaving would be one more reminder of how stupid he'd been. Splitting up seemed almost inevitable. It had become evident in Caroline's smiles. Henry lathered and dragged the razor down his cheek. His skin felt like it was being ripped into pieces.

He'd begun counting her smiles the day after they'd returned from Wales. The first day, he'd counted eight. The next thirteen days, she smiled an average of just over seven times a day. On Sunday, when they spent the whole day together, he counted thirteen smiles. If they did stay together, he calculated he'd see Caroline smile 70,494 times, including Sunday smiles, before he retired. Assuming he retired at sixty-seven—the age his father had—and assuming she stopped working too, he'd have four years of complete days with her before he died. If she continued to smile with roughly the same regularity, he'd get an extra 18,980 smiles, for a total of 89,474.

Eighty-nine thousand smiles! That number seemed large. But it was an absurd, nonsensical number, like the number of hours scientists said it took to bicycle to the moon. He had a hunch the average was dropping, too. He might have let himself, with all the counting, become paranoid. But if the average continued to drop, the number of her remaining smiles would be dramatically lower.

Henry kept at it with the razor, setting his teeth at the pain. His face streamed with blood. He resisted the urge to count something. He'd been counting too much as it was—while he dug, while he drove, even while kissing. He calculated the number of summer days they'd likely spend together, the number of evening films they'd watch. Each number depended on the all-important number of days he had left, 11,365. Each number depended on the assumption that they would marry and stay together until he died.

Henry kept shaving until the beard was gone. He washed and dried his face with a towel, startled at the young man staring back at him.

*   *   *

"Beautiful," Caroline said, holding his face in her hands. "I mean, you're the most handsome man in Sussex. Look at the angle of those cheeks. Look at that chin!"

She led him back upstairs to his mirror. He blushed and let himself be fussed over. "Look at you," she kept saying. "Look how handsome you are."

"Please," he begged. "Let's do something else with our day." He brought her back downstairs and onto the sofa. It was no use. She kept staring. "I know I'm making you upset, but I can't help it. You have to admit you look better."

"Yes, I admit it. I'd just rather not dwell on it, that's all. I shaved. I didn't climb Mount Everest."

She laughed and kissed him. "I won't talk about it any more, then. But it's taken ten years off you."

It wasn't true, Henry thought—he still only had 11,365 days. He looked at the photo of his parents on the mantle. Too early, his father had been robbed of his allotment of love. His chest tightened. He tried to get up, to leave his mother's sofa as it had been months before, a relic in a museum. He didn't have the strength to move. The sitting room seemed to be darkening, closing in.

"Henry! Are you all right? My God, you're shaking."

He clutched the arm of the sofa. "I can't breathe," he said. His chest seized, and he thought for certain he was about to die.

* * *

The Black Ram stood empty. All the regulars had stayed out of the rain, as if by joint decree. The hours crept by. The refrigerator hummed louder than normal, and an awful stillness hung in the air. Sid preferred working to standing around, but tonight only Oliver Marsh was in. It wasn't much different than being alone.

Sid looked at his watch. It was only ten. "I'll lay money on it, Oliver—it won't be just us tonight. I've got a sense about these things."

Sid talked to Oliver more than anyone in the pub. He knew it was strange, but recently he'd been telling the man about his wife, eight months pregnant and giving him fits. Oliver hadn't seemed to mind. He sat on his stool like a ghost, his skin pale and pockmarked. Occasionally he lifted his pint glass to his mouth, and that was about it.

Crossing his arms, Sid looked out the window at the slanting rain. "I'd lay a fiver on it," he said. It so rarely happened it was almost mythical, the pub empty all the way to closing. Never mind the rain, or that times were difficult. Rain and difficult times were all too common in Chalk. So when the door creaked open and Darren Roberts stuck his head inside, Sid shot Oliver a smile. Even if it was a feeble pulse, the village had one. He could have sworn Oliver smiled back, but it was probably his imagination.

Sid waited while the teacher took off his coat. Darren hardly ever came to the pub, and he couldn't recall what it was the man drank. "What will you have, then, Darren?"

"Cider, please," Darren said. He looked like he was deciding where to sit.

Choosing the snuggery was anti-social in an empty pub, but Sid could tell Darren wanted to drink alone. He craned his neck in that direction and seemed in a bad way. Finally he took Dick Miles' stool in the corner by the door. It was a draughty spot. Dick liked it because he was the gatekeeper on the estate, and he was partial to doors of all kinds. Darren already regretted his choice—it was clear by the way he rubbed his knees. He'd tried to get as far from Oliver as possible without being rude, and he'd landed in the one spot where he'd be forced to look at the man's face.

Sid rolled a cigarette behind the bar. He was about to step outside with it when he noticed Oliver's empty pint glass in front of his mat. He poured the first half of a new Guinness, and the door opened.

Trevor Nelson stormed to the bar. "Bloody goddamn rain," he said, by way of greeting.

Sid let Oliver's Guinness settle while he pumped Trevor's lager. All of a sudden he was busy. "Another wet night."

"Wet? It's a goddamn downpour!" Trevor took the stool directly in front of the taps, as if worried someone might confiscate them. "Hello, Oliver," he said. "I hope things are going well with you." Trevor paid for his beer and noticed Darren in the corner. "Well, well. What are you doing here, Mr. Roberts?"

"What do you mean?" Darren said, scowling.

"Isn't it a school night?"

"Fuck off," Darren said.

Trevor was silenced by that. He took his time with the first sip of his drink. "Prickly pear in the corner, Sid."

Sid ignored the comment. He poured the rest of Oliver's Guinness and put it on the mat. "Two pounds forty, please, Oliver. Thank you."

"You never shut up, Trevor," Darren said, staring down the length of the bar. "Always jabbering, you are. Can't a man have a quiet drink?"

Trevor raised his glass. "Sir, you may proceed with as many quiet drinks as you see fit. I get the feeling you need them."

That seemed to be the extent of it. It wasn't polite for Trevor to have needled Darren, but the teacher had clearly been testy. Behind the bar Sid drifted toward Darren's stool, as if to send a message that he sympathised. There was a great deal to be sympathetic about—the rain, the pitfalls of sharing a bar with Trevor Nelson, the fact that they all lived in Chalk. He thought Darren would leave after one, but the teacher returned his pint glass empty in short order.

Sid flicked on the cider tap. He had a bad feeling about this. It was only a matter of time before Trevor's restraint ran up. Darren had just returned to his seat when sure enough, Trevor raised his glass toward the corner.

"Strong stuff, that ladies' cider. I can tell you're a drinking man."

Darren sat forward. His eyes were badly bloodshot. "You don't have manners, do you?"

Trevor cocked his head. "Me? I should say not."

"Bloody rude bastard, you are. It was your doing, making me the fool at Beverly's service."

Trevor stared at him. "What in hell are you on about?"

"You don't remember. Or you're acting like you don't. You made me look bad in front of Caroline."

"You didn't need my help."

Sid put his hands on the bar. "Gentlemen," he said, "this is your first warning."

"You really think you had a chance with her?" Trevor said. "I don't think she goes for Nancies."

Darren stood up. "Take that back."

Trevor pushed back his stool. "I won't. Come on, then."

"Gentlemen! Sit down this instant."

Darren had already come forward with a big looping right. Trevor blocked it. He whipped the teacher round and shoved him face first against the bar, but not as hard as he could have. "Nancy," he said. "Learn to fight." Darren squirmed, but Trevor held him fast. Oliver sipped his Guinness, watching.

"Sit down, please, gentlemen, or go outside," Sid said. "Not in the pub."

"Learn to fight," Trevor said again. He jabbed his finger in Darren's face.

Darren drooled on his shirt. His face was red. "Let me go. You don't understand."

"I do, mate. I understand too well."

"Now, now," Sid said, gently. The men were past the danger zone, or they wouldn't have been chatting. Still, he couldn't remember the last time he'd seen a scrape like this. He started wiping the bar around Darren's head. "Caroline's a rare bird for Chalk. We all know it. No need for arguments."

Trevor released Darren and sat down. Darren brushed himself off. He went back to his stool by the door, his eyes darting, his thinning hair strewn about his forehead. He seemed to be deciding whether to stay or go home. "I'm a schoolteacher," he said. "I don't know what I..." His hands shook as he smoothed out a fiver on the bar. "One for yourself, Sid. And one for you, Trevor." He pulled out a ten. "And whatever Oliver's drinking as well."

Sid took the ten and started on the drinks. "Thanks, Darren. Very decent of you."

Trevor nodded down the bar. "It certainly is."

There was a silence. Trevor drank his beer in one go and motioned for another. "The parish gravedigger has our teacher now. There's consolation for you!" Suddenly gloomy, he dropped his head to his empty glass.

Sid gave Trevor his next lager and waited in front of his stool. "Two pounds thirty for that one, Trevor."

Trevor sat up and dug into his pockets. "One for Darren as well."

"I don't think I should," Darren said. "I mean—I've just started on this one."

"I don't know what's worse," Trevor muttered. "Thinking of her alone, or with him."

"Try seeing her all day, every day," Darren said. "In those outfits."

Sid could picture it. Oliver Marsh picked nervously at the pockmarks dotting his face, as if picturing it as well.

"And she listens," Trevor said. He sat up a little. "She listens instead of talks!"

"You ought to try it sometime," Sid said.

"You think they'll last?" Trevor asked him. "Caroline and Henry Bale?"

Sid shrugged. Caroline would pass through eventually, he thought, like a storm. "They seem happy enough, don't they?"

"A woman like that can turn your life around," Trevor said. "Turn you into a better person. Henry got bloody lucky, the bastard."

"He's a good chap," Sid said, putting his hands on the bar. He'd defended everyone in the village at one time or another—even Trevor.

"He shaved his beard off," Darren said. "She got him to do that, I'm sure."

"Beards grow back," Trevor said, smiling a little. He looked out the window. "And rain continues to fall."

"Maybe I will learn to fight," Darren mumbled. He made his hands into fists.

Sid looked outside along with the others. There was something unsettling about this rain, something ominous. He checked his watch. "Last call, gentlemen," he said, "and then I'm going out in that to smoke." Almost in unison, three pint glasses slid forward, and he went round to pick them up.

* * *

The rain continued into April. Henry tried to remember when he'd seen a day without it. He and Caroline had just eaten supper, and as was their custom these days, they sat on his sofa reading—he with the current issue of *Waterfowl*, she with a book of poetry. Jackie slept in the wicker basket by the fire.

Late February, Henry guessed, when they'd last had a day without rain. He tried to count the number of days that was, but Caroline kept catching him tap his finger. She'd become concerned with his behaviour, he could tell. Lately he found himself wishing for the kind of evenings he'd spent with Jack. It might have been nostalgia for nostalgia's sake, but a part of him longed for the quieter life he'd once led. He winced as a shot of pain caught him in the back.

"Are you all right?"

He stayed motionless on the edge of the sofa, waiting it out. "It's nothing," he said. When she touched his shoulder he flinched.

"It's your back again, isn't it?"

There she was—probing him, making him talk. "Just tired," he said. The phone rang, and he gingerly made his way across the sitting room. It was a man's voice on the other end.

"Henry Bale? This is Marshall Moss. The undertaker here in Kington. Derrick Watkins has fallen ill, and we've a grave that needs digging Friday. Derrick gave us your name..."

"Kington? The parish church?"

"That's right. A new double. I know it's a bit of a drive."

"Not too bad to Kington," he said, though he knew it was. It was just like Derrick to plan on falling ill on a Friday. "What time's the service?"

"Half one."

"Yes, I'm free," he said, checking his calendar book by the phone. "All right."

"I'll make it worth your while, Mr. Bale. What's your normal fee?"

"One hundred twenty for a new double."

"Same as Derrick, that is. I'll throw in an extra twenty for your trouble?"

"Fine. Will the grave be marked?"

"It's the next spot in the row along the north hedge, which the vicar's designated for new burials. You'll see. The casket's six-five by twenty-four, plus your clearances. Bloody wet digging, these days. You have an electric pump?"

"No need," Henry said, writing down the dimensions. "I'll be using my bailer, most likely."

"It'll be bloody wet digging," Moss repeated.

"Don't worry," Henry said. After twenty years, didn't he know how to dig in the rain? He hung up. Instead of returning to the sofa, he stayed near the phone table in the dark.

Caroline sat perched forward, her eyebrows knitted. "Is everything all right?"

"Of course it is."

"What are you doing over there? Why do you sound so gloomy? Aren't you going to come back over and sit next to me?"

He slinked over to the sofa. As soon as he sat down, she took his hand and stroked it. Her eyes still melted him half away. "Henry," she said, looking at him searchingly, "does it depress you sometimes, digging graves?"

"Not really." It was true—his job never really bothered him. It was only recently that he'd been preoccupied with death, and with dying as a whole. Even so, he didn't exactly feel depressed. He didn't know what the word for it was.

"Still," she said, rubbing the top of his hand as if he were sick, "it can be grim work, can't it?"

The phone rang again. It was Hetherington, booking him for Monday and Tuesday of next week. He wrote down the appointments and went back to the sofa, where Caroline had been listening to his schedule fill up. "Always busy in wet weather," Henry said, shaking his head. Jackie stretched in the cot, and he pointed at her. "Look how she's grown," he said, trying to change the topic. "Jack sprang up like that."

"Henry, why do you dig?"

He sighed. "I've already told you. It was my father's job."

"I know. But why do you?"

"People don't stop dying, do they? The phone kept ringing after Dad retired, that's all. It's steady work. Like teaching."

Caroline kept searching his eyes as if he needed special understanding. "I've never looked at teaching that way," she said. "I love it, most days."

"Fair enough. But not everyone can do what they like. I wasn't the best student, for one reason or another." He wanted to be alone. He would have been sitting in his armchair right about now, watching television and falling asleep. "Dad says I didn't leave myself many choices."

She kissed him on the cheek. He hated it when she did that because it made him feel like a child. "I think it's wonderful what you do."

He stood up. "Wonderful? It's not wonderful while you're digging, I'll tell you that. Especially in this weather!" He stoked the fire with the poker, though it was fine.

"I can imagine."

"Maybe you can, maybe you can't." He was starting to sound like his father, encouraging the very pity he spurned. He stoked the embers with rough stabbing motions. Smoke billowed from the hearth. "My work's no more difficult than anything else."

"I should say it is," she said. She smiled weakly. "I'm proud of you for what you do. And it can't be easy, psychologically. Do you think that's why you're getting these anxiety attacks?"

He hung the poker back on the hook. He wanted her to leave, but he didn't know how to ask. "I don't think about it much, to tell you the truth." He kept staring into the flames.

"Not even when it's someone you know?"

"We all have to go sooner or later."

Caroline put down her book. She crossed her legs and folded her hands on her lap. "Henry. I want to know something, and don't be upset with me for asking. Do you believe in God?"

"I don't know."

"But you've never attended much church, have you?"

She'd trapped him again. This time she'd made him admit that he had no philosophy to speak of. "No, I haven't. What about you?"

"That's why I'm asking. I've been thinking about it lately. I don't know why, maybe because of all the time I've got on my hands here."

"So you believe in God?"

"Not a traditional one. I try to pray once in a while. If that's what you call sitting still and trying to look inside yourself."

"Good for you," Henry snapped. The whole subject irritated him. "How can anyone know if God exists, traditional or no? You've got so much time on your hands? Then I suggest doing something with yourself!"

Jackie sat up and barked. Henry realised he'd been shouting.

"I don't like being screamed at," Caroline said. She inched away from him, like she was about to run. "You're acting like my father, you know. Always trying to find some sinister motive to a simple conversation."

"Really? And how would I know about that? You never talk about your father."

"He can be just like this. He yells, like you're yelling now."

"Wonderful," Henry said, stuffing his hands in his pockets. "Now I'm like your father. Why do you get to analyse me all the time, but you never talk about yourself?"

Caroline blinked at him. "Talking takes time. He wasn't abusive or anything. You don't have to get upset with me."

"I'm just sick and tired of it." Henry didn't remember the last time he'd been in an argument like this—an argument that pulled him apart—but he felt like giving in to it. He didn't even know what they were arguing about any more. "I'm sick of your fucking pity."

"I'm not pitying you, Henry. Don't be ridiculous. Your face is all red and contorted. And don't swear at me, please."

"You don't smile as much as you used to. I've been counting, and I know!"

"Counting my smiles?" She smiled now, as if caught. "What are you talking about?"

"Never mind," he said, turning back to the fire. He took a deep breath. "I think I need to be alone right now, Caroline."

There was a long silence. "All right."

"God knows you won't stay in Chalk long," he muttered, speaking as much to himself as her. "Time on your hands—that's rich. I've got the reverse problem. Why don't you go back to that boy Trent. He's got more life in him. The only reason you're with me is to play the teacher and the mother and to pity me." He turned, and his face went pale. She stood by the door with her jacket on, her purse in her hand.

"I had no idea you were keeping so much inside," she said.

He rushed toward her, suddenly frantic. He'd done it. He'd fallen straight down the hole he'd tried to dance around, ever since they'd met. "Don't listen to me," he begged. "Please…"

"Maybe we moved too quickly," she said. "Stupid of me not to realise."

She went to the door, and he followed her. Now he dreaded being alone. "Please, Caroline. Don't leave. I'd rather die than be without you." He reached for her arm, but she slapped his hands away. She opened the door and turned as if taking him in for the last time. It was all he could do not to fall on his knees and beg her forgiveness.

"Just for the record, Henry, I love you. I never pitied you at all until now."

Henry looked at the carpet and waited. When he heard the door close and the gate clang shut he couldn't raise his eyes, not even to look at his dog.

NINE

All the roads to Kington were closed. Henry left the van beside a farmhouse and set out on foot across the fields, pushing his wheelbarrow along the public footpath.

After a mile of trudging through mud and climbing turnstiles, Henry arrived in Kington exhausted. The church sat on a hill, and the car park beside it resembled a lake. A few sheep had abandoned the waterlogged pastures to roam the graveyard. On the churchyard gate, a sign in red lettering read, *CAUTION: Ground subsistence due to recent heavy rainfall. Please take extreme care while walking through burial ground.*

Derrick picked a fine day for a hangover. Even the birds seemed in hiding. Henry spotted the area for new graves beyond the spruce trees and parked his wheelbarrow on the next empty plot. It would have been nice to rest, but there wasn't time. He took the measurements out of his pocket and read the name. "Here we go, Charles Young," he said.

To keep the grave dry, he'd brought a canopy. The wind played havoc with the tarpaulin as he fastened it to the tent poles, and rain found its way in anyway. He started to dig. The spade went in easily enough, but the soil dripped. By the time he'd carted the excess away—nine wheelbarrow loads to the edge of the churchyard—it was ten o'clock. He wasn't even two feet down. The rain kept coming, with no sign of letting up.

The hole started to fill with water. It took twenty minutes of bailing to get it dry. "Now then," he said, panting, "watch out, you goddamn rain." He dug a sump at the foot of the grave where water could collect and kicked the spade to the head. He dug wildly, taking out double portions. The mound grew.

Henry worked steadily, and soon he'd thrown off his waterproofs to keep cool. The rain could bucket from the sky—he'd be finished by the time it mattered. In no time, he'd cleared two spits. He picked up his pace, and even the sump stayed dry. The walls of the grave rose level and clean. A twinge tickled his right shoulder, but he ignored it, digging as if possessed. Then like a bullet, pain ripped down his back.

"Oh, God," he said, gasping. "Oh, no." It was bad this time. He kept his boot on the edge of his spade, and the pain kept coming in waves, making it hard to see. Groaning, he dropped to his knees.

His shoulders locked solid. His feet went numb. Time passed, and the pain locked his back like a metal cage. What would happen if he couldn't dig? He'd be in a fine mess, kneeling inside the hole when the casket came! He tried getting to his feet. Each time, his muscles seized.

Water kept seeping in. Henry cried out for help. He didn't call too loudly—just a few words, offered to the wind. A little later he was shouting at the top of his lungs. The only response was the rain, thudding against the tarpaulin.

At the foot of the grave, the sump overflowed. He was kneeling in three inches, then four. He started to shiver, to really panic. He had to get out. Gritting his teeth, he got up on one foot, but his boot slipped, and fresh bolts of pain shot up his back. Screaming, he fell to his knees. When the blackness went away, when he could finally see again and his mind cleared, the water had risen to his waist. It was absurd, but he was drowning.

"Help! Help me, someone!" He wasn't self-conscious any longer, only scared.

A crack formed on the grave wall. Henry put his hand against it. The crack grew sideways, as if thinking about where to go, and then it shot down in a straight line. The wall crumbled.

Overhead, the canopy collapsed. A wave of water rushed into the grave, filling his clothes. Gasping for air, Henry lifted his chin above the water. A shoe floated by his face. He thought of his father. He thought of Caroline at his door with her jacket on. There was a gurgling sound. Henry knew what it was before he saw it, and then the next corpse in the row surfaced in front of him, face down in the water, its reddish hair matted with mud.

* * *

Trevor kept his car up on the banks of the road. He drove alongside fences and hedges and walls. He was drunk.

The roads had become rivers. The hills were saturated to overflowing. Even Trevor's ears felt wet. The rain had found its way through the rubber lining of the car windows and crawled down his neck onto his shoulders. Maybe God did exist, as Chris Crawley had argued. How else to explain this flood, testing him to do the right thing?

Trevor kept circling Kington on the bypass roads, seeking an open way into town. Finally he parked beside a closed bridge, got out, and ran.

It had taken a marathon drinking session with Chris Crawley, but eventually he'd come to the conclusion that Henry didn't deserve what he'd done to him. The drink and the guilt made him weep and confess. Chris had shoved him into the car, demanding he drive to Kington straight away. He needed to remedy the situation, Chris said, especially for the family of the deceased going into the ground.

Now as he splashed along the bridge Trevor could see the Kington steeple beckoning him over the treetops, holding out the possibility of forgiveness.

"The Lord is my saviour, the heaven so high above..." He kept singing his favourite hymn from childhood.

On the other side of the bridge, the water stood higher. Soon he was wading. Broken tree branches floated with clothes and aluminium cans. Tremor scrambled up on a dry bank to rest. A lift was what he needed. He held out his thumb and waited. It took a long time before he remembered the roads were closed.

*　*　*

Derrick Watkins battled an unusually severe hungover as he rammed his wheelbarrow through the muddy sheep pasture. His toes had developed blisters inside his wet socks, and his jeans had soaked through to the second pair. To top it off, the wheelbarrow kept jamming in the mud. In the end he carried it on his back, all the way up the path and through the churchyard gate. Then he threw down the wheelbarrow and fished in his pocket for a cigarette.

Derrick had risen early, unable to stay asleep. He'd woken on the downstairs sofa in his rambling farmhouse, surrounded by books, the curtains drawn. It was his favourite place to sleep after a night of drinking, coasting in the pitch black straight through to noon. But after just a few hours of sleep he'd sat up, wide awake, squinting as if sunlight streamed onto his face.

It was guilt, Derrick knew. In the muddy churchyard he found a bent cigarette and tossed it away. He'd never woken with that sort of guilt, in all the years he'd lived, even with his habit of drinking to excess and speaking his mind. What was guilt, anyway? Why did he suddenly care what he'd done to another man? The more he thought about it, the harder it was to sleep.

He searched his other pocket and found a cigarette in acceptable condition. The wind blew out his first match, but when he peered across the churchyard he didn't bother lighting a second. He left his wheelbarrow at the gate and despite his hangover he hurdled the headstones like a deer.

"Bloody...fuck!"

The hole had broken into a gaping mess. For some reason Henry had left, abandoning a giant crater, swirling with muddy water, clothing, and pieces of wood. A tarpaulin attached to a tent pole flapped in the wind like an errant sail.

Derrick scanned the churchyard. The man was nowhere to be seen. Had he gone back for his pump? It wasn't possible—he would have run into him on the footpath. Besides, his wheelbarrow was still there, parked beside the hedge.

Derrick checked his watch. It was just gone eleven. The service started in two hours. Had Henry ducked into the church? He reached for another cigarette and stopped. A head floated on the water.

That would be Dick Simmons' head, Derrick thought—the man who died three weeks back. But even as he thought it, he knew he was wrong. Dick had red hair, and this had black. The forehead was still pink, too. He took a step closer to the hole, and the head turned slowly under the water. The chin pointed up to the sky, and the lips puckered for air.

* * *

Henry thought the splash came from another wall caving in. Grave water filled his mouth.

He'd been repeating words and phrases in an effort to stay calm. He'd remembered the complete verses to two hymns, along with the Lord's Prayer. If God saved his life, he promised, he'd start attending church and try to be a better person. Then an arm circled his waist. There was a great sucking noise, like bathwater draining, and he felt himself being lifted out of the water.

He flopped on the muddy ground like a fish. He coughed and he spat until the taste of the grave was gone. Then he saw Derrick Watkins.

"You gave me quite a fright." The gravedigger stood over him. Mud streaked down his face. "What the hell were you doing, Henry, having a swim?"

"Me? What are you doing here?"

"Never mind that. Why were you inside that grave?"

"My back went." Henry sat up on the mud. Little spasms trickled down his spine, but he could move.

Derrick kept hovering over him. He seemed torn between anger and sympathy. "Well? And how long were you in there?"

"An hour, maybe."

"Jesus. You could have drowned."

"I know." Henry moved the parts of his body, taking inventory. "It was awful, Derrick. Just awful, not being able to get out."

"You'd better change into some dry clothes. What happened to your beard? You didn't lose that in there, did you?"

"I shaved it."

Derrick headed for his wheelbarrow. Henry stood up and went running after him, his Wellingtons sloshing, his lungs filling with clean air. "I thought you were ill."

"Lucky for you I got better." From his wheelbarrow Derrick took out a pair of dry trousers and pullover. "Here. Change into these while I get my pump into that hole."

Henry held the pullover to his chest. It was going to be too small for him. "I've never seen a grave wall give way like that."

"Must have been an underground runoff," Derrick said. He attached a rubber hose to his pump. "I was afraid of something like that."

"Is that why you're here?"

"Of course! You think I came to pass the time? Now hurry up and change. This weather isn't letting up. We've got to build a jamb in that grave."

"You saved my life, Derrick."

Henry looked up at the sky. He started to pray but didn't know what to say besides thanks.

Derrick threw his pump into his wheelbarrow. He pointed toward the hole, his finger shaking. "There's two graves to dig now, and Dick Simmons to rebury. Go on. Change into those clothes. You're a fat lot of good to me, shivering like that."

"All right," Henry said, smiling. "You don't have to get angry at me." He walked the muddy path to the church. At the door, he emptied his Wellingtons and wrung out his socks.

*   *   *

The Kington church smelled of ammonia, and the stained glass windows streamed daylight across the pews. In his wet socks Henry slapped down the nave and ducked into the shadows of the chancel to change. Derrick's trousers and pullover reeked of cigarettes. But the clothes were dry, and as he came back over the chancel rail Henry kicked his feet in a little dance. He was alive.

Remembering his promise, he stopped at one of the pews on his way back out. He pulled out the red-padded kneeler and lowered himself down. "Almighty God..." He clasped his hands, his voice no louder than a whisper. "Thank you for sending Derrick to save me." He said the Lord's Prayer again, and at the end he added, "Please let Caroline understand me."

The cross above the altar stared down at him mutely. Taking his wet clothes, Henry slid the kneeler back and started down the nave. The church door opened.

"Henry!" Trevor Nelson said, rushing toward him. "Derrick told me what happened—thank God he came along when he did." Trevor patted his shirt pockets. "You wouldn't have a cigarette?"

Henry blinked at him, confused. "What are you doing in Kington?"

"This is one of my favourite churches, you see. Wait! Did you say you had a cigarette? I've been running for miles."

"I don't smoke, Trevor."

"I've done something terrible," Trevor said, dropping to his knees. "I have a confession to make!"

Henry kept walking. "I've had a long morning," he said. A part of him was still in the grave. He certainly had no patience for Trevor Nelson right now. But before he knew it Trevor jumped to his feet and blocked the door.

"Get out of my way, Trevor. I mean it. I've got a grave that needs digging."

"It's because of me you almost drowned."

Henry wiped his mouth with the back of his hand. "What? You saw me in that hole and didn't do anything?"

"I paid Derrick to dig that grave wide. That's why the wall collapsed. Then I told him to pretend to be ill, so you'd have to dig the next one and get—"

"You what?"

"It was a prank, Henry. It's true. I swear to God, here in this church. It was because of Caroline. Chris told me to find you and apologise. It was me, Henry! I got Derrick to dig his last grave wide. With all the rain I knew it would make for messy digging, and—"

Henry punched him. Trevor collapsed, his hand to his nose.

"You deserved that." Henry said, panicking a little at Trevor moaning on the floor. "You're lucky I don't hit you again. You all right? Trevor?"

The vicar entered the church. He was an elderly man with a shrill voice. "What's going on here?"

"I'm the gravedigger today," Henry said, hiding his bundle of wet clothes behind his back. "Filling in for Derrick."

"Why is this man on the ground?"

"I hit him. I won't do it again."

Trevor kept moaning. He was dripping blood all over the clean floor. "I've got a hanky," Henry said, searching the pockets of his overalls. "But it's wet."

"Stay away from that man," the vicar told him. "Get back." He produced a clean white handkerchief from the sleeve of his robe. "Now put your arms at your sides," he told Trevor, kneeling behind him, "so I can plug that nose."

Trevor did as he was told. He leaned back against the vicar's chest and regarded Henry smugly from the comfort of holy cloth.

✳ ✳ ✳

Working together, the men finished the grave by the time of the service. The ground around the hole was muddy, but considering the state of the churchyard, it didn't look out of the ordinary. Derrick transferred Dick Simmons to his original plot and shored up the wall with a network of wooden jambs. Trevor, sporting a bandage across his nose, kept pace with the bailer. Henry did the lightest work. Taking care not to re-injure his back, he hauled away loads of wet soil, quietly stewing.

Henry didn't want to hold any grudges. He knew that the cost of bitterness was high, that it was too small a community to engage in feuds. Toward Derrick he still felt a strange gratitude, considering the man had technically saved his life. Though he was still angry at both of them, Henry hoped his hours near death yielded lessons he wouldn't have had otherwise.

Trevor insisted on telling Caroline what had happened. It was essential to his redemption, he explained to Henry, as Derrick split off in one direction and they walked in the other, over the fields in the direction of their cars. Henry tried to dissuade him, but it was no use. Trevor was heading to Caroline's whether Henry liked it or not. Wary of what Trevor might do or say on his own, Henry decided to follow him to Bates Farm to oversee the "confession."

Caroline didn't invite them inside. She stood outside on her step, blocking her door, her hands on her hips. Trevor told her what he'd done with the vicar's bandage still taped to his nose.

"It was because of me that Henry suffered," he said, hanging his head. His clothes were covered with mud. "But also because of you. Maybe if you hadn't treated me so rudely." He looked up and winked. "You see? Henry suffered because of us both. We're jointly to blame, Caroline. We make our own little team."

"Hardly," Caroline said. "Disturbing the dead? That was your plan to get my attention? You two are quite a pair."

"But what did I do?" Henry asked. He still hadn't changed out of Derrick's clothes. The trousers barely reached his ankles, and the pullover had started ripping at the shoulders. "My back went out. I nearly drowned!"

"You're in the wrong as well. Fighting in a church."

Henry stamped his feet in the cold. Caroline was still angry with him from the night before. "It was hardly a fight," he muttered. "I told the vicar I was sorry."

"What is it about the men in this village?" Caroline pointed her face at the sky.

Trevor got to his knees. "I'm sorry, Caroline. I wanted to confess. There are other things to apologise for. Should I keep going?"

"Stop it," Henry said.

"Or go on if you like," Caroline said, "but do it somewhere else."

"He wants you to forgive him, Caroline," Henry said.

"First sin, then forgiveness," Trevor said, getting to his feet. "After that is redemption."

"I don't feel like forgiving you," Caroline said. "I don't believe you are genuinely contrite."

"Unredeemed, and free to sin again! But what about your confession, Caroline? Haven't you considered how selfish you've been, descending on Chalk without considering Darren and Henry and me? What about us?"

"Shut up, Trevor," Henry said. It was too late—Caroline went inside and slammed the door.

Trevor stared at Henry significantly. They stood together in silence until Trevor slinked off into his battered Citroen. He started up the car and rolled down the window. "Hey, Henry. Want to grab a pint?"

Henry ignored him. As Trevor drove off he waited on Caroline's step, hoping for her to come back out.

*   *   *

The next day, Henry rose before dawn. His back sore, his head crowded with images of death and promises to God, he walked to Bates Farm and waited under the same oak Trevor had chosen. The rain had abated, but not by much. Under the branches, he huddled into the darkest, driest pocket he could find. Time passed under the dripping leaves—too much time, it seemed—and Caroline's bedroom light stayed off. Had she gone out last night?

As daylight appeared through the clouds, Henry crept out from under the tree. He couldn't bring himself all the way to her door. For a while he just stood in the middle of the road, getting drenched. He had a vision of himself stuck there, his back frozen solid, while the rest of Chalk woke up. Stupid, he thought, checking his watch—it was only a quarter past seven. Caroline was probably still asleep. He went back under the oak.

Half an hour later her light went on, followed by shadows behind the curtain. Unable to wait any longer, Henry went to the door and knocked. Still in her nightgown, Caroline opened the door. She smiled as if expecting him, handed him a towel to dry off. They went into the kitchen, where Caroline made tea. As she poured it from the pot he stared at the hands that had touched his face only two days ago. It took all his self control not to seize them and hang on.

"I miss you," he blurted. "There. I said it."

She laughed a little as she looked out the window at The Beacon. "You're such a jumble of nerves," she said, pulling her nightgown together and tying the sash.

"What do you mean?" It bothered him, the way she'd pulled her nightgown closed. Wasn't she being overly modest? He looked at that nightgown, drawn like a straightjacket round her waist, and knew he was doomed. "You've changed your mind about me," he said. Henry stepped toward her, then retreated to where he'd been standing by the counter.

"Henry, stop your brooding. You've been acting so strange lately. How long have you been counting my smiles?"

"What do you mean?"

"You told me the other night. You can't deny it now. And what is this nonsense about not being able to live if we broke up?"

He tightened the towel around his neck. "Maybe I just say things."

"Henry. You never just say things. If you could see yourself right now! You act cornered when I ask you the slightest question." She crossed her arms, as if chastising a child. "If we can't talk to one another, how are we supposed to function as a couple?"

Her hint of a future made his heart jump. He wanted to leap across the kitchen, but he stayed where he was. "I do try to talk. I just get uncomfortable."

"You shouldn't be uncomfortable around me."

"I'm not like you, Caroline. Don't you understand? I'm past forty. I'm over half finished." He looked at her hopefully, as if she might tell him it weren't true.

"I don't care about your age," Caroline said. "I love you."

These words should have cheered him, but her closed nightgown told him otherwise. "I love you, too," he said.

"We have this problem," she went on. "You were right the other night. You wanted to be alone."

"I didn't. Not really."

"Yes, you did. And I couldn't accept that. I've thought about it, and I've come to the conclusion that we moved way too quickly. You're… we're just not ready."

"But—"

"I want to keep growing. I want to keep learning. And I want to be with someone who can communicate with me."

"All right," he said, coming toward her. "Let's talk. Let me ask you a few things," he said, talking now for the sake of it. He took her hands and faced her. "Tell me why you don't see your parents. Tell me your favourite childhood memory—"

She pulled her hands away and pointed across the kitchen. "Henry. Please stand back over there."

He retreated to the other end of the counter. The humiliation was almost unbearable. "I knew you wouldn't waste any time moving on. Why are you so reckless, Caroline? Why did you come to Chalk?"

She lowered her eyes like horns. "You think I'm reckless for coming here—to Chalk?"

"You need to be constantly searching for something new."

"Isn't everyone?"

"Not that I know of."

"Well, they should be. Even if they're happy they should be—it keeps us alive, Henry. And there's nothing wrong with my parents, they just don't define me. I believe in defining myself. They've never left Nottinghamshire."

"I'd never left Sussex until a few weeks ago. Not once. How did you ever get on with me?"

She looked down at her hands. "Perhaps you remind me of the fundamentals I've missed. You're old-fashioned, but you're willing to try new things, too. Most people aren't. You're different because you think. And you let yourself feel."

There was a silence. He reached for his tea, but he'd drunk it all. He hated being this vulnerable. If she wanted him to make love to her, he would. And if she wanted him to go dig a dozen graves, he'd do that instead.

"Henry. Tell me what's happened in your head. Tell me what's really bothering you."

He stared at the linoleum and wished he hadn't been born. He wanted to tell her about the terror he felt, the compulsions. It was all because he loved her. It was because he couldn't bear to think of it ending with her. Now she was the one person he couldn't confide in. It would only drive her further away.

"I've been moody lately," he said. "That's all."

She shook her head suspiciously. "You're not telling me what's on your mind. A psychologist might help, Henry. I know you don't like talking about it, but there must be a reason for these moods."

"You bet there's a reason. It's called getting older."

"No. More than that. I'm worried, Henry, that you're using me—us—as the solution to certain issues that you're tackling."

"I have no idea what you're talking about. You sound like a psychologist yourself. Maybe I should just keep talking, even if what I say amounts to nonsense, filling each silence with words. How about that?"

"I think we should take some time off."

Henry stood there with his head down, waiting to hear the rest, knowing the words before they were spoken.

"It's best, Henry. I've thought about this, and I think we just rushed into things. It was my fault as much as yours. Let's try separating for a month or so, then see where we are."

"A month? You might as well break up with me right now, if that's what you want to do."

"If we're meant to be together, we will be. In the meantime, let's use this month to think about things."

"Think about things? What does that mean?" He looked up at her, his eyes streaming. "You're too young, Caroline—you don't realise how valuable a month can be. I can't do it. I can't wait a month for the same result."

"Henry." Caroline walked across the kitchen. She put her arms around him and her head against his chest. "Trust me on this," she said. "If it ever seems like you can't do something, it's proof that you should try."

TEN

Even as he approached his house Henry dreaded what it contained: the brown armchair, the walls, the television.

There was always the pub. Sid would be behind the bar, ready to pour a pint. The idea scared him—so easily he could become a regular, and the regulars all had problems. He was trapped. Everyone in Chalk would soon find out. He'd have to stay indoors to avoid the glances, the questions, the jeers.

At his gate he wanted to turn back, to beg Caroline to change her mind. He had no graves to dig today, nothing to do. Without Caroline, without work, what could he do? He had nothing but time, and nobody to share it with. Caroline was right. Their relationship only covered a hole in his life. But what was the nature of this hole? He had no idea what its dimensions were, let alone start to fill it up. The hole existed long before Caroline arrived.

Only yesterday Henry had emerged from a water-filled grave, excited to be alive. It was high time to offer prayers inside St. Margaret's, to remember his promise. Instead he opened his gate and hurried inside. He sat in the armchair and turned on the television. Here he was, resuming the life he hated, even as Jackie stared at him from her basket. He wanted to go to sleep, to forget. Eventually he'd nod off, only to drag himself upstairs and collapse. He might as well get it over with now.

But it wasn't fair—up in his room, the huge bed only reminded him of what he'd lost. He switched to the guest room where his father slept. It was the coldest room in the house. The window faced Mrs. Tilson's drainpipe. A single bed lay pushed against the wall between an old nightstand and a wooden dresser. Henry flopped on the unmade mattress, still in his clothes. He stared at the radiator against the wall and followed Caroline's instruction to think.

*   *   *

In his white robe Reverend Pierce whisked up the nave, passing the congregants in their stalls. Henry sneezed beside the door. He squinted through the shadows, wondering whether to choose a stall or stand. Reverend Pierce stopped in front of him.

"Is something the matter, Henry?"

"Not at all," Henry lied.

"A problem with the churchyard? One of the graves?"

The congregants had turned in their stalls to stare. "Nothing like that," Henry said. He spotted Kevin Yapton up front with his wife and daughters, and to their left, in the other front stall, Penny Pierce beside Karen Bates. William Harvey waited at the organ, his feet on the pedals, his hands on the keys. Oliver Marsh sat at the back.

"I believe I'm in time for the morning service," Henry said.

Reverend Pierce placed a hand on his shoulder. He took him to a bookshelf beside the door and took down the red-jacketed Book of Common Prayer, together with the blue-jacketed hymnal. "Good to have you with us," he said, placing the books in Henry's hand. "Sit wherever you'd like."

The door opened. Behind Henry, Darren Roberts came inside, blinking in the cold and dark. "Goodness," the vicar said, clasping his hands. "We've a busy morning."

Henry ducked into a stall on the left. He chose it because that's where his house stood, the third on the left, as he came into Chalk. He closed the stall door behind him, and when he sat down, cobwebs covered the knees of his trousers. William Harvey started to play the organ. Reverend Pierce seated Darren in the stall opposite Henry's, then proceeded to his lectern beside the altar. He opened his Bible and bellowed, as if speaking to a great crowd.

"Here begins the first lesson from the second chapter of the Book of John."

Henry thumbed through his book for the right page. Before he knew it, the vicar had finished the lesson and started another. He tried to join in, but he kept sneezing. By the time he'd stopped, the vicar had moved on to the Book of Common Prayer. Henry flipped through the pages frantically. When he finally joined in with the others, he could barely follow the meaning of his words.

Reverend Pierce faced the organ and sang. The congregants joined in—thin, timid warbles rising from the stalls—and as they did, a swallow circled a chandelier and disappeared. Henry tried to understand the hymn, but he was trying harder to sing on key. Was attending church always this difficult? He looked across the aisle. Darren was glaring at him.

After the hymn, Reverend Pierce made a sign of the cross. He went to the pulpit, pulled his robe above his ankles, and started climbing. Soon he disappeared in the rafters. A spider crawled across Henry's shirt, and he brushed it off.

The vicar's hands appeared under a reading lamp. "Friends. Though we are now well into March, abiding memories from our New Year celebrations have lingered. The brilliant—" Reverend Pierce stopped. The door opened and creaked shut.

The congregants turned. Trevor Nelson, smiling sheepishly, searched for a stall.

"As I say, the brilliant fireworks from The Beacon and the wonderful weekend services that followed are not joys we'll soon forget. These are cheerful times. But there are inevitable sorrows. The annual spring floods have come, and we have seen some horrendous damage to our farmlands. Sometimes we look back, for solace, but let us also look forward with hope! Our lives are in God's hands. He dwells in eternity, where there is no past nor future."

Henry had a cramp in his neck. The pulpit was too high on the wall. There was nothing to see but the vicar's hands anyway, so he decided to listen to the sermon with his head down. Then he realised he might look like he was asleep, so he lifted his eyes to the cross instead.

"…in God's eyes, the reason for life lies in the giving and receiving of love. Any act of kindness, however small, will never rust or decay…"

Henry's mind drifted. He wondered if Derrick ever went to church. He kept thinking of Caroline and wondered what she was doing. He searched the shelves of his stall and found a scrap of paper, folded at the centre. The writing on it was oversized and looping, like a child's: *Fuck church and fuck God and fuck all this rot.*

Henry heard the sound of footsteps. It was Oliver Marsh. He'd moved to the stall behind Henry's. He gripped the partition with both hands and shook it like an ape in a cage. Henry turned back around.

"Love is our key," the vicar continued. "Our guide to living! It is the great commandment Jesus gave us: 'Love one another.' There is no time like the present to celebrate this commandment…"

Henry put the paper back where he'd found it. A child must have written it. He'd completely lost track of the sermon now. Then he realised Reverend Pierce might find the note after the service and suspect him of leaving it there. He took it back and stuffed it into his pocket.

"We ask ourselves, 'What am I doing with my life? What am I here for, anyway?' God created us for the glorious purpose of growing into his likeness, knowing Him, loving Him."

Under the lamp, one of the vicar's hands reached for the switch. As he descended the pulpit the rest of him gradually appeared—his shoes, the bottom of the long white robe, his torso and head coming down. William Harvey began to play. The vicar took a hymnal from the lectern and began to sing.

Suddenly there was a loud squeak. Henry wheeled. Oliver loomed in the aisle.

"What is it?" Henry whispered, shrinking back. "What do you want?"

Oliver leaned over the door of Henry's stall. Up close, his face looked drained of blood. Deep gouges and pocks littered his neck, cheeks, and forehead. He dropped a cloth collection pouch over the door and shook it, jingling the coins inside. Henry fumbled for a pound. Oliver winked as he dropped it in—so slightly it might have been a tic—and continued down the nave for the Yaptons.

*   *   *

For the sake of his career, Darren liked to attend the occasional service. He stayed a few minutes after, lingering by the door and chatting with the Yaptons about their two children, asking after Penny's health, offering to walk Mrs. Bates home. A teacher could do a lot worse than appear at church.

While the little group assembled by the hymnals, Trevor Nelson slinked out the door, followed by Oliver Marsh. Darren hadn't expected to see either of them at the service, let alone Oliver, acting in something of an official capacity. The shopkeeper and his wife he knew were regulars, along with Karen and Penny.

Soon the gravedigger came tentatively up the nave. His massive shoulders were bunched around his neck, like he'd been beaten by sticks. Perhaps the inevitable had happened at last. It would explain Caroline all last week, staring into the distance during playtime. It would mean the opening he'd been waiting for. Darren's excitement grew, but he still needed proof.

The gravedigger kept limping forward. His head was bowed, his eyes lowered. It was how the man used to look. Darren suppressed a smile, held out his hand. He asked after Henry's health, and his father's. Henry didn't reply with more than a few mumbled, incoherent words. The look he received from the sunken eyes almost made him sorry for the man. The door opened, and he was gone.

"Broken heart," Penny said. "But we knew it was coming, didn't we, Karen?"

Karen Bates shrugged. "From the start."

Mr. Yapton pulled his daughters toward him. They stared at their shoes and elbowed each other. Their mother lowered her chin. "To tell you the truth, Mr. Roberts," she said, "we aren't at all convinced your new teacher belongs here. Are we, Kevin? I mean, if that's the kind of life she leads."

"You must excuse me," Darren said. "I'd forgotten the time…"

He said his goodbyes and hurried out the door. He followed the gravedigger from a distance, all the way back to the man's house.

* * *

Henry didn't know what he expected—a vision, an unexpected shudder like he'd had looking at the cross inside the church. He stood under his mother's willow and waited. He knelt on the ground and prayed in broad daylight.

Henry had gone home after the service and brought back some cutting shears to clip the grass around the headstone. The plot might as well have been a stranger's now. His recollections were so dim they were practically imaginary. How much could any child be expected to remember? The willow needed pruning. The lower branches almost reached the ground. Two hundred years old, the tree probably was. He'd have given a great deal for that much time.

Henry trimmed around the memorial and brushed the grass away. He stuck his fingers inside the carved letters of his mother's name. Soon there wouldn't be anyone left with memories of Evelyn Bale. Then her life might not have happened. She'd be completely forgotten one day, like the people buried in the older part of the churchyard, the dead with the unreadable names.

Fuck God, the note had said.

He kept trimming the grass until it was even. He'd felt obliged, after the service, to do something. In his sermon Reverend Pierce said everyone had an obligation to love each other, to live as if they might continue beyond their lifetimes. It was a comforting thought, at least for a minute or two. Now, out in grey afternoon, the idea held less credibility. Henry couldn't say that he lived for any purpose at all.

Maybe that was the hole in his life. He had no idea why he existed. Did anyone? For a moment he felt relieved, knowing the hole's nature. But it wasn't a hole, it was a chasm. He had to fill it with something more substantial than fear.

Some cleaning solution would make the letters on the headstone truly stand out. He had some at home. Henry stood up and held out the shears. He could see the future clearly—the crumbled ruin of the church, the graveyard overgrown, neglected for centuries. Then, in the end, there wouldn't be any vegetation at all. The sun would die and the Earth would freeze. Did his mother's headstone matter?

Henry took the shears with both hands. He lifted them high in the air and wondered what they would feel like in his stomach. Voices shouted obscenities in his head. Pictures flashed across his mind—his father sobbing under the willow, Jack dead, Jackie dead, Mrs. Tilson dead, Caroline in a casket, waiting to go underground.

He heard footsteps. It was possible, Henry thought, that he was going insane. Darren Roberts came across the mounds toward him, waving like an old friend.

* * *

Drinking tea on the patio, Caroline could hear the boys play football behind the church, taking advantage of the dry Sunday. She tried to picture who they were, based on their shouts.

It was selfish of her, Trevor said, moving to Chalk. It hadn't struck her as true until now. She badly wanted Henry beside her. It hadn't even been a full week, and she missed him more than she thought she would. Maybe Trevor was right, maybe it wasn't appropriate to pursue a man she liked, and to fall quickly in love. Perhaps it was better—truly better, in a moral sense, for a woman to sit around like a frightened sheep.

Caroline sat up. She placed her bare feet on the cement and listened. From the direction of the churchyard, someone was screaming.

She slipped on her sneakers. It was a child's voice. Caroline ran down to the road, passed the school, and came into the churchyard through the front gate. The noise had come from the creepy one, the oddest one of all, the man in Chalk who never spoke. She'd thought it had been one of the children but they were out there kicking the football across the mounds. It was the madman who stood under the stained glass windows with his mouth open, his pockmarked face hideous and pale. He turned and pointed. Then she saw Henry and Darren, facing each other under the willow.

Caroline waited on the path, catching her breath. Henry was holding a knife. "Stop!" she cried, running across the mounds. "Get away from each other!"

"Caroline," Darren said, greeting her with his simpering smile. "What's the matter?"

She saw they were both dressed for church. It was only garden shears that Henry held, covered with grass. "What are you doing, Henry?"

"Tidying up Mum's grave," he said.

Darren nodded. "And talking, too."

Henry stepped toward her, then turned onto the path. "See you in a month," he said. He walked across the churchyard with long, steady strides, leaving her with Darren.

"Twenty-five days, Henry," Caroline said.

*　*　*

It was eight at night by the time Henry reached the pensioners' home. The desk nurse stood as he came through the door. "May I help you?" she asked, acting as if she didn't recognise him.

"I'm Henry Bale. You've seen me before. I'm here to see my dad."

"This isn't a scheduled visit." She opened her appointment book and ran her finger down the page.

"I can't always schedule a desire to see my father."

The nurse wrinkled her nose. "I'm sure you understand we're a little short of staff. It's Sunday evening, and it's late."

"I don't care about the staff. I just want to talk to my dad, if that's all right."

"You say you don't care, but who's going to wake him up? Who's going to get him dressed?"

Henry started for the door. "I'll wake him. I don't care if he's dressed."

"Stop," the nurse said. "I'll see what I can do. Sit down, please."

Henry waited by the door while she made a few calls. "He was asleep," the nurse said, putting down the phone. "Now that we've woken him, he'll be making quite a fuss. A floor nurse will get him ready, and you'll just have to wait. This isn't a hotel, you know—you can't just come by without ringing in advance. Hang on, don't go in there by yourself!"

The pensioners' home was uncomfortably hot. Against the far wall, a man sat slumped in a wheelchair under a flickering fluorescent light. Henry turned down the first hall. An elderly woman in a bright green nightgown pushed a stroller toward him. Across the hall, a nurse came out of a darkened room. "Pardon me," Henry said, "can you tell me—"

"Sshh," the nurse said, closing the door. "Now, what is it you want?"

"Frank Bale. Where is his room, please?"

She pointed down the hall. "Room ninety-four."

He kept going, passing a series of open doors. Each room dispensed its own odour—urine, perfume, microwaved popcorn, sweat. His father's room was closed. At his father's room, Henry knocked and opened the door.

A nurse beside Frank's bed smiled. "You must be Henry."

It was even hotter in the room. Frank sat on the edge of his mattress, a sheet circling his waist. His bare chest was sunken, his arms thin as twigs. "Dad," Henry said, "I need to talk to you."

"Look here," Frank said to the nurse, straightening the hair on his head. "I don't have to visit anyone, you know. It's after eight!"

"I know, Frankie. I know."

"Why is he here? What gives him the right? I was asleep!"

"Henry's your son. He's come all this way to see you tonight. Now we must be brave, Frankie, and slip on our socks."

Henry waited in a chair beside the bed. Frank grumbled and swore and even kicked a little, but the nurse eventually got him dressed. She placed his legs into his trousers, slipped on his shirt. "Be a good boy, now," she told him. She helped him down to the other chair and left.

"You shaved off your beard," Frank said.

"The teacher put me up to it."

His father brightened. "I heard you were seeing her."

Henry folded his hands in his lap. "Tell me what you did today."

"You must be joking."

"I'm not, actually. Caroline says it's important to talk about the little things."

Frank snorted. "All right. This morning I spent an hour trying to get out of bed on my own. By the time I called for the nurse, I'd soiled myself. The next thirty or forty minutes involved her cleaning me. I don't think you'll want those details, Henry, and I'm very sure Caroline doesn't either. At some point there was food. It was horrid as usual. Then I lay here in this hot little hole, and I watched the telly until I fell asleep."

"Why do you sleep so much? Don't you have anything else to do?"

Frank wiggled in his chair. "Did that teacher really put you up to this?"

"I came on my own," Henry said. He looked away. "We've hit a rough spot."

"I should have known."

"That's nice, Dad. A fine father, you are."

"I was a fine father." His hands shaking, Frank rolled up the sleeves of his shirt. "Take a look at these arms," he said. They were bent at the elbows. "Look at the state they're in—I can't straighten them! I dug and I dug, every day I was able. I dug more than you'll ever dig. You don't know the meaning of work."

"Yes I do."

"No you don't. You work for money—I worked to put food on the table. Don't talk to me about setting examples. I raised you. On my own, mind you, after Evelyn was gone."

Henry felt the old anger rising. He didn't feel like getting in the way of it. "When, exactly, did you raise me, Dad? When you sat in that armchair each evening without a word?"

"Go to hell," Frank said. He rolled his sleeves back down. "Get out of my room."

Henry stayed in the chair. "Not yet. I want to ask you a few things."

"Like what?"

"After mum died. Why didn't you ever remarry?"

"None of your goddamn business. I married once, at least. That's more than you'll ever do."

Henry crossed the length of the tiny room. He leaned down, his face inches from his father's. He could smell the old man's breath. "All your life, you did the least. Why didn't you ever take a different job, or move anywhere new? What the hell did you live for, anyway?"

"Shut up," Frank said, raising his fist. His upper lip curled over his teeth. "You want to feel a dad's touch?" He lowered his hand. "No. You won't make me do it. I never did hit you, and you can't get me to do it now." Gripping the arms of the chair, he tried to stand.

"Hold on," Henry said.

His father arched his back and kept pushing. His arms wobbled. Henry backed away. "Stop it! Just sit with me for five minutes, will you?"

Frank made it to his feet. Henry tried to help, but his dad pushed him away. "I don't need you," he said, lurching toward the bed. His legs buckled. Crying out, he collapsed to the floor.

Henry knelt beside him. His father was panting and covered with sweat. "Should I get a nurse?"

"For yourself, maybe." Frank tried to stand. He swatted away Henry's hands. "Leave me alone." They batted at each other like children. Eventually Henry took his father in a bear hug and hoisted him onto the bed. He hardly weighed anything.

"You're sure you don't need a nurse, Dad?"

Henry sat beside him on the bed. Frank lay on his side and faced the wall. "No. Go on now, Henry. I'm worn out." He didn't sound angry any more, just defeated.

"One more thing. You can sleep the rest of your life away, I don't care. But I want to know if you believe in God."

"You can't be serious."

"Answer the question."

Frank sighed. He and placed his palm against the empty wall.

"I don't know what I believe. Sometimes there's a god. Other times not."

Henry wondered if he too would be this way, at the end. "But doesn't it ever bother you? I mean, not knowing?"

"It bothered me once."

"Aren't you pretending now? Pretending that you don't care?"

Frank turned on his back. He had his blue eyes wide open. For a moment he looked like a young man considering an important question. "Henry, what's going on?"

"Lots of things, Dad. I went to church this morning, and—"

"What? Church? What the hell for?"

"My own reasons. I found this in one of the stalls." He gave his dad the note he'd found.

"Oliver," Frank said, sitting up against his pillows. He held open the note and shook his head. "Up to his old tricks."

"What? Oliver Marsh?"

"I used to find these all the time. Stuck to the memorials. On the front door of our house. Inside my wheelbarrow once."

"Does Reverend Pierce know?"

"Everyone knows. Oliver's been leaving these about for years."

"Everyone?" Henry snatched the note back. "But Oliver was there on Sunday! He does the collection!"

"He's batty, Henry. The whole village ignores him. Where have you been the past twenty years?" Frank grinned. "Going to church, visiting your dad unannounced? Sounds like quite a woman."

Henry went to the door. "I'll leave you to sleep now," he said. He turned out the lights. In the bed there was only a small shape curled up, the sheets pulled around its neck.

"I'll tell you something, Henry."

Henry waited by the door. "I'm listening."

"Sometimes I wish I'd remarried. But I knew—I just knew nobody would suit me like your mother. She was a wonderful woman. She loved you very much." Under the sheet, Henry could see the figure starting to shake. "You have no idea how it hurt. I didn't want to live…"

Gradually, the room went silent. "Maybe it's not too late, Dad. I mean, what about Mrs. Tilson? You two get on well together."

He listened. "Dad?" From under the sheet, he heard the sound of a snore.

ELEVEN

In early May, the village walls turned a shinier shade of grey. In the fields the hardening mud protected seeds of grass. People began walking the roads for enjoyment. Even Lord and Lady Wembles came out of doors to attend a Sunday church service. Mrs. Tilson filled her bird feeder more often. And in the warmer, lengthening evenings, Henry found it increasingly difficult to sleep.

They were on him like flies after the separation—people he rarely spoke to, like Karen Bates and Darren Roberts, wanting details. It was better to remain indoors. He stopped shaving again. He confined himself to his bedroom and sitting room and left the house only to work. With the improved weather, grave digging slowed. The sick and aged postponed their deaths to feel the sunshine, see their relatives one last time. Spring would have been the perfect time to go on holiday, if Henry had been inclined. But these days Henry saw death everywhere, in every person and every thing. The sun only illuminated its face.

Everything made sense, alone. Before Caroline, Henry had only occupied space, like a headstone marking a hole. Falling in love had awakened him to this. Now that they were broken up, most of his old patterns resurfaced. Henry passed entire evenings looking at the wall. He often slept in the guest room for its smaller bed. He tried church once more, but the lessons and hymns made for too much effort. And then there was Oliver Marsh. What sort of vicar allowed regular blasphemy in church?

In a village the size of Chalk, Henry had expected to run into Caroline, but he never did. He gave up tracking how long it had been since they'd separated. Counting sunsets became a waste of time without anyone to share them with. When the month passed, he barely realised it.

His mind started drifting during work. He would be standing in the grave, studying the trees, only to remember the time. Rushing to get done, he'd leave a hole shallow, or wet along the bottom.

One morning, digging in the churchyard at Glynde, Henry heard shouts. He ducked inside the grave and listened. It seemed to him that the shouting came from underground, from all of the dead people who wanted to live again. He leaped out of the hole, thrashing his spade like a sword. But it was only two boys playing nearby. Henry scared them, and they ran away to hide. After he went back to work, they gathered some dirt clods, crept around the headstones, and pelted him in the back.

* * *

Up front in the mobile library, Leslie Whittaker sat patiently beside her supervisor, James Cripley, as he brought the minibus in front of The Black Ram. A single mother in her thirties, Leslie trained as a library assistant as a break from counter work at Woolworth's.

"We don't like to waste time," Mr. Cripley said. "Bring the ladder down so people know we're open." He turned off the engine and reached into the glove box for his rolling papers. Mr. Cripley's silver hair was styled in stiff pomade. A recent stroke had flattened the right side of his face.

"I'll fetch the footstool right now, Mr. Cripley."

"There are those returns left to shelve, too."

At the back of the minibus, she took down the ladder and placed the footstool on the pavement. Never mind his stroke—Mr. Cripley was a bastard. He even smoked in front of children during story time.

"That ladder down all the way?" He turned in his seat, losing some tobacco to his shirtfront. "Someone falling, that's all I need. Now don't forget there's the activity log to prepare." He licked his cigarette shut. "You might think you've got a few minutes to spare.

But in a few minutes, we're going to be so busy we won't be able to move."

"On my way," Leslie said, keeping her voice bright. She couldn't believe anyone lived in this tiny village, let alone borrowed books. But someone had already started climbing the ladder—a woman with a blue scarf around her hair, carrying a basket.

"Morning, Mrs. Pierce," Mr. Cripley said, poking his head over the seat. Leslie stepped against the nonfiction so they could see each other.

"Morning, James. No Jenny today?"

"Married, of all things. Moved to Hastings."

"Married!" Mrs. Pierce searched Leslie's face, as if holding her responsible. "That is something!"

"You never appreciate someone until they're gone." In the driver's seat Mr. Cripley lighted his cigarette while his hands shook.

"Can I help you find something?" Leslie said.

"I just have the one return," Mrs. Pierce said, hesitating. She took a book from her basket, its cover down.

Leslie took it. *Rapture in Monaco*, the title was. "I'll just get your return slip," she said.

"She'll need a return slip," Mr. Cripley shouted.

"On my way," Leslie said, as cheerily as she could. A clipboard hung from the peg behind her seat, and as she took it down a woman in curlers came up the ladder.

"Morning, Mrs. Bates," Mr. Cripley said.

"Morning, James. Hello, Penny. Lovely day." Seeing Leslie, she frowned.

"Jenny's been married," Mrs. Pierce said.

The woman put her hand to her mouth. "Married? We won't be seeing her again."

"Moved to Hastings," Mr. Cripley added. "We're doing our best to cope." He wasn't halfway through his cigarette, but he started searching his shirt pockets for rolling papers. "Bloody hell," he muttered. "I'm out!" He opened the glove box and began rummaging.

Leslie reshelved Mrs. Pierce's book. Smoothing her skirt, she took a step in the vicinity of Mrs. Bates. The minibus was getting cramped. "Anything in particular I can help you find?"

"No thank you, luv. Just browsing this morning."

Leslie jumped. A tall, broad-shouldered man filled the doorway.

He had wild black hair and a beard. "Good morning," she said, composing herself. He had a book tucked under his arm. The two older women huddled together in the corner as he came inside.

"Hello," he said. He didn't look at her, and he didn't look away either. He hung his head and searched the ground.

"Is that you, Henry?" Mr. Cripley said, glancing over his shoulder. He took his last drag, flicked away the butt, and continued searching the glove box. "Did you like that one, then?"

Nodding, the man held out his book. Leslie took it. She noticed that he wasn't bad looking.

"Get Henry his return slip, Leslie," Mr. Cripley said.

"Coming," Leslie said, hurrying to the front. The man's book— *Trees and Shrubs of Sussex: An Adventurer's Guide*—was six weeks overdue. The man seemed so tortured, she wanted to do something nice for him. "Don't worry about the late fee," she whispered, as she brought him the return slip.

The man opened his mouth as if to say something. He turned in his muddy boots and started back down the ladder.

"What a state," Mrs. Bates said, shaking her head. "Did you see that hair?" They went to the top of the ladder and watched him walk along the road. Leslie re-shelved the book, straining to hear.

"We knew it wouldn't last."

"He's worse than he was before he met her."

"Looking more and more like his father, he is. That woman should be ashamed of herself."

"I hope she stays, for our sake. We're getting used to the income."

"Damn it!" Mr. Cripley barked. He had the whole glove box out on his lap. Suddenly he gasped. A rolling paper had stuck to the back of a receipt, and he peeled it off.

The women walked down the ladder together. They hadn't bothered to say goodbye. Leslie opened the library catalogue and ran her finger down the botany section. They'd be coming back to Chalk in two weeks. She decided to set aside something special on trees.

* * *

Shoring walls, patching holes and flood banks—each Spring, the same rebuilding. After the flood, the great flood, the vicar thought, what a smell would have pervaded the world, clean and redolent with the beginnings of life. He kneeled by the fence in the vicarage garden with a box of nails and a hammer. His work jeans were ripped, his shirt covered with tree dust. Debris from the garden—broken branches, mostly—lay in a pile by the compost heap.

Reverend Pierce's front fence had lost two planks to the wind. He'd taken a couple of boards from the back fence as replacements. "Robbing Peter to pay Paul," Penny had said as he'd carried them through the house. If men needed reminding of any inadequacies, wives were happy to oblige.

The vicar stood up and lined the planks between the fence posts to make sure of the length. He knocked away the broken bits of wood with the side of the hammer. Winter destroyed, Spring pieced back the fragments. The church was meant for that. More activity in years, St. Margaret's had seen. Perhaps Caroline Ford would be good for the village in the long run. Reverend Pierce stuck some nails in his mouth. Every once in a while a lesson was needed, Pascal's wager considered. Better to be a foolish believer than to bet on a godless world and be wrong. Darren Roberts and Trevor Nelson found out. Henry Bale would learn it soon enough.

He looked up the road toward the pub. He couldn't allow himself a pint yet. Three o'clock it was, and too much work in front of him. It wasn't much, just a couple of boards and some leaves to rake, but the tasks that should have been easy never were. He took the nails out of his mouth and studied the first fence post. Then he looked up and saw Henry in the road.

"I thought you might want a hand with your fence," the gravedigger said.

"I knew I prayed for a reason," the vicar said. Henry didn't smile. He might have emerged from one of his own graves. "Are you as handy with a hammer as you are with a spade?"

Henry looked at the ground. "No."

"It's a simple matter. I mean, I thought it would be. That gap, there. Those two boards..." Henry was already lifting the first one. He handled it like a toothpick. "I'll just nip inside," Reverend Pierce said. "Be right back."

He crossed his garden and opened the door. "Penny?" He heard the television in the bedroom upstairs. "Penny, darling?"

The bedroom door opened. "Yes?"

"Can you please prepare some tea for the sitting room?"

"What? For whom?"

"For Henry Bale. He's out in the garden mending the fence." The vicar waited. "Penny?"

"He won't want to come in for his tea. He's odd."

"Are you sure about that?"

"Well, why don't you ask him? In the meantime I'll get the tray ready."

Outside, the gravedigger had already finished nailing in the first board. He was working on the second. "Henry," the vicar said, "would you like to come inside for tea after you're done?"

Henry paused, the board in one hand, the hammer in the other. He had the nails in his mouth. "No bother," he said.

"Shepherd's pie—that would be a bother. Tea is not."

"I only wanted to mend your fence. To be a better person."

"Henry," the vicar said, "please come inside. Just for a few minutes."

The gravedigger placed the hammer on the fence post and shook his head. Reverend Pierce remembered how it was for Henry before Caroline came. The man hated conversation of any kind. Of course he wouldn't want to sit down for a cup of tea. As Penny came outside with the tray, calling to them across the garden, the gravedigger took nails from his mouth.

Reverend Pierce placed a hand on his shoulder. "You've always been a good person, Henry. You may not see that right now, but it's true."

"All I see is darkness." The words came out softly, spoken by a man barely alive.

✻   ✻   ✻

The Brighton train inched out of Glynde and picked up speed on the straightaway through the lettuce fields. With every mile from Chalk, Caroline felt incrementally saner. Still, as she looked out at the farmland hurtling by, and as she pictured Henry having tea in his armchair, she almost felt she was betraying him.

She'd waited at his gate a few nights back. The flicker of his television visible through the curtain, she'd stood in the road and imagined herself inside. Why had she pushed him away—because of his odd behaviour? Because she couldn't abide the force of his declarations of love?

Tonight she was weak with loneliness. Trent's band played at a club called The Greenlight, and a reunion with old friends presented an opportunity to gauge the past four months in Chalk.

After she arrived at the Brighton station, Caroline took her time getting to the nightclub district. She lingered at a café and visited one of her favourite bookshops. By the time she reached the club it was loud and smoke-filled. It didn't take long for her coat to get splashed with beer. Still, after Chalk, she felt returned to civilisation.

All the evenings she'd spent drinking vodka tonics at Trent's gigs crystallised in a single glance at the stage. She caught glimpses of the band as she wormed her way through the crowd—the lead singer with his spiked hair and wide, pouting mouth, the electric guitarist prowling the stage, the tall bassist, motionless except for his hands. Boyish and handsome, Trent banged at the drums with dizzying speed, his head thrown forward like a boxer. As always, the music was barely tolerable. Trent wrote it. He'd had a relatively tame upbringing, but the lyrics painted a tortured, misunderstood adolescence.

Caroline found Trent's best mates Rex and Sally at a table near the stage. Sally had shoulder-length red hair and a nose ring. She owned a vintage clothing shop. Rex, her boyfriend, was a skater with sideburns and a soul patch. He wrote articles on youth culture for an on-line magazine. Tonight he was wearing a black stocking cap and a tee shirt that read *Girls Kick Ass!* Across the table, one of Caroline's classmates from university sat smoking a cigarette. Her name was Madeline. She wore heavy black eyeglasses, though she could see perfectly well without them, and she had on her usual low-cut blouse. Caroline always suspected Madeline fancied Trent—and here she was at The Greenlight, occupying the chair closest the stage.

Sally threw up her arms. "Caroline! It's been ages!"

"Hi!" Caroline shouted. The dance floor jammed, she pressed against the table to avoid getting trampled. Sally pulled her by the arm to an empty chair. Rex kissed her on the cheek. Across the table, Madeline smiled thinly.

"How's your new teaching job?" Sally shouted.

"Where are you again?" Rex said.

"Chalk!" Caroline took off her coat. Madeline, she noticed, was examining the dress she'd put on. "It's sort of near Springmer."

Rex looked at her blankly. "Springmer? Chalk?

"I told you. The country," Sally said, squeezing one of his cheeks. She rolled her eyes. "He never listens."

Caroline laughed. "How's the shop?"

"We've got new inventory in—lovely old suits that I'm selling to all the lads. Come and see! Are you back for the weekend?"

"Just for the night," she shouted. The song came to an end. If she remembered correctly, it was the final number of the set.

Sally followed her gaze. "He asks about you, you know." A spray of beer shot across the table, and she brushed off her shirt. "Bloody animals."

Rex stood up. "What are you having, Caroline?"

"Vodka tonic, thanks." She reached for her purse but Rex waved her off.

The set finished, everyone applauded. Caroline watched Trent file offstage with the rest of the band. "You dating someone out there?" Sally asked.

"For a while, I was. An older man. A gravedigger."

"A gravedigger?" Madeline's eyes widened. "Literally?"

Rex came back from the bar and set down the drinks. "Caroline was seeing a gravedigger," Sally told him.

"Bizarre," Rex said. "He ever take you along to work?"

"I never asked," Caroline said, laughing. She knew they'd be curious—not everyone could go out with gravediggers—but she couldn't help wondering what Henry would have thought. "There's a great deal to him, actually. And I don't mind Chalk."

Caroline sipped her drink. Her friends had become distracted by an announcement about the next band. One of them hadn't stopped texting since she arrived. She wondered what she was doing in Brighton, sitting with a skater in a stocking cap and a girl with a nose ring. Where, if anywhere, would she ever feel at home?

Trent came through the crowd toward their table. His tee shirt was torn at the neckline, his face flushed. He kissed Caroline's cheek and slumped beside her. "You turned off your mobile. Just back for some noise, are you?"

With one glance at her ex-boyfriend Caroline remembered the endless nights she'd spent in his messy flat, smoking and drinking among his band members, surrounded by piles of rumpled clothes.

"Noise?"

"That's what you called our songs, last time I saw you." He looked round the table, creating a bit of drama as always. "It was the last time we spoke, Caroline—not counting your lovely letter telling me it was all over between us."

There was a long silence. "I didn't come here to watch you make a scene," she said.

He threw his head back. "Ha! You're still busy scolding people like children."

"Be gentle, Trent," Sally said. "She just got here."

Fidgeting in his chair, Trent turned away. On the stage a couple of men were breaking down the microphones and the guitar stands. "So how's that place in the countryside?" he asked. "How's the school?"

"Some days it seems I've moved to the moon," Caroline said. She looked at the drumsticks poking out of Trent's back pocket. She had an urge to touch them once more. She reached for Trent's back pocket when a voice shot across the table.

"Caroline's found a bit of village romance," Madeline said. She looked at Trent significantly. "An older man."

Caroline narrowed her eyes. "It's a welcome change, maturity."

"You came back to share your latest exploits?" Trent asked.

"Of course not."

"Then what are you doing here, anyway?"

"Trent," Rex said, putting his hands in the air. "Chill."

"I'll get us a drink," Madeline said, heading to the bar.

"You're right, Trent," Caroline said, searching his eyes. Anything that might have remained between them had gone. "I don't know what I was thinking. I suppose I wanted a bit of company, that's all." She stood up and reached for her purse. It had been a long time since she'd felt this alone, this hollow.

Sally took her hand and pulled her over to the next table. "Talk to me" she said. "Tell me what's happening."

"Talk?" Caroline laughed bitterly as she put her purse down once more. "Okay, let's talk." She glanced around the club as if to find herself in one of the young women in the club. "I once thought that talking might have helped." Sally leaned in to hear more, but it was no use. The next band had took the stage, and the sound of their electric guitars drowned out Caroline's voice.

*   *   *

Henry stood under the oak and watched Caroline's bungalow. It wasn't late, but her lights were out. Perhaps she'd turned in early. He leaned against the trunk and imagined Caroline asleep. Her hair would be down, her arms bare. How easy it would have been, had he been in bed beside her, to watch her while she slept.

Footsteps approached from The Beacon. He couldn't get caught like this. Henry ran from the tree and kept going, past his front door, running anywhere, he didn't know why. He stopped at The Black Ram and ducked inside. The pub was empty. He took Oliver's seat in order to face the door.

He hunched forward in his coat. He wondered what that woman from the mobile library had thought of Chalk. Had it been his imagination, how she fancied him? More than anything, she made him miss Caroline. He missed her so much he didn't want to be alone.

"Quiet pub," Sid said, entering the bar. He brushed away bits of sandwich from the corners of his mouth. He poured a pint of Cuckoo and placed it on the mat.

After some beer, Henry felt better. He drank the pint and ordered another. He could feel his cheeks flush. After the second pint, he ordered a third. "I'm going to get good and pissed," he declared. "Why not?"

Sid didn't appear to have heard. He was checking the taps, wiping the runoff from the nozzles. Henry wanted to ask him a question or two, just for conversation. He didn't know much about the man. "You married, Sid?"

"I am. A baby on the way as well."

That was that. How stupid he must have sounded. He'd known Sid for years. When he looked at his watch, he was stunned. He'd only been at the pub ten minutes.

The door opened. Seeing Henry in his customary place, Oliver froze a moment, then took a stool at the middle of the bar. Those pockmarks on his face were one thing, Henry thought, but what kind of person wrote such vicious notes?

Henry placed a twenty-pound note on the mat. "Another Cuckoo please, Sid. And a Guinness for Oliver, whenever he's ready." He didn't know why he said it—the words just came of his mouth. "Whatever you're drinking as well, Sid."

"Cheers, Henry," Sid said. "Thanks very much."

After the pints were poured and placed, and the business of

clearing old glasses taken care of, a painful silence returned to the
bar. Henry struggled for something to say. Oliver, of course, could
hardly be expected to say anything. Sid and Oliver probably thought
he was bribing them with drinks for a bit of company. The awful
thing was, it was true.

Reverend Pierce came in clean-shaven, his hair combed in neat
rows. He had today's *Times* in his hand, folded to the crossword.
"Evening," he said, sitting beside Oliver.

"Evening, Reverend," Sid said. The barman reached for a mug
made of dull pewter, suspended on a hook above the bar.

Placing the crossword so that Oliver could look on, Reverend
Pierce clicked his pen and set to work. Oliver leaned to his right,
peering at the clues. Watching them made Henry's head spin. How
could they sit together? Maybe nobody really knew anyone in the
world, not even in Chalk.

Henry finished his pint, and a fresh one took its place. "Sorry, Sid.
I don't think I'll have another, thank you."

Sid's eyebrows knitted. "Oliver sent it over," he said.

"Is that so?" Henry hadn't heard Oliver say anything. "Cheers,
Oliver, thank you." Oliver shifted on his stool, as if to acknowledge
Henry's thanks, and the pub became quiet again. The only sound
was the vicar's pen filling the squares.

Henry started on the next pint. He was getting drunk, just as he'd
planned. He barely flinched when the door flew open, and Trevor
Nelson came into the pub, followed by Chris Crawley. Chris held the
door, and Vickie Eckleton came in next, arm-in-arm with a woman in
a feather boa. The whole group surged toward the bar as if blown by
the wind, slurring their words and talking at the same time.

"Four Tetley's to go, please, Sid," Trevor said. He leaned over the
bar, a ten-pound note in his hand.

"Make two of them lagers," Chris said.

"Five Tetley's then," Trevor said. "And one lager."

The woman in the boa plopped down beside the vicar. "Not to
go," she said. She was tall and angular, with mouse-brown hair and
tortoise-shell eyeglasses. "That's my money he's got, and I'm not
going anywhere. Where's the loo?" Reverend Pierce peered at her
over his reading glasses. "In there," Sid said, pointing as the woman
stumbled off.

Chris grinned. "Looks like we're having a pint here first."

Sid lined up their glasses. "You're just in time, too. Last call, everyone."

"Just in time?" Trevor pulled Vickie onto his lap and kissed her. "Pardon me, vicar, but I'd better not waste any."

Clearing his throat, Reverend Pierce pushed his mug to the edge of his mat. "One more, please, Sid," he said.

Trevor surveyed the length of the bar. "Is that you down there, Henry? You didn't tell me you were coming tonight!"

Henry couldn't help but laugh. "Since when do I tell you what I'm doing?"

In an instant Trevor had joined him. He threw his arm around Henry's shoulder. "Vickie Eckleton's out tonight!" Trevor shouted. "Isn't she the most gorgeous girl in Chalk?"

"She's a fine catch," Henry said.

"Smoke?" Trevor held out his pack of cigarettes.

"Thanks." Without knowing why, Henry took one. They went outside to the front step.

"I know things with Caroline didn't work out," Trevor whispered. "You were pretty keen on her, weren't you?"

Henry took a drag of the cigarette and stifled a cough. "Things have come to a halt," he said. He was drunk and wanted to talk. "I don't know why I screwed things up…"

Trevor patted him on the shoulder. "It's all right, mate. At least you're not Darren. I'm here for you, if you ever—"

"Leave Henry alone, Trevor," Chris Crawley called outside. "Stop antagonising him."

"I'm fine!" Henry said. He looked into the pub and smiled. "I'm fine, everyone. Really!"

Vickie raised her glass. "We know you are, Henry. Just tell Trevor to shove off when he gets annoying. That's what I do."

Trevor kept his voice at a whisper. "I hope you're not still angry with me, mate."

"What happened with Caroline would have happened anyway. I shouldn't have hit you. But it's funny—after Kington, things jumped out in the open. Maybe it's a good thing."

They finished their cigarettes and went back inside. "You knocked some sense into me, too!" Trevor said. He tilted his head at the lavatory. "What do you think of Vickie's friend? If Chris doesn't get on with her, she's available."

They sat back on their stools. Henry stared into his beer. "I'm still in love," he said. He couldn't help it—the drinks made him emotional.

He wanted to get it all out, as fast as he could. "I started counting things," he said. "Do you know I actually calculated how many days we had together before I died? She had every right to run."

"She's a teacher, Henry. She gets paid to confuse people. In a few months she'll be in some other village, maybe back in Brighton." The woman with the boa came out of the lavatory. "This is Lucy," Trevor said.

"Very nice to meet you," Henry said. He couldn't help staring. Her figure nicely pushed against the limits of her dress.

"Lucy's divorced," Trevor said. He dodged her as she tried to slap his face.

"Christ, you're rude," she said.

Henry laughed. "He gets away with it, somehow."

Lucy smiled at him, adjusted her eyeglasses. "From Chalk as well, are you?"

"Lucy," Trevor said, "don't be forward. Henry's shy."

As Henry tried to deny it, Reverend Pierce looked up from his crossword. "I suppose it's true," Henry admitted.

"Shy's all right," Lucy said. She loosened the boa, exposing the length of her neck. "You must be hot in that coat, Henry. It's roasting in here."

Trevor winked and patted Henry on the back. "Where the devil's my pint?" he said, joining Vickie and Chris at the other end of the bar.

With Trevor gone, Henry didn't know what to say. Thankfully Lucy didn't seem to mind talking. She told him she lived in Eastbourne and had a managerial job at a bank. Chris Crawley kept glancing over, so Henry polished off his pint. "I should be off," he said. "It was very nice meeting you."

Lucy grabbed his arm. "Come with us," she said. "We're off to Trevor's next."

"Tonight? I shouldn't," he said. "I've had too much to drink."

Lucy squeezed his knee. "You seem sober to me. Stay here. I'll see what Trevor thinks."

Henry tried to stop her, but it was too late. There was a flurry of activity as everyone grabbed purses, hats, and coats. Trevor pulled Henry from the stool, and Chris held open the door once more. Carrying multiple bottles to go, they piled into Trevor's Citroen.

Henry wedged himself into the back between Vickie and Lucy. He had the dizzying sensation of not knowing what would happen next. As they pulled out of the car park he craned his neck and looked back at the pub. Oliver Marsh stood at the window watching them, his hands pressed against the pane.

* * *

Trevor pulled his Citroen into the courtyard. The group tumbled drunkenly out of the car. "Welcome," Trevor said, leading everyone into the kitchen.

Henry hung back. The small kitchen smelled of bacon, beer, and cigarettes. Rusting water pipes ran along the walls. The cooker tilted in a corner, coated with burnt cooking oil. A square wooden table sat in the middle of the room like a stage, surrounded by chairs. On it stood a bottle of whiskey, half full.

Trevor started opening cupboards. He found a few clean drinking glasses and banged them on the table. Henry wandered into what looked like a sitting room. There was an old sofa, framed portraits on the walls, and two antique armchairs, most likely from the Wembles Estate. An old black-and-white television lay face down on the carpet, as if kicked over in a rage.

Henry retreated to the kitchen, toward the signs of life. "Sit down," Chris said, pulling out a chair.

"How's the garage these days?" Henry asked. He tried to keep the room from spinning as he sat down.

"Mobbed," Chris said. "Everyone's bringing in their cars for holiday tune-ups."

Trevor pulled Vickie and Lucy down to the table. He lined up the glasses and poured five whiskeys. "Now then. Time for us to get good and pissed."

"That's nice," Chris said, taking a sip. "And even better with a sidekick." He opened his beer.

"Hey," Vickie said, "can you do this with your hands?" She stretched her fingers back until they touched her wrists. "I'm double-jointed."

Chris tried, but his fingers didn't get far. "Aaargh," he said. "That hurts."

Trevor laughed. "Your fingers are fat sausages, that's why."

"I've got a question for the men," Lucy said. "Do girls only go for blokes who are self-confident, or do blokes become self-confident when they know that girls like them?" She put her hand on Henry's arm. "You first."

"I wouldn't know," Henry said.

"Henry's modest," Vickie said. "He would never admit he's good-looking."

"But he is handsome, isn't he?" Trevor said. "Even with that beard growing back."

Lucy poured herself another drink and threw it back. "What is it you do, Henry?"

"I'm a gravedigger."

Lucy looked round the table. "As in, out in cemeteries, digging graves?"

"That's right," Henry said, as everyone nodded. He couldn't tell if she was intrigued or frightened. "Over twenty years now."

"Mark my words," Trevor said, "we'll all need Henry's services one day."

"I thought gravediggers were a thing of the past," Lucy said. "I mean, don't they have machines?"

"In cemeteries they do," Henry said. "But there isn't room for any heavy equipment in churchyards."

"I think it's wonderful what Henry does," Vickie said. "People are fragile during funerals."

"Just imagine how crowded those old churchyards are!" Trevor said. He made shovelling motions with his hands. "See, you need to dig a narrow hole, but deep enough that—"

"Can we switch subjects?" Lucy said.

"We used to be called sextons," Henry said. Everyone had been talking about him as if he weren't there, and now he wanted to explain his job himself. "We walked in processions wearing black robes."

Trevor poured another whiskey. "A better time, that must have been. Religion's been replaced by psychology!"

"I'm not so sure that's a bad thing," Lucy said. She took off her boa and held it in her hands.

Trevor finished his whiskey in one gulp. "I have to admit I've been attending a bit of church lately."

Vickie stroked his hair. "There, there. You're working on things."

"I don't deserve you, Vickie. I don't deserve to live."

Chris placed his arms, big as logs, on top of the table. "Stop this right now, Trevor."

"You're my best friend, and I don't deserve you." Trevor tipped his glass back, but it was empty. As he reached for the bottle, he slipped and hit his forehead on the table.

"My God!" Lucy said.

A smile crept across Trevor's lips. "I'm influenced by the devil! You know what I'm capable of, Vickie. I'm a heartless son of a bitch."

Vickie stopped stroking his hair. "Don't do this, Trevor. Not in front of company."

Trevor just laughed. "You see! My own girlfriend, begging me not to talk!" He took a swig from the bottle. "I made it bad for you, Henry. I bet you cursed me inside that grave."

"What's done is done," Henry said.

Trevor pounded his fist on the table. "Like I said—people have to be careful. I have the capacity for evil."

"Stop hitting the table, Trevor," Chris said. "You're scaring people."

"Here I am," Trevor said, "drinking myself into the ground. I need to be purged of the devil!" With two quick blows, he punched himself in the forehead. There was blood.

"Stop!" Vickie shrieked.

Trevor collapsed onto the table. Vickie put her arms around him, frantically groping his face.

"He likes to hurt himself for attention. He'll be fine by tomorrow," Chris said. He reached for another bottle of beer.

"That man needs therapy," Lucy said. As she took a cigarette out of the pack, her hands shook.

Henry left the table and drifted into the sitting room. The alcohol had worn off, and only fatigue was left over. He went over to the frames on the wall. They held maps of Chalk, some of them reprints from five hundred years back. Nothing much had changed—the Wembles' land had been subdivided, but that was all.

When he returned to the kitchen, Trevor lay bent over the table with his head in his arms. Vickie leaned over him, whispering. Chris and Lucy had moved their chairs closer. Nobody seemed to notice Henry walk out through the kitchen door.

* * *

An hour later, Henry was lost. This close to home, he would have thought it impossible. If he started off the wrong way from Trevor's, he still should have reached something familiar. All around him in the fields, sheep stood huddled together.

Henry broke into a run. On his left, the fields narrowed. The hedges rose. When he stopped to catch his breath, a noise surfaced like wind rushing through trees. He went to the hedge and stuck his head through. A horn sounded. A car whizzed in front of his nose, and then another. He thought he was dreaming. It was the A-27.

"I don't believe it." He hadn't passed through Glynde, had he? Surely he would have noticed an entire village! He must have turned at a fork without knowing it, diverting him onto an access road. If it was the A-27—and it couldn't be anything else—he'd walked six miles from Chalk. Henry pulled his head out of the hedge and went up the road. Yes, there it was—the entrance to the motorway, just around the bend.

He sat on a patch of grass and listened to the cars roar by. The sound was actually reassuring. He remembered what Caroline once said about feeling more connected to people in cities than villages. He hadn't understood what she meant until now. He set off for home, watching for the fork in the road. About two miles later he found it—right in front of his eyes, before the road turned to Glynde. For the first time in years, he decided to sing out in the open.

"Keep me to thee, gentle and mild…"

It was the hymn the woman sang by the grave at Burgess Green. The words had stayed in his head. Good music, the vicar once said in his sermon, carried elements of the eternal. Then it was as if the world were stripped of colour. Henry understood what all words and music was for, what people were meant to do until they stopped breathing: they had to search.

Trevor's house was dark. Henry kept walking toward a corridor of towering silver firs that stretched to Wembles Manor. His chest tightened. What if the search was in vain? What if God never existed? Beside the Wembles gate, a figure darted away.

"Who is it?"

Henry squared his shoulders. "Is anyone there?" He moved on and tried to ignore the footsteps behind him.

At the turnoff to The Beacon, a man came down the footpath toward him. It was William Harvey, his blond hair bouncing.

"A brilliant night for a walk, isn't it?" William said. He'd almost passed by when he turned back. "We've missed you at church."

"Oh?" Henry kicked at the ground. "I've been meaning to come again."

"I won't pester you. I just wouldn't feel right about not inviting you back."

William continued along the main road. Henry hesitated—he needed a place to think, and he didn't want to go home. He walked past the school. Behind him, there were footsteps.

Henry wheeled. Oliver Marsh ran toward him, out of breath. "It was you all this time, following me?"

Oliver put his hands in his pockets. He turned and shrugged, as if he'd just come out for a stroll. "It's not right, Oliver, do you know that? You followed me to Trevor's, didn't you, then waited for me to leave! Why?"

Henry had the feeling Oliver could speak. The man's mouth twitched.

"What is it you want, Oliver? Come on, out with it."

Oliver shrugged again. He looked about to run. "You can talk, can't you? Come on. Don't pretend any longer."

"You're the one pretending," Oliver said. He had a voice as high as a child's.

Henry almost laughed out loud. Now that he heard Oliver speak he couldn't be sure it happened. "What do you mean?"

"Singing hymns like a believer," Oliver said. "You're only doing it because of her." He pointed behind the church. "She's on the bench alone," he said.

*   *   *

After all that had transpired this evening, Henry almost felt calm as he crossed the churchyard. Caroline had on a dress. He didn't want to know why. He only wanted to sit beside her as they'd done on so many previous nights.

"Lots of people out and about," Henry said, glancing around for any signs of Oliver. "Probably the weather."

Caroline faced the headstones, her hands in her lap. "Aren't you happy to see me?"

Henry sat down and feigned indifference. "We're finally enjoying some dry days," he said, stretching his arms.

She stared at him, her lips trembling. "The month is up."

"I suppose you're right."

"Remember when we met, Henry—right over there, beside that hedge?"

She took his hand. He started to pull away. When he glanced at her legs beneath the dress, instantly he knew it had been a mistake. He could practically feel them wrapped around him.

"You look like you did that day," she said, squeezing his hand, "with a beard and messy hair."

Henry managed to get his hand back. He turned from her on the bench.

"I went up to the pub tonight," she said. "Right before closing. Sid told me you'd just left—you and Trevor and Chris, with Vickie and another woman."

"He did, did he? Well, what if it's true?"

"You don't have to explain."

"I wasn't explaining."

"Have you seen other women, Henry?"

He shrugged. "I don't know if that's any of your business."

"I went to Brighton tonight, Henry. Do you know it only made me realise how much I wanted to come back to this spot?" She put her hand on his cheek. "I wasn't being fair. I kept asking you to talk, to tell me your feelings. But I wasn't prepared for what came out of your mouth."

He wanted to act distant, but he couldn't. He buckled under her touch. "I liked it, Caroline. I liked it when you pushed me. I was worried about dying." He took a deep breath and plunged forward.

"Because you love me?" She smiled. "I think I understand."

"Let me finish, Caroline." He left the bench and waved angrily at the trees. "Even right now, I worry about something happening. Something falling from the sky. I know it's ridiculous, but it's true. Take that, for instance," he said, pointing at the willow. "It's nothing more than a tree. It'll outlive us."

Caroline laughed. "I'm not laughing at you," she said, as he turned around. "I'm just so happy that you're talking about it."

"But talking doesn't make the fear go away. And I don't want to get drunk every night to forget. I don't want to forget."

"The time apart didn't help me, either. But—do you think it helped us?" She was staring at him again—he could tell even when he looked away. "I love you, Henry," she said, coming over to him, "You need to find meaning in your life."

"I dig graves for a living," he said.

"You've never missed a day of work. You care about people, Henry, even if the people you care for are dead."

Henry put his arms around her and before he could stop himself he kissed her. In some ways, it seemed like no time at all had passed between them. Together they turned toward the headstones and the graves he'd dug. Henry had to admit it—he was proud that tomorrow, somewhere in Sussex, he would wake before dawn and dig another.

TWELVE

Henry had heard of some unusual names, but nothing came close to Pigsbottom. Under the lamp at the telephone table he copied the deceased's measurements from his schedule book, and the name kept him laughing all the way out to the van. Then the sight of the tools, and the wheelbarrow, and his muddy boots reminded him that a man was dead. He went back inside the house and up to his closet. He brushed off the suit he hadn't worn since Beverly Smith's funeral.

At Springmer, Henry stopped at a florist's for half a dozen carnations. On the card he wrote, *Rest in peace - your gravedigger*. He kept his suit in the van, and after digging the Pigsbottom grave, he changed in the back, among the tools. Inside the church he sat away from the mourners, not wanting to intrude. But he listened to the sermon, the tributes, the personal testimonies, and he prayed for the man's soul along with everyone else.

After the committal Henry placed his carnations beside the other flowers on the mound. A woman approached from the church. She was the widow, Henry knew—he'd seen her at the front of the procession. She was in her sixties, a woman married one week and a widow the next. Standing at a distance, she gave him a tight smile.

"My husband," she said, "told me that someone who attended his funeral would be an enemy."

"I'm just the gravedigger," Henry said.

"My husband was often a hateful man. Did you know that?"

"I'm sorry." Henry waited. "I can't say that I knew him at all."

"He was my husband for thirty-nine years!" The woman looked over at the church. Some of the mourners had assembled in the car park. "And I can't say that I knew him either."

"There's good in every man," Henry said, and as she looked at him with surprise he realised that he actually believed it.

* * *

By the middle of May, Henry and Caroline had resumed where they'd left off. Henry shaved his beard again and went to Glynde for a haircut. He continued buying carnations for the deceased. He stayed in the churchyards long after the mourners had gone, and he scraped the lichen and lime from the letters of the older headstones. The people of the parish began to notice.

While digging in Burgess Green, Henry noticed a stack of headstones beside a hedge. He thought of all the people they belonged to. He thought of mass burials and paupers' graves, and without warning something shifted inside, and he leaned over the side of the hole to retch. What were used headstones doing on church grounds, piled up like bricks? Climbing out of the grave, he went over to the hedge. Most were in good condition.

At the vicarage door Henry knocked before he realised it was six in the morning. He waited inside the garden between beds of begonias. A brass nameplate beside the door said the vicar was called Desmond Folsom.

A light went on upstairs. There were thumps inside the house and finally the door opened. In the shadows there appeared a shrinking, mole-like man, his head buried in his shoulders, his fingers curling around the edge of the door. A woman stood behind him with her hair in curlers. She clutched the back of her husband's nightgown and blinked at the sun.

"Morning, Reverend. I'm Henry Bale, the gravedigger for today's service. Sorry for waking you, but I've a problem in the churchyard."

The vicar opened the door a bit further. "Did you find the marker?"

"Yes."

"Hetherington gave you the dimensions?"

"Yes, Reverend. But there's something else. Maybe you're not aware, but there are some discarded gravestones under the boundary hedge. Eight of them."

The vicar peered around Henry in the drive, as if to make sure he'd come alone. "We can't do anything about that at the moment," he said.

Henry kept his voice steady. "You know about them, then."

"Of course. Overcrowding, you see."

"But I've never seen them before. I've been digging here ten years."

"That's because they were in the apse." Behind him, his wife kept blinking and clutching his nightgown. "I'm trying to get the church in order, Mr. Bale, and we're a bit short on space. I had the warden move them out of doors."

"What were those headstones doing in the church to begin with?"

The vicar just stared. "They must have fallen down. It's certainly not anything for you to worry about."

"Pardon me, but it is. We have a service today, and they're out in the open. Anyway, it's not just about hiding them. Where are the graves they belong to?"

"The deceased will be listed in the burial registry. Nothing to fear about that. But we can hardly replace the headstones now, can we? There isn't room."

"No room?"

"I'm surprised you've never come across this sort of thing," Reverend Folsom said. He started to close the door. "If you'd be so kind…"

"I've seen plenty of things," Henry said, thrusting his chin forward, "but I've never seen this level of neglect."

There was a silence. The door stayed partly ajar, and the vicar's voice came quietly through the opening. "All right. What would you have me do, Mr. Bale?"

Henry pointed to the churchyard. "The relatives have a right to know what's happened. The dead themselves have rights. Arrange to have those headstones put back, Reverend—back above their proper plots!"

"You must be joking," the vicar said, his voice gaining strength. "That churchyard is six hundred years old. If I did what you suggested, you wouldn't be able to use the path. We bury on top of existing graves, you know that. In London, we had eight deceased per cubic meter!"

Henry felt his stomach turning again. "Excuse me," he said,

leaning over the flowers.

The door swung open all the way. "Goodness gracious," Mrs. Folsom said.

"He's being sick all over my begonias."

* * *

The vicar's wife brought a pot of tea into the sitting room and stood over Henry as he drank it, as if to make sure it stayed down. Then she crept back to bed.

Reverend Folsom had changed into trousers and a polo, and as he sat in his leather armchair he tilted his head at the packing boxes in the corner. "We've only just moved here," he said. "It's difficult deciding where to put things." He dropped his hand to the side of his chair, where a Springer spaniel watched Henry while licking its paws.

Henry balanced on the edge of the sofa, shifting his weight on the newspapers the vicar's wife had asked him to sit on. He'd left his boots outside. The tea, at least, had calmed his stomach. "Where were you before Burgess Green?"

"North London. Quite a change, coming here. Now you're from Chalk, is that right? Where exactly is that?"

"It's hidden. A place with very little to recommend it, I'm afraid." He put his hands on his knees. "Reverend, I'm certainly not here to argue. In fact, I hate arguments. But in this case—"

"You don't have to explain. It's a deplorable state of affairs."

"You mean, you agree?"

"Of course! I'd love our church to have more room. But we must place those headstones somewhere." The vicar sighed. "Mr. Bale. John Hetherington told me you were the epitome of reliability. That's all anyone can ask for, these days. But he also told me you've started to do more than you're paid for. I hope this isn't what he meant."

"I can't speak for Hetherington." Henry felt his ears turn red. "Perhaps I've just begun to notice things."

"What sort of things?"

"Examples of carelessness."

The vicar nibbled his lips like a rabbit. "In all your experience, have you ever squeezed in a new grave where there wasn't quite room? In between a couple of older headstones, for instance?"

"Of course!" Henry shouted. "But those are abandoned headstones. Overcrowding doesn't excuse that!"

The spaniel sat up and barked. "Raymond," Reverend Folsom said, squeezing the dog's mouth closed. "Raymond, hush. And Mr. Bale, please listen. Everyone who dies in this parish has a God-given right to a churchyard burial. Only the Church of England can change that. Meanwhile, there is simply a shortage of space. If the older headstones break or fall, we move them aside to create room. We can hardly turn people away, can we?"

"All right, Reverend," Henry said, "you may be right about church issues in general. But you're just shifting the blame. What will be done with your churchyard? The headstones under your care?"

"In a way the headstones are mine, and in a way they're not. I'm not the one who presided over the burials."

"How do you expect me to dig Mr. Milburn's grave with discarded headstones nearby? What would his family think?" Henry leaned forward on the sofa. "I'll tell you what they'd think—they'd worry about his soul, that's what."

Reverend Folsom rubbed the end of his nose. He seemed to be regretting recent choices he'd made—moving out to the country, answering the door, inviting Henry inside. "There's always the cellar, I suppose. I haven't yet seen it, but there's bound to be room."

"The cellar."

"It's the warden's day off." The vicar ran a finger under the collar of his shirt. "We'll have to move them ourselves."

*　*　*

Reverend Folsom unlocked the cellar door and pushed. Nothing happened. Leaning into it with his shoulder, he pushed harder. The door nudged open, and a gust blew into the churchyard, carrying the smell of stale air.

Together they banged the door open all the way. The vicar flicked a switch along the wall, and a light bulb hanging from the ceiling flickered on. He took a step down the cement staircase, his nostrils twitching. "I'll just take a look," he said.

Henry paced on the grass. The sun rose above the treetops, and as he counted the graves, the churchyard seemed to shrink. There were only sixty-three headstones. If the vicar was right, there had to be sixty dead beneath those, and sixty more beneath those. How far down did the dead go?

A muffled voice cried out, as if from the bottom of a mineshaft. Henry went to the top of the stairs. "Was that you, Reverend?"

After a moment Reverend Folsom appeared at the top step, panting. "I'm afraid there's no room," he said.

"What do you mean?"

"No room! See for yourself."

Henry slipped by and descended the cement steps. The air grew cold and damp. "There's another light at the bottom if you need it," the vicar called down.

At the bottom, Henry gasped. He couldn't go any further if he tried. From one end of the cellar to the next, hundreds of headstones had been stacked to the ceiling. The level of organisation was almost sinister.

Henry wanted to go back up, but he forced himself to stay. He had a feeling he'd never see anything like this again. It seemed important to take it all in—the stacks of crumbling stone, the smell, the spiders. The cellar concealed a secret that must have spanned generations. Henry had an urge to count them, but he didn't really want to know the exact number. All he could do was stand on the step and shiver.

He thanked Reverend Folsom for his time and finished Percy Milburn's grave. It was too late to find a suitable place for the headstones by the hedge. Henry collected some branches and covered them from sight. The Milburn family didn't seem to notice. For the service Henry changed into his suit and placed his carnations on the mound. *Rest in Peace*, the note card said, thought he knew it was a lie. The deceased in Burgess Green weren't resting peacefully at all.

* * *

What if St. Margaret's cellar held headstones? The thought ate at Henry as he sat in his armchair. "Maybe a human grave is no different than a dog's," he said, waking Jackie in her cot. "But people deserve to know the truth!" He reached for a pad of paper and wrote a letter to the *Sussex Sentinel*.

Dear Editor,

In the cellar of the Burgess Green Parish Church lies an alarming number of neglected gravestones. Families of these deceased have the right to know. I am a gravedigger and have seen it with my own eyes.

Yours sincerely,

Henry Bale,
Chalk, E. Sussex

P.S. Reverend Folsom is not necessarily to blame. He has inherited the situation.

That evening as they sat on the sofa after supper, Henry told Caroline about his day. She seemed more curious than horrified. "A bunch of headstones? Who started it?"

"I don't know. It had to have been a vicar from a while back. During the first war, maybe." He showed her the letter.

She read it over slowly, then handed it back. "You're being very civic-minded, aren't you? How many headstones are we talking about?"

"I didn't count. There had to have been more than a hundred. I can't get them out of my mind, Caroline." He sat there holding the letter, unsure whether to post it or not.

"Why did it bother you?" When you're dead, you're dead. You've said as much."

"I said I didn't know what happens after you die. Anyway, it's probably against the law, what they've done." He put the letter on the coffee table. "I'm posting that tomorrow, and that's the end of it."

She looked at him doubtfully. "There might be publicity, Henry."

"Of course!"

"I don't mean for the gravestones." She sat up, swung her legs around, and faced him. "Are you ready to have reporters coming round? You want your photograph in the paper?"

He retreated to the arm of the sofa. "You told me to find meaning in my life, and now that I have, you—"

"You're right," she said. No matter what you believe, churches shouldn't hide that sort of thing from the public."

"That's what I think. Why were you disagreeing with me just now?"

"I wanted to know how you really felt."

He looked about the sitting room, as if just hearing what she'd said earlier. "But...reporters here? Wouldn't the newspaper just send someone to Burgess Green?"

"They'll want to talk with you as well. A conscientious country gravedigger, writing a letter of complaint—you'll be the story, not the cellar. The vicar will resent you for meddling, too."

Deflated, Henry stood up and went to the fireplace. "Here I am, following my instincts. All you've done is find fault."

Caroline got up and blocked him from the hearth, as if to prevent him from plunging into a remoter part of himself. "I agree with you, Henry. And I'll support you, no matter what you decide, because I love you. I only want you to be aware of the consequences."

"I care about this, Caroline. I don't know why, but I do. I dig graves every day, and I have to believe my work is more or less permanent. Is that just a delusion?"

✳ ✳ ✳

It had been three weeks since the reporter from the *Sentinel* came to Chalk. A pushy young woman from Brighton, she'd interviewed Henry for twenty minutes and left. Henry had practically forgotten about it until this morning. He was out of dog food, so he walked up to the shop. Still, he considered turning back when he saw the crowd inside. On the newspaper board facing the road, the headline in bold black letters read, *Gravedigger Reveals Burial Space Crisis.*

The butler, Roger Lowry, stepped out of the shop with a stack of newspapers under his arm. "The Wembles will be so proud," he said, nodding to Henry and hurrying on.

"It's him!" someone inside shouted.

"Get back!"

Trevor came out onto the road, his arms outstretched. He looked on the point of tears. "You've put Chalk on the map," he said, guiding Henry inside. Darren Roberts moved aside to let them through. "The man of the hour," he said.

Reverend Pierce, standing on top of a box of potatoes, raised his hands. "Let's all hear it," he said, "for our very own Henry Bale."

Everyone broke into applause. People came at Henry from all directions, clapping his shoulders and pumping his hand—Chris Crawley, Vickie Eckleton, William Harvey, Penny Pierce, Sid Book, Karen Bates.

"First time Chalk's been in the papers."

"It took courage, that."

"Such a nice photo, Henry."

"He qualifies as a celebrity, I should think."

"I saved the last copy for our local hero," Mr. Yapton announced. He held an open *Sentinel* above his head. There were two photos, side by side—one of Henry beside Jackie's cot with his arms crossed, and another of the headstones in the Burgess Green cellar.

"Oh, dear," Henry whispered. Flashbulbs went off in his face. Kevin Yapton whisked around the counter, the paper in his hands. He gave it to Henry and bowed. "On the house."

"That's not necessary," Henry said, digging in his pocket for change. "I just came in for some dog food."

There was a roar of laughter.

"Typical Henry!"

"As pure as they come."

"It's only dog food he's here for! Who's going to get it for him?"

"Leave it to me," Darren Roberts said. He placed twenty pounds on the counter. Henry protested, but Kevin Yapton hurried behind the counter to make the sale.

It was half an hour before he could leave. The events of that day had to be repeated, the inevitable rumours discredited. After turning down invitations to The Black Ram, Henry finally squeezed out the door. He hadn't even had a chance to read the article.

At home, a sheet of paper had been taped to Henry's door. The looping black letters were in Oliver's hand: No hell is hot enough for the likes of you!

* * *

It felt strange to be in the armchair and studying a photograph of himself by the mantle. He had his arms crossed and his lips pressed together, as the reporter had requested.

GRAVEDIGGER REVEALS BURIAL SPACE CRISIS

The cellar of St. Anne's in Burgess Green holds a dismal secret: dozens of gravestones, neatly stacked. A crisis of churchyard overcrowding has too long been ignored. Indeed, the crisis would have continued unobserved were it not for the attention of gravedigger Henry Bale of Chalk, whose detective work began on 3 June, starting with a pile of eight headstones in plain sight outside the church.

"When I saw them lying by the hedge, I was appalled. I had to enquire at the vicarage," Mr. Bale told the Sentinel.

Mr. Bale, who has been digging graves in Sussex for over twenty years, was later led into the church cellar by Reverend Desmond Folsom, who hoped to find room for the headstones there. Instead, both men discovered the grim scene. "I think the vicar was just as shocked as I was," Mr. Bale said.

Reverend Folsom, who moved to Sussex from London in April, admits the problem should have been addressed long ago. "Unfortunately," he said, "Burgess Green is not the exception."

Morris Wheaton, a Chartered Town Planner, told the Sentinel that funeral activities are nearly impossible to police. "Most churchyards don't even have grave numbers," he said. "Families don't own the graves, whereas in County Council cemeteries people can lease cemetery plots for 50 or 70 years."

The effect of time is especially evident in older churchyards such as Burgess Green's. Here, the burial ground has risen in some places to the level of the fence. Cremations, which have soared from 6% in 1951 to 73% in 2006, have eased the spacing burden. Still, undertakers are forced to improvise. Some churchyards in heavily populated areas have resorted to squeezing new graves between spaciously laid older graves, reclaiming unused space, or raising land by up to 15 feet to place new graves on top of much older ones.

Until such a practise is authorised, however, one can only wonder what the newly bereaved might expect. "People should be informed if their headstones might land in a cellar," Mr. Bale said. The Home Office and the Church of England said the matter is under review and refused further comment.

Henry read the article a second time. All things considered, the reporter had done a fine job. He only wished his photo hadn't been used.

The telephone rang—it was Hetherington, and he was angry. "I never expected this, Henry. After all the work I've sent your way."

"The article wasn't about you, John."

"Do you know who's been ringing me all morning? Relatives of people dead for decades, wanting to know if their ancestors' graves are in that cellar. How am I supposed to know?"

"I'm sorry about that."

"You might be enjoying a bit of fame, Henry, but I'm not very popular. A family business, this is. You're only as good as your name. I've had six cancellations just today."

Henry leaned against the telephone table to steady himself. "I only wanted to do something about those headstones," he said.

"Maybe you did, maybe you didn't. I'm certainly not sending any more of my business to a publicity monger." He hung up.

"That's it, then," Henry said, the phone still in his hand. What was he going to do for work? He rang Reverend Folsom, but the line was engaged. The vicar would be thumbing through the church registry right now, reassuring people that their loved ones were safe.

"But they're not safe!" Henry slammed the receiver down. "No one is!"

Jackie left her cot and ran barking to his feet. Henry tried the vicarage once more, and the vicar answered. "Reverend Folsom— it's Henry Bale. Has it been a difficult day for you?"

There was a silence. "It certainly hasn't been easy." The vicar sounded more weary than angry.

"I was afraid of that. I didn't mean for you to be named."

"It would have been nice to get fair warning that a reporter would be coming round. There are some frightened people in my parish thanks to you. Frightened for their fathers and mothers, frightened for themselves."

"I'm sorry for that. I didn't think things through properly, I suppose."

"People ought to do a lot of thinking before writing letters to newspapers." He hung up.

Jackie kept barking as the doorbell rang. She was still barking as he opened the door. There was nobody there. He wondered if it was Oliver. Henry went out to his gate and Jackie followed him, sniffing the grass. The road was empty. He came back inside and Jackie shadowed his feet. In all the excitement, he'd forgotten to feed her.

The phone rang again.

"Mr. Bale? It's Charlie Cotton. We met a few months ago in

Burgess Green?"

Jackie was still barking. "Be quiet," Henry said, "you'll get your food. Excuse me, Charlie, I was speaking to my dog. Hello?"

"I'm here. I say, Henry—you saw those headstones? They were really down there?"

"I'm afraid so."

"I must have dug fifty alone in that churchyard. Did you happen to see any names?"

"I didn't, Charlie. I just stood there until I couldn't bear it any longer. Frankly, I didn't know what to do."

"Henry, listen. I'd like you to dig my grave when the time comes."

Henry winced. A twinge rippled across his back. "Pardon me?"

"It's important to me, knowing everything is done proper. You understand."

"I do, Charlie."

"You remember how I dig my graves, do you?"

"Deep," Henry said, "by a foot. Bowed at the midsection."

"I knew I could count on you. Thank you, Henry."

When he hung up, the phone rang again. "This must be some sort of joke." It was Frank. "What the hell were you thinking?"

"You should have seen that cellar, Dad. It was so organised, so evil."

"Any press is bad press. I suppose Hetherington's rung up."

"I don't think he'll be using me in the future."

"Christ. You may as well go on the dole now."

"What do you care? I thought you wanted me to change careers." Jackie pawed at the carpet by the door. "Stop it, Jackie!"

"This is my name, too. Everyone's going to think I brought up some sort of activist. I didn't break my back for forty years to have you—"

Henry hung up, ran to the door, and opened it. "Stop, you bastard!"

Oliver leaped Henry's front wall. Jackie barked and tried to wiggle through the gate, but Henry brought her back inside. Another note hung on his door. *Idiots care about rocks. Gravestones are rocks. Therefore, Henry is an idiot!*

Mrs. Tilson came out to her garden with a bag of birdseed. "Lovely article in the Sentinel," she said. "Never mind what your father thinks."

"So you've been talking to my dad, have you?" Henry snapped.

"How nice for you!" He decided to go after Oliver, even if it meant making a scene. The man was always at the pub. Halfway to the gate, he stopped. "I'm sorry, Mrs. Tilson. I hadn't meant to be rude."

Standing on her tiptoes, she poured birdseed into the feeder. "You needn't say another word about it."

"My phone's been ringing nonstop, you see."

"Media coverage." Mrs. Tilson shook her head, as if she'd been in similar predicaments. "Mind you, I'd certainly like to know if my headstone might land in a cellar. But as I say, we won't discuss it further."

Henry stayed at the wall. Now he did want to talk about it. "I just couldn't let it go unreported," he said. "Probably Caroline's influence." Mrs. Tilson didn't seem to have heard. He said it again, a little louder. "Caroline's changed me!"

She looked at him and nodded. "You've always been a good man, Henry." Taking her birdseed, she went inside.

Henry looked toward Bates Farm. Caroline was the one person who hadn't rang. She obviously had better things to do than read the *Sentinel*. Stuffing Oliver's notes in his pocket, Henry headed to the pub.

* * *

Oliver sat alone at the bar behind a Guinness. "I've had enough of this," Henry said, coming toward him. "You might have badgered my father, but I'm not going to put up with it."

Looking right at him, Oliver yawned. Henry leaned over the bar. "Where's Sid?" He half expected to see the barman on the floor, bound and gagged.

"The psychological problems you have," Oliver said, in his high feeble voice. He took a long drink from his pint. "We're the same age, you and I. But you wouldn't know that, would you?"

A thumping noise came from the back of the pub. "You can't grow a conscience in your forties," Oliver said. "Who cares about a few headstones in Burgess Green? Your father wouldn't have."

"What's that noise back there? What have you done with Sid?"

"For years, you hadn't the slightest appreciation for grave digging. Sickening to watch, it was."

"Shut up, Oliver."

"You may be taking the moral high ground now, but what about when you acted like it was just another job?"

A loud clanging shook the floorboards. "At least I don't run around like a child," Henry said, "leaving idiotic notes on people's doors."

"At least I can remember my own mother."

Henry stormed to Oliver's stool, fists clenched. "Don't say another word, Oliver. I swear I'll—"

"I've heard you under the willow," Oliver went on. "Trying to remember the littlest things. Comical, really. How do you know it's not an empty plot?"

The door to the lavatory opened. "Sorry to keep you waiting, Henry," Sid said. "Just fixing the loo." He put a spanner down on the beer mat and washed his hands in the sink. "Cuckoo for you?"

Henry sat down. He counted seconds in his head to relax. "Not just yet, Sid, thank you."

"You sure? I'll just be a minute, if you change your mind." Taking his spanner, he went back into the lavatory.

"I don't want to hurt you, Oliver," Henry said. "I really don't. But if you keep bothering me—"

"It's for your own good," Oliver said.

Henry took the notes out of his pocket and shook them. "If you believe these, why do you bother attending church?"

Oliver grinned. "Reverend Pierce thinks I'm a believer."

Henry put the notes back in his pocket. "He's not that stupid."

"The things he lets me do would surprise you. He made me a warden, Henry! But don't worry—Chalk has no burial space crisis."

"What? How do you know?"

"Think about it." Oliver finished his pint. Then he walked behind Henry's stool and out the door.

Sid came out of the lavatory. "Your first drink's on me, Henry," he said, pouring a pint of Cuckoo. "Quite the excitement, that newspaper article." He pointed his rag at Oliver's glass. "Gone?"

Henry nodded. He wondered if anyone else knew that Oliver talked. "Say, Sid—I just realised I don't know the first thing about the man. His parents, for instance."

"Oliver? He doesn't exactly volunteer any information." Sid wiped the length of the counter, shaking his head. "Both of them went tragically, I heard, when he was just a boy. Raised by his grandmother, Oliver was. She's gone too, now—just last year."

Henry tried to picture Oliver all alone inside the old Huntsman's cottage he was rumoured to occupy. Weeds swarmed the front garden, taller than the wall. "I don't recall digging a grave for Oliver's grandmother. Where's she buried?"

Sid shrugged. "I haven't a clue, Henry." He placed his hands on the bar and leaned forward. "You're not collecting material for another one of those newspaper articles, are you?"

Henry picked up his drink and stood up. "I wrote one letter, and now I'm done with it. I couldn't care less about Oliver's bloody grandmother. I was only making conversation."

"All right, Henry, all right. No need to get steamed."

Henry drifted into the snuggery. He sat by the empty fireplace and wished Caroline were beside him. He wondered what kind of man people thought he had been, the past forty years. He wondered how he would know what to believe in next. Gradually the room went dark.

Henry was tired when the armchair beside him moved. He kept his eyes on the floor until he felt her hands. "You've done it," Caroline said. She pulled him on his feet.

"You started something, and it became larger than yourself."

Henry put his head over on shoulder and closed his eyes. Someone over at the bar had started to sing. It was a woman's voice, singing a song from his childhood that he'd forgotten. The song made him sad with nostalgia, with memories of a time when his mother read him stories and he never had to question whether or not they were true. He held Caroline close and together they turned in a circle.

THIRTEEN

In July the sun lingered longer in Chalk's sky, as if to reassure people of its warmth. Henry was busier than ever. Hetherington had switched to Derrick Watkins, but it made no difference. Other undertakers came forward, hired by families asking for Henry by name. These undertakers removed the memorials before he arrived. Their bearers stepped carefully around his mats. At the end of each service, Henry found bonuses slipped into his fee.

The burial scandal at Burgess Green gradually died away. The report from the Home Office never materialised, and people forgot about the headstones in the church cellar. But fresh faces appeared at St. Margaret's on Sunday mornings. Often elderly or infirm, the new congregants struggled out of their cars after driving miles to find Chalk, the home of the gravedigger who dignified the dead.

Henry wasn't often there to greet them. He prayed at home, doubtfully, without skill. Generally content, he made only petty requests. Generally virtuous, he confessed sins of little consequence. He prayed for the deceased. He prayed for favourable digging weather. When he felt a pang of pain above his hip, he prayed for it to pass.

Caroline watched him, he could tell. She found reasons to come upstairs, to pass the bedroom as he knelt on the carpet. If he prayed in the guest room, he sensed her at the door. Every night he knelt in his pyjamas, his hands clasped. He never heard anything that resembled an answer, but he wasn't going to be caught unprepared on the day it came. He suspected his search was pointless. What sort of God didn't bother answering a simple prayer?

When the urge struck—in traffic on his way home, the dead

time accumulating like dust—he counted. He kept track of the days he had left to live. He calculated the average days per week he and Caroline made love. When the counting took on a life of its own, when he couldn't stop the numbers from spinning in his mind's eye, he found refuge in the church. He snuck across the road and into a stall. He knelt and recited The Lord's Prayer until the counting subsided. It was the closest he came to believing.

To keep his promise to be a better man, Henry continued to attend funerals and bring carnations. He roamed the churchyards with his scraper, and he cleaned the letters of the older graves. He couldn't help nosing around a little. He pushed open forgotten doors, investigated tool sheds, peered under hedges. Sometimes he went at night to avoid suspicion.

*　*　*

At night the shapes slowly took form—the chandeliers and empty prayer stalls, the vicar advancing up the nave in his white robe. There was stubble on his chin.

"You perform Sung Evensong alone?" Henry asked. William Harvey wasn't at the organ.

Reverend Pierce adjusted his robe. "Not many people come in the evenings, I'm afraid."

"But there's nobody here. Nobody at all!"

"It's better than it used to be, Henry. When I first came to Chalk I didn't have a single congregant, not even Sunday mornings." Reverend Pierce checked his wristwatch. "But Sung Evensong has been conducted every week here for over four hundred years. It's the church's way of saying that things may change in our lives, but God is always present."

Henry looked up at the altar. He tried to imagine Chalk's previous congregants—earlier versions of Trevor Nelson and Kevin Yapton, a seventeenth century Oliver Marsh. "I came at night because I didn't want a crowd. But I didn't expect to sing alone."

Reverend Pierce opened his prayer book. "Look," he said, pointing to the top of the page. "It's an antiphonal service. I'll sing the first part, starting with the third chapter of Exodus. Then you follow. Then, starting with Psalm 89, I'll sing alone. Got it?"

"I don't know the notes."

"Don't worry. I'll sing your parts with you." The vicar checked his watch again. "Right. If you're ready, Henry, let's proceed."

Henry chose his usual stall. Reverend Pierce followed from the rear of the church, and he passed Henry's stall without looking over. Then, turning at the chancel rail, he began to sing.

Henry kept his eyes on the cross. Having Reverend Pierce singing straight at him in an empty church made him painfully aware of himself. Other times, he almost forgot he was there. He sang with his hymnal held high and let the vicar guide him through the notes. He wanted a sermon and he didn't know if he was going to get one. Perhaps it was enough for now to repeat these ancient words, to have the outward bearing of a believer.

At the end of the service they recited the Lord's Prayer. Henry stayed on the kneeler a while. The quiet of the church calmed him.

Up at the altar, the vicar cleared his throat. Henry hoped he hadn't stayed longer than he should have. He opened the stall door and hurried out. It seemed strange to leave without saying goodbye, but he didn't know how appropriate it was to linger. The vicar caught up to him. "Lovely night," he said, as they came outside.

Henry looked up at the steeple. Some of the shingles had fallen off. What would happen if the whole thing collapsed? "Reverend," he said, "are you satisfied with our church?"

The vicar followed Henry's gaze. "It's not going to make any guide books. But a church is mostly a place of work."

"What sort of work?" They came through the gate and stood side-by-side in the empty road.

"To keep alive our communication with God. It never takes much to make the church relevant—a war, a plague, an economic collapse." Reverend Pierce looked at him. "Or, on a smaller scale, just a series of personal discoveries."

The vicar sighed heavily. "I have more congregants on Sunday mornings than ever before. The problem with relevance is that we must work that much harder to keep it." He glanced up the road toward the pub. Then he lowered his head, opened the gate to his vicarage, and started home.

* * *

"I'm handling a family that's requested you personally," Hetherington said on the phone. "You can always refuse, I suppose."

"Go on," Henry said.

"Charlie Cotton died yesterday."

Henry sat on the carpet beside the telephone table. It didn't seem that long ago, Charlie ringing him up. "When's the service?"

"Tuesday next week. In Burgess Green, of course. The wife's making all the arrangements."

Henry hesitated—he'd have to see Reverend Folsom again. He'd have to walk by that cellar door, knowing what lay beneath. "I don't know," he said. "My schedule is pretty full." But it was a gravedigger that needed burying, and he'd already practically agreed. "I suppose I can see my way to doing it," he said.

"Good. Now don't go snooping round that church. And no staying after to clean the headstones, or any of that rubbish you've gone in for. Reverend Folsom wants you to steer clear."

"I've seen all I need to in that churchyard," Henry said.

"Good. Then I'll see you—"

"One thing I forgot to mention, John. My rate's gone up. All the attention from that article in the newspapers, you see. A hundred and fifty pounds now."

"I'm not paying that."

"Right. Make it one seventy-five, then."

"Listen, Henry, if you think you can—"

"No, you listen, John." Henry stood up and leaned over the telephone table, stabbing the air with his finger. "Twenty years I dug for you. Not once did I miss a job. Why didn't you ever move the memorials off like the other undertakers? Yours is a family business, you say? So is mine. How many times did my father prepare a perfect grave and make you look good?"

"All right, Henry. Take it easy." Hetherington sounded exhausted. "What's come over you, anyway? One seventy-five it is. Just have the grave ready, please—and stay away from the church?"

* * *

Caroline stood at the door and searched the faces of her pupils as they filed out, as if to find answers in their expressions. It had come quicker than she'd thought—the end of term, six weeks of summer holiday, the completion of her contract. She'd passed the test she'd given herself by moving to Chalk for the length of the term. Now Headmaster Briggs wanted to plan the following year.

Could she permanently settle in Chalk? She and Henry discussed marriage in a general way, talking around the subject as if it only applied to other people. Caroline wasn't sure what she'd say if he proposed. But if she signed a second contract, wouldn't she be entertaining the idea?

On her way to Briggs' office she stopped at the hallway window and looked across the road at the row of tenant cottages. Henry would be having his tea right now, perhaps napping in his armchair. If she stayed in Chalk, each day would be a repetition of this moment. She would cross the road after work to find him inside his tiny house, watching television or sleeping with his head tilted sideways. She knocked on Briggs' door and he called her in.

Caroline took the chair across from his desk. She crossed her legs and sighed with exaggerated weariness. "Well, that's over, anyway. I thought the term would never end, and now—here it is!"

Briggs folded his hands on top of his desk. His combed white hair glared in the sun from the window behind him. His office was cluttered with files and reports and letters, stacked on the floor surrounding his desk. Years ago someone had sent him a postcard from New York City, and the faded photo sat taped to the side of his computer, its sides curling inward. "I do hope you've decided to stay on, Caroline," Briggs said.

Caroline tried to be direct as Briggs. Her thoughts, though, were anything but clear. "I need more time, I'm afraid. I should know next week, if that's all right."

"More time." Briggs raised his eyebrows. It was his method of extracting further information.

"That's right." Caroline had nothing further to say, so she left it at that. The headmaster hadn't advertised, she knew, for anyone else.

"I'm tempted not to give it to you," Briggs said. "Education isn't something we take lightly here. You see, it's all we have."

She leaned toward his desk, searching his eyes for the understanding she thought they'd shared. "Are you implying something, Robert? It's because I don't take the job lightly that I need more time."

"You've had months."

"And they've gone quickly."

"Most people think one week in Chalk is an eternity."

Caroline laughed. "Maybe I like to suffer."

She thought the joke would make him smile. The corners of his mouth didn't even twitch. "If you want more time, then let me know what it is you're considering."

"Okay." She spoke slowly, trying to order her thoughts. "I'm happy teaching here. And the students seem pleased…"

"I think they are, yes. And Darren is full of praise. If we weren't pleased, the offer wouldn't have been made."

"I appreciate that. But there are other concerns." Her eyes darted to the window overlooking the road. "It's personal."

"Love," Briggs said, still motionless.

"That's right," she said. "A few days to think about it, and—"

"A few days—to think about love?" He tapped his desk. He straightened the postcard of New York and it curled in again. "I know something of love myself. A love of learning, and the school's function in the village. You have a week to sort out your situation. If you decide you want to stay, the position is yours."

"I appreciate your understanding, Robert." Collecting her things, she left his office and hurried down the hallway. She didn't want to go home. She didn't want to go to Henry's. Somewhere in Chalk, she needed a quiet place to think.

* * *

Henry dragged the box of keepsakes out from under the guest room bed. He sat on the carpet and recognised his father's old denim coat, worn at the shoulders and permeated by the smell of firewood. Frank used to build a fire each night while Henry's mother prepared supper. Right next door it would have been.

The box held some jewellery, a bundle of photographs, a letter wrapped in string. Henry didn't feel right about handling the letter just yet. The photographs were mostly of his parents—holding suitcases beside the Vauxhall, at the beach in swimming outfits. Henry almost didn't recognise his father for the grin on his face. His mother couldn't have known how near she was to death.

The postmark on the letter was dated two years before Henry

was born. He took it out of the envelope and studied his mother's handwriting.

Dear Frank,

Far too long since I was last in your arms. Could it only have been last night? I take back what I said. I love you, and you know it. Sometimes words come out of my mouth that have no meaning.

Henry looked away from the page. He didn't want to know what his mother intended to take from his father's memory, let alone a future son's. He returned the letter to the envelope. What was he supposed to do with these keepsakes when his father died?

One of the photographs showed a children's cricket team in front of The Black Ram. Henry found himself at the end of the second row, his arm around the nearest player. Names were written along the bottom of the photo in his mother's hand. He tried to imagine her writing them, asking which boys were which. One of the names in particular stared back at him—Oliver Marsh.

Oliver stood at the other end of the second row, away from the group and turned sideways as if alarmed by a sudden noise. Henry went to the window and looked across the road at the churchyard.

Chalk has no burial space crisis, Oliver said. How would he know? Henry thought of Oliver following his dad and leaving notes in the wheelbarrow, on the door, on the headstones. He thought of what a troubled man in Chalk might do with his spare time—a man already considered insane, with only a grandmother for company. Oliver had been made a churchwarden. He'd have all the keys to the church.

Oliver could have worked at night. He could have dug up any graves he liked and taken the bodies down to the cellar. Once the thought found its way into Henry's mind, it stayed. It wasn't going anywhere until disproved.

Henry ran down the stairs and nearly tripped over Jackie as she lunged at his feet. He left his front door standing open. For the first time, he leaped the gate.

*   *   *

Caroline shivered as she entered the prayer stall. Since when was a cold church a refuge for lost souls? She turned over the kneeler. Then, as if kneeling itself had power, shame overwhelmed her.

"This is nonsense."

Her voice betrayed her and wobbled. Since she listened to all her feelings, she listened to this one too. Shame called into question all she'd done, everything she had yet to do. Perhaps the church only evoked memories from childhood, when she'd been forced to attend services and confess her sins. The building was old and draughty, like religion itself.

Caroline closed her eyes. She recited the Lord's Prayer, but deep down she meant none of it. The whole thing made her uncomfortable. It reminded her of an experience she had with a deranged person in a Brighton coffee house.

The lady had been wearing a red dress two sizes too small. Makeup streaked across her cheeks. She was muttering to herself and writing in a notebook with big block letters. Caroline saw as she passed the lady's table—each sentence a declaration, like I AM A SINNER, and I WISH PEOPLE WOULD BE NICE TO ME. When she'd finished, the lady ripped each page into little squares and quietly wept. Caroline couldn't bear to watch, so she left. Walking home, her face turned damp, like clay. All her life she wanted to believe people in pain deserved sympathy, and all she'd managed to do was flee.

Now, kneeling and confronting her shame, Caroline fought the same urge to get quickly away. It wasn't cold in the church, but she kept shivering as if to convince herself it was. She opened the stall and headed for the door. She walked behind the church, where the sun blanketed the grass.

God was just another word for nature, Caroline thought, not some bearded old man in the sky. But did these words really carry more meaning than the Lord's Prayer? Along the path she passed the older headstones and pictured Henry bent between them in the rain, his spade flying. No wonder he grappled with anxiety. No wonder he dreaded death.

Henry knelt under the willow with his back to her. She saw him as she neared the gate. She should have gone to him, but her face had gone damp again. What kind of man cried over his mother, thirty years after her death? The sight of him made Caroline want to run from the confines of Chalk.

* * *

His mother's memorial stood in its original place. The ground soil near the tree, Henry could tell, hadn't been disturbed in years. He still needed to see the church cellar. Oliver could be capable of anything.

Henry left his mother's grave and approached the cellar door knowing full well it would be locked. He jiggled the handle, pushed as hard as he could. His hand flew into the doorjamb. A cut opened on the knuckle of his thumb. It wasn't going to be pleasant, digging with that. Sucking on the wound, he turned to see if anyone had seen him. Then he walked around to the front door.

Inside the church, Henry hurried up the nave and over the chancel rail. There had to be a spare set of keys somewhere.

The green carpet had been worn away between the lectern, the altar, and the pulpit. It was the path the vicar walked each week. Henry remembered the day his father had knelt in front of the altar, right under the cross.

How could you have taken her, Frank had cried, the woman I loved, the mother of a seven-year old child? He'd pointed to Henry at the chancel rail, and while he'd waited in vain for an answer Reverend Pierce had too.

At the back of the chancel stood the Wembles Chapel, separated by a curtain. Henry slipped inside. It was dark, but he could make out the crucifix on the wall, the alabaster effigies of George and Anne Wembles.

Henry tried the wardrobe. The latch clicked open, and inside he found some musty choir robes on a rail. Henry held a sleeve to his nose and smelled the mouldy velvet. He drew the robes aside. At the back of the wardrobe stood three hunting rifles, leaning on their stocks.

Henry took them out of the closet, one by one. They had nicked barrels and splintered handles. They were undoubtedly Reverend Pierce's from the days when he'd been a game hunter and shooting partner of Sammy Wembles. Henry had seen the vicar come home from the Wembles Manor with a line of pheasant over his shoulder. He put the rifles back and searched the drawer at the bottom. There was nothing. Nothing of any significance, anyway—just some candles, pencils, and matchboxes, a Brighton Downs horse racing form. A box of bullets sat half-opened, as if the vicar had snatched a handful on his way to a hunt. It would have been the perfect place to find a set of cellar keys, only there weren't any. He started to leave when he noticed the book in the opposite corner.

The book sat face up on a prayer stool. The words *Burial Registry* were embossed on the cover in gold lettering. The spine was threadbare, but still intact.

The pages crackled in Henry's hand. They were yellow and brittle, filled with entries in black ink. The earliest entry, the death of a Reverend William Marten, dated to 28 January, 1609. For four hundred years the entries continued down each page in a remarkably consistent hand, as if made by the same person. Then he understood: the book was old, but the writing wasn't. The entries had been re-copied as recently as a few months ago, judging by the addition of Beverly Smith.

The recent pages listed the familiar names—Nelson, Wembles, Bates. Henry turned to the year of his mother's death and there she was, Evelyn Bale, dutifully recorded with the date of birth in parentheses. It was just a name, but it was satisfying to see it nonetheless.

At the beginning were the names nobody remembered— Oxenbridge, Wolsey, Pye. Farmers, they would have been, or artisans attached to the Wembles Estate. There was nothing further about them, nothing but names and dates, and as he saw their descendants disappear Henry wanted to know if they'd been generous or petty, friendly or rude, loved or ignored. Now they'd been reduced to ink.

He skipped ahead to the more recent deaths in Chalk, the ones he and his father buried. He counted them—starting in '52, they'd buried 103 Chalk residents. Prior to Beverly Smith, there was Steven Philpott, Chris Crawley's eleven year-old nephew. He'd been swimming with a friend and died of a heart condition the doctors diagnosed after his death. Before that was Margaret Harvey, William's mother. Then there was Susan Briggs, Robert and Tracy's mother, who died at eighty-one while watching television. The most disturbing part of the book was the front, the long unwritten chapter filled with blank pages.

Henry sat on the kneeler and started over from the beginning. Some years had no entries. One year had as many as seventeen. Starting from 1609, the average number deaths per year came to just over two. This year, only Beverly's name was listed, but it was only July. There was still plenty of time for the average to be reached.

Henry didn't find a single Marsh in the registry. He started to check again when a noise on the other side of the chapel curtain made him stand up.

*　*　*

"A bit dark back here," Reverend Pierce said. "Not the best reading environment."

"I wasn't exactly reading, Reverend." Henry lowered his eyes. Why did he always lie to vicars?

"A very old book, that registry," Reverend Pierce said. "Did you find anything of interest? Recognise some names?"

Henry put the book back on the kneeler. He stood facing the vicar beside the effigies of Lord and Lady Wembles. "Not really," Henry said. "I mean—a few names, yes."

"I do appreciate your zeal. And the effect you've had on attendance." The vicar straightened the sleeves of his robe. "You've been reaching people. And your extra work in the churchyards means a great deal."

"Reverend, please don't think I came back here just to snoop."

"Feel free to look round all you like! Chalk has no burial concerns, as I'm sure you're aware."

Henry turned to the tiny window overlooking the rear of the churchyard. Through the dirty glass, he searched the older headstones, tilting in the sun. "To tell you the truth," he said, "I've been curious about that."

"Only in beauty lurks the potential for evil. Only in the pretty places, like Burgess Green, do churches contend with overcrowding. People leave Chalk more often than they move here."

"Reverend, I hope you don't mind me asking—I noticed the registry's been updated recently."

The vicar nodded. "Oliver has an enormous capacity for monotony. Recopying those entries must have taken the better part of a week."

"Oliver did that?" Henry couldn't help his voice from rising. "Don't you think it unwise, letting him do something so important?"

"Oliver's a warden, Henry."

Henry cleared his throat. It was now or never. "You may not like what you're about to hear, Reverend. Oliver has been leaving nasty notes on my front door. I found one here in the church as well."

Reverend Pierce threw his head back and laughed. It was an enormous, resounding laugh. Even Reverend Pierce seemed surprised, and he stopped abruptly.

"I can't imagine what's so funny," Henry said.

"You remind me so much of your father, Henry."

Despite himself, Henry smiled. He leaned against the effigy, then caught himself and stood up straight. "I do?"

"Your dad comes to church rarely, as you know. The first time... well, I don't have to tell you about that. A very dark day. The second time was to complain about Oliver."

"When was this?"

"He would have been a little older than you are now. Oliver, of course, was just a lad. Your dad arrived on a Sunday morning in a suit and tie, and he sat by himself in one of the back stalls. He waited until all the congregants had left. Then he politely informed me of Oliver's pranks."

The vicar strode over to the wardrobe. He opened the door, swept aside the choir robes, and took out one of the rifles. "Don't give it another thought," he said. "I'll take care of Oliver." He tucked the stock against his shoulder. He pointed out the window, peered down the sight, and pulled the trigger. There was a click.

"But—what are you going to do?"

"I'll tell him to stop! Oliver's harmless, Henry. Don't worry."

Reverend Pierce put the rifle back in the wardrobe. Together they left the Wembles Chapel.

"It was a terrible thing when his parents died," the vicar said. "His father wasn't overly fond of the Anglican church, but he was always ready with a smile. A self-taught botanist. He was struck by lightning in his front garden during the most lovely spring."

"My goodness," Henry said. They walked down the nave to the door. "I don't know why I never knew."

"Oliver's mother went not long after. Probably suicide. Oliver picked at his skin, the poor lad, until there was nothing left. He stopped talking. He was angry at the world, angry at God. Considering his predicament, I never objected to him coming round the church, or even those notes of his. He became obsessed with churchyards, graves, that sort of thing."

The vicar held open the door, and they took the path to the gate. Flowers had sprung up. The afternoon sun felt hot on his face and Henry shook his head at how little he knew of his own village.

"You coming up to the pub?" the vicar asked.

Henry stared across the road. His front door stood open.

"I must have left my house without thinking.'

Henry ran across the road. His garden lay in ruins. There were piles of dirt and clumps of grass scattered from one wall to the next. Someone had been digging.

"Harmless? This is harmless?"

It had to have been Oliver. Henry started to call over the vicar, to show him what Oliver had done. Then something moved near Jack's mound, and Jackie lifted her head with a bone in her mouth.

* * *

Caroline paid for her wine, greeted Reverend Pierce, and found a seat in the snuggery. She only wanted to be alone. But it was no use—soon a man had taken the facing chair. "Afternoon," he said, as if he'd been invited. He looked about seventy. The lapels of his blazer were dusted with cigarette ash, and the hair in his nose came out in clumps. "I'm Roger Lowry," he said, after she stared at him.

"You live in Chalk?"

"At the Wembles Estate." He made it sound like it was the best place in the world. "I'm Head Butler."

"You live in the manor itself?"

The man smoothed his shirtfront with the tips of his fingers. "My wife and I have had an entire wing to ourselves for forty-five years. The best view in Chalk, I don't mind saying." He burst into laughter. "Not that there's much in Chalk to see!"

She smiled. "It's a small village."

"Up at Bates Farm you must have a view of The Beacon. Mind you, tourist prices." He winked. "Are you pleased it's the last day of the term?"

"Hang on—a village this size, and I've never met you. How is that?"

"People keep to themselves if they want to. That's the beauty of Chalk." He burst out laughing again. "The beauty of Chalk!"

She looked sideways at him. He seemed to be toying with her.

"Do you think you'll be back next year?" he asked.

Caroline reached for her drink. "I was just thinking about that."

"None of my business, I suppose. But supply teachers from Brighton typically don't last."

"Pardon me, Mr. Lowry." She turned and stared at the wall.

"As I say, none of my business," the man went on. "We never had children, my wife and I, so I take it upon myself to look out for the people of this village, as I do the Wembles family. I take it, Miss Ford, as my job."

"The village needs protecting from women like me, is that what you're saying?"

"We must watch after our schools. As a teacher, you're in charge of the village's future, aren't you?"

Caroline fumed. She agreed with him in theory but was too angry to admit it. Anyway, the butler seemed more interested in baiting her than actually having a conversation. She slugged down the rest of her wine. She planned on leaving but her pride took over—she wasn't about to be chased out of the pub. "Would you like another, Mr. Lowry?"

"I thought you'd never ask."

She took their glasses up to the bar. In charge of the village's future—the comment rattled in her mind as Sid poured the drinks. "Here we are," she said, returning to her chair.

"Excuse my bluntness," the butler said, taking his beer. "I had no right to be rude."

"It's my choice to put up with you."

"I'm sure you find me annoying. Most people do. But I'll tell you something—I find you very good-looking. There, you see? I knew you'd find me annoying."

He leaned forward and touched her knee. "The gravedigger Henry Bale."

"What about him?"

"My age gives me liberties, Miss Ford. Let me ask you—how do you feel about him?"

She swatted his hand away. "This is an interrogation! I don't mind having a drink and answering your questions, as long as you keep your hands to yourself. If you want to know, I'm sort of taken with him."

"Sort of?"

"All right, I am taken with him. I love the man. There."

"I thought so." The butler leaned back in his chair. "Then why consider leaving? You're in love. You like your job well enough. You're just not sure about Chalk?"

"You have nerve, telling me what I'm thinking."

"I don't lack nerve, Miss Ford. I'm old and childless, and I'm having drinks with an attractive woman." He took out a tobacco pouch, rolled a cigarette, and licked it shut. "But I would advise you of something. Take pains to secure your future. Look at me—look at my face. I'm past seventy, and I've still got my teeth. My hair is thick as a brush. It's not my diet, as you can see. It's because of marriage. It's only by virtue of my wife that I'm worth a damn."

Caroline stood up. "Excuse me," she said, putting down her wine glass. "I have to go."

The butler nodded without looking up. "Of course you do."

* * *

Reburying Jack's remains took the rest of the afternoon. When he'd finished, Henry went inside for his tea, shooting angry glances to Jackie's cot. Chalk didn't need Oliver to cause destruction when it had a Jack Russell.

After his tea, Henry rang Caroline to invite her on a walk. He took Jackie even though he still harboured a grudge. By the time he set out, the stars had emerged. It was a warm night. A breeze blew over the village wall, carrying with it the smell of wildflowers. Caroline came to her door in jeans and a silk scarf plunged into the neck of her jumper.

He waited while she pulled her hair back in front of the mirror. It was still hard to look directly at her, as beautiful as she was, and he paced in her sitting room while she got ready, sneaking glances. They set out and went straight up the path. They took Jackie off lead, and she ran ahead of them to sniff under the shrubs for fox.

Henry told Caroline about his day, but he could tell she wasn't really listening. At the top of the hill, he gave up talking and tried to kiss her, but she broke away.

"Give me a moment before you seize me like that," she said. She glared at him as if he were a stranger. "What do you want with me, anyway?"

"What do you mean?"

"Answer me."

Puzzled, he strode up the path in the dark, only to turn back. "I want us to be together, of course." Jackie ran to his side, her tongue hanging in the wind.

It reminded Henry of the first time he and Caroline met, right on this path. She had run all the way down the hill while he'd stopped to collect his thoughts.

This time his thoughts were clearer. He came straight to her and put his arms round her waist. She needed the reassurance now, not him. He held her tightly while the breeze blew her hair around. "I love you, Caroline. You know that."

"I know," she said. "But I didn't tell you about my day yet. Briggs wants to know if I want to renew my contract."

"Well—why not?"

Her eyes watered in the wind. "Remember when you bought your bed? How you were worried I might get the wrong impression and be scared off? I don't want you to get the wrong impression, either."

"You're wondering about our future?"

When Caroline nodded it was as if time came screeching to a halt. For so long he'd been afraid of losing her, and now his fears fell away, if only for an instant.

FOURTEEN

In the morning moonlight Henry pushed his wheelbarrow up the churchyard path. Reverend Folsom's marker pointed to a plot beyond the lower branches of a walnut tree.

Henry paced off the outline of Charlie's grave, taking care to bow the midsection. The soil was warm and easy to move. He told himself not to think of the headstones inside the church for fear it might affect his digging. The hole grew quickly. As the morning flushed with sunlight, he worked under the walnut's shade.

When he finished the spit Henry unbuttoned the top of his overalls and stopped to rest. He stretched his arms above his head and leaned to each side. The exercise was Caroline's doing. It had been helping his back. He looked at his watch, closed his eyes, and counted a minute in his head.

"Fifty-eight, fifty-nine, sixty."

Henry checked his watch and leaped out of the grave. He'd counted a minute on the nose.

"Not exactly proper conduct."

Henry swung around. Oliver Marsh leaned against the tree trunk. "You gave me a fright," Henry said, lowering his spade. "What are you doing here?"

"A gravedigger's burial," Oliver said. "I'm paying my respects."

"Don't you leave any notes in there," Henry said, pointing his spade at the church.

"Charlie dug more graves than anyone in Sussex."

Henry scanned the headstones, as if for confirmation. "How do you know?"

"You're not the only one who counts things." Oliver nodded

at the hole. "If I were digging that one, I wouldn't be taking it so lightly."

"Don't worry," Henry said. He paced beside the grave. "I'm taking my time, keeping things clean. I've got carnations waiting in the van. But I don't need to explain all of this! Go away!"

Oliver picked at his neck with his fingernails. "I have a right to be in the churchyard."

Henry remembered what Reverend Pierce told him of Oliver's past. "I suppose you're not harming anybody," he said.

Oliver left the shade of the tree. He wandered the churchyard a moment, then came up to the hole and squatted on his heels. "How are you digging it, then?"

"Just like he asked." Henry put his hands on his knees and looked in the grave. "Bowed, here at the midpoint. I'll make it nice and long. And a foot deeper, too."

"Good."

"I'd better get back to work."

Henry hopped back in. With Oliver watching, he dug more vigourously than he normally would have.

"You should be this considerate with all your graves," Oliver said.

"Not everyone sees it that way."

"You haven't thought about it the way I have. You haven't done research."

Henry stopped digging. "Research? Some people, Oliver, believe in God. They plan on going to heaven, and the bodies they leave behind are just remains."

"You count yourself among the faithful?"

"Leave me alone." He went back to digging out the spit.

"Let me ask you something," Oliver said. "Why do people want to be buried in churchyards if it's just their remains? Why do vicars bother blessing the ground?"

Henry sighed. "I never said our remains don't matter. Listen, are you going to stand there all day? You're making me self-conscious."

Oliver went back to the tree and sat under it. "The way a man digs is an extension of his personality. Take Charlie Cotton. To compensate for his stature, he dug each grave deep. He also added a flourish—that midsection bow, as you put it. Then there's Derrick Watkins. He's all over the map, a different hole for each hangover. But he's fast, Derrick. He'll appear at ten in the pouring rain and have a double ready by noon."

Henry went to the head and started digging his spit backwards. "Don't you have anything better to do than watch gravediggers?"

"Maybe I'm in training."

Henry looked up. "What's that supposed to mean?"

"Don't worry," Oliver said, smirking. "I'm not after your job. Not yet anyway. Now, about you—you're as reliable as they come, but you've only recently started to care. You can forget those bloody carnations. It's the grave that matters. And scraping all those gravestones is a waste of time. A good stone will only last a few hundred years, so who cares about keeping up the letters?"

"I like to honour the dead." Henry reached into the soil and removed a rock. "People pay their respects, Oliver, and they want a clean path to walk on, a pleasant place to sit. They want to read the names."

"You've only recently believed all that to make yourself feel better. People put up too many monuments to themselves. Why don't you spend more time shoring up those walls, mixing sand in for a more compact fit? You don't want Charlie to bob to the surface after a record winter."

"I liked you better when you were quiet all the time. Go away!" With his spade, Henry flung dirt toward the tree.

"Hey!" Oliver said, getting to his feet.

Henry flung another spadeful—harder this time—and it splattered the front of Oliver's black turtleneck.

"Stop it!" Oliver's voice squeaked even higher. He looked like he was near tears. "This was my dad's."

"You've been wearing that damn thing for years," Henry said. "It's high time you changed. You're not the only one to lose loved ones. Now go away, once and for all, or—"

Henry put down his spade. A woman, dressed in black, came barrelling across the churchyard toward the grave.

* * *

"Henry Bale, I take it?"

Still inside the grave, Henry glanced at the walnut tree. Oliver was gone. "That's right."

"Maggie Cotton," the woman said. She squared her shoulders at him. "I'm Charlie's wife."

"My sympathies, Mrs. Cotton."

Mrs. Cotton looked round the gravesite, as if searching for something out of place. She was probably in her seventies and still solidly built. "Charlie had a high regard for you," she said. "I don't know what I would have done if you'd fallen ill." She opened her handbag and handed Henry two of Charlie's cigars. "Can you find a place in the grave for these?"

"Of course," Henry said. He put them in the back pocket of his overalls. "A lovely day we're having."

"It is lovely," Mrs. Cotton said hopefully. "Charlie would have appreciated this sun—hated digging in it, mind you." She gave a little laugh. "He always preferred digging in autumn, Charlie did—said his spade just flew through the soil." She looked at the end of the grave, and her voice broke. "That's where his head's going, is it?"

Henry moved into the middle. "It is."

She looked quickly away. "Well! That tree gives you some shade."

Henry put his arms above ground and leaned on the grass. "I'm thankful for it," he said. He brushed stray dirt toward the mound, and he could sense Mrs. Cotton watching. "I've got my fresh mats waiting in the van. It'll be a clean service. And Hetherington's a good undertaker, for what it's worth."

"I know he is. He always paid Charlie on time. You can't ask for more than that, these days." She took a deep breath and let it out slowly. "Do you like the outdoors, Henry?"

"I don't think I could work in an office. Stuck behind a desk."

"Charlie was the same!" Mrs. Cotton said, smiling. "I suppose you'd have to like working outdoors, wouldn't you, to suffer the rain. Not to mention the blazing sun."

Henry scraped some mud from his boot. "That's probably right," he said.

"But the problems Charlie had with his back!" Mrs. Cotton straightened her back herself. "Such a sight! The shape of it all mangled and bent in the evenings. Do you have problems with your back, Henry?"

He picked up his spade and leaned on the handle. "I feel it, now and then. Been lucky, really. Only once did it really give out."

Mrs. Cotton's eyes widened. "Gave out on you, did it?"

"Well, it did," Henry said. "I had to be helped out."

"Oh, dear! Was it while you were digging?"

He nodded. "It's all right now, Mrs. Cotton. Nothing to worry about."

"A gruelling occupation." She glared at Henry, her anger almost giving way. "Even Charlie said so. When he retired, he said he didn't know why he'd kept on all those years."

"There's never any winning with grave digging, my dad used to say—only not losing."

"I heard your father was a gravedigger. How long did he keep on with it?"

"Almost forty years. Not quite as long as Charlie, I don't think."

"My Charlie could work with the best of them!"

She took a couple of steps along the side of the grave. Her eyes kept darting to the head. "Thank you, Henry," she said. She squatted in her heels and held onto him a moment, her hand inside the hole.

*　*　*

In his best trousers and a clean Oxford, Henry entered the lanes of Brighton. He walked with his head thrown forward and avoided eye contact. Each lane stretched longer than Chalk itself. It was the last place he wanted to be, out among the crowds, but he had to take advantage of his opportunity to shop. Tonight, Mrs. Tilson had invited them to a dinner to celebrate Caroline's term ending. Henry had to collect his father in two hours.

Halfway down the first lane, a man in a pink pig costume stood under a neon light. Evidently he was meant to attract people into one of the jewellery shops. The pig and the light caught Henry's eye, and he stopped to sort through some of the rings on the table outside. He didn't see anything particularly wrong with the jewellery, but he followed an instinct to keep moving. He passed clothing stalls and eateries. Soon the storefronts stood back from the road. Window displays held jewellery on mannequin hands and velvet cushions.

He started to go inside one of the nicer shops when a voice made him freeze. "Henry, stop! Stop this right now!"

Behind him, a woman led a small boy by the wrist. "That's disgusting, Henry," she said. The boy reached for an ice cream cone on the pavement, and she dragged him away.

Gathering himself, Henry stepped into the jewellery shop.

Everywhere he looked, there were diamonds. He leaned over a display case against the wall.

"A brilliant stone, that," a salesman said, creeping across the carpet. He looked like a thug, with his tacky suit and enormous gold watch. He pointed to the ring under Henry's nose. "You know what you're looking for. Now I'll just nip back and open that case."

"I didn't say I wanted you to," Henry said. "I'm not ready!"

Panicking, Henry rushed to the door. He ducked down a smaller lane to catch his breath. After a moment he kept on, passing bookshops, studios, and art galleries. Just before the main road, a small jewellery shop sat above a florist's. He went up the stairs and inside. Thick Persian carpets lined the floor, and antique lamps hung from the walls. In one of the display cases a diamond ring caught his eye.

At the front of the shop, a young couple were arguing in front of the saleswoman. The ring was too expensive, the girl kept saying. But they'd been looking all day, her boyfriend complained—he was tired of shopping. Henry waited as long as he could bear it.

He left the shop and took the stairs down to the lane. He walked with the crowds toward the train station and ducked into the first open café. At the counter he became disoriented and ordered a coffee instead of tea. Even his chair by the window annoyed him—hard and angular, it had been designed for appearance, not comfort. Outside, people came and went without looking at one another, barking into mobiles and texting with their heads down as they walked. How had Caroline lived here? He wondered if she was too young, if she hadn't lived long enough to know what she wanted. Maybe Chalk was only a temporary holiday from this, her true home.

"A gorgeous day!" came a voice behind him.

"Lovely and warm," someone replied.

Henry had to admit it—the day was warm. And his coffee actually tasted good. Only an hour, he'd been looking. And who would have thought he'd be looking for an engagement ring at all? Henry retraced his steps to the jewellery shop above the florist's. The young couple were coming down the stairs now, holding hands.

The saleswoman followed Henry to the display case. There it was in the middle row, a silver band with a round, bright diamond on four prongs. "Like a beacon," Henry said. He didn't ask the price. He just pointed at it and smudged the glass. "That one," he said, "that one there."

* * *

The lobby of the pensioners' home was full. After signing in, Henry sat beside a family of four along the wall. Adjusting Caroline's band, the saleswoman told him, would only take a day or two. Henry had measured one of her rings while she slept.

Frank came crashing through the double doors in his wheelchair. He was fresh from a bath and wore a suit.

"Cow," Frank snapped at the nurse pushing him. "Let me out!"

"Sit still, Frank," the nurse said. She nodded across the lobby, and Henry stood up.

"Let me out!" Frank pulled the hand brake, and the nurse continued forward and scraped her knee. "That's what you get for not letting me out," he said.

"You nasty man," she said. She bent over, rubbing her knee. "Keep this up, and you'll never come back. You'll have to stay in Chalk!"

Henry ran to the door and opened it. People were staring. "Come on, Dad," he said. "Be a good sport."

"Go to hell." With a grunt, Frank propelled himself from the wheelchair. He'd taken two steps when his knees buckled. He fell to the floor in a heap.

Henry stood over him. "You all right?"

"I'm fine. I'm not going in that goddamn chair."

"How are you going to get out the door, then?"

Frank rolled onto his back, kicking his legs like a tortoise. "Maybe I'll roll. Leave me alone, for God's sake."

"Mrs. Tilson's waiting for us. She's made ham."

"I don't care. Tell her to stick it up her bum."

Someone in the lobby laughed. Henry wheeled. "So you think it's funny, do you?" he said, addressing everyone at once. "A poor man on the ground? Just wait until your legs don't work!"

His father took his arm. "Easy, lad. This is my home, now. Show some manners."

✳ ✳ ✳

Caroline wore a summer dress—a blue one that barely reached her knees. As they stood in Mrs. Tilson's garden, Henry could tell the dress tormented his father. The old man found comfort in criticism, and with Caroline there was little to find fault with. Leaning on his walker, his head down like an elderly mule, he lurched inside.

A porcelain tea setting waited on the coffee table. Mrs. Tilson had left out various toys, as if hoping her sons might bring her grandchildren for a visit. They hadn't been to Chalk in over a year, Henry knew. He made his way to the sofa and sat down. Mrs. Tilson placed Frank at the head of the table in the dining room, though dinner was some time away.

"Right," Caroline said, clasping her hands, "what can I do to help?"

"Nothing at all," Mrs. Tilson said. "You just sit down with Henry and keep him from any mischief." They had a little battle to demonstrate their resolve. Caroline removed her cardigan to show she was ready for work. Mrs. Tilson blocked the kitchen with her arms crossed. In the end Caroline sat on the sofa as she was told.

After a moment, Mrs. Tilson came back out of the kitchen. "Come to think of it," she said, "I'd like some company in here." She took Caroline's hand and led her into the kitchen.

Henry waited on the sofa, listening to the clattering dishes. He wondered how many evenings like this he might have had if his mother hadn't died. Would she have liked Caroline? As he looked round the house, he imagined how he could have grown up. He might not have been so shy. He might have left Chalk like most of his friends from school. At the same time, he probably wouldn't have met Caroline at all. In dying when she did, his mother was very much alive, right down to the woman he loved.

"Now then," Caroline said, as she came back to the sitting room. She put her hands on her hips. "What will you have, Henry? There's beer. Or I can make you a gin and tonic. We'll be having wine with dinner…"

"Is there Cuckoo?"

"You can't find that in bottles," his father said. He slumped forward at the table. "Fancy you not knowing that, Henry."

There was a silence. "I never needed to know it, I suppose. But it's good of you to point out my ignorance, Dad."

Caroline gave a nervous laugh. "You can try a different beer. She has Sam Smiths and McEwans."

"I'll have a McEwans, thank you."

"Frank?"

He raised his eyes at her. "Gin and tonic, please."

Caroline went back to the kitchen. Henry waited quietly, looking at his shoes. He counted a minute in his head and then another. The house started to smell like ham.

"Here we are," Caroline said, breezing back into the room. She placed Frank's gin and tonic on the table. "Try it. Tell me if it's all right."

Frank took the glass with both hands. He sipped it and smacked his lips. "Wonderful."

Henry moved down on the sofa. Caroline handed him his lager and sat beside him. "Not long now," she said, kissing him.

Frank turned to them. "Very pretty, that dress."

Caroline smoothed it with her hands. "Thank you."

"I was going to say something earlier. Not that it matters, coming from an old man." Frank swallowed half his drink. "I say, Henry," he said, "what's taking you two so long to move in together?"

"Shut your mouth, Dad."

They sat in silence a while. Henry sat fuming with his eyes lowered. "I'll just check on Mrs. Tilson," Caroline said. She squeezed Henry's hand and went back to the kitchen.

Frank watched her all the way to the door. "She's got a lovely way about her, Henry."

"I know, Dad. Just don't say anything about our relationship. Please."

"I only mentioned it because I thought you made a nice couple."

"No, you didn't think. You didn't think at all. Just keep your mouth shut!"

Finally the women came back—Mrs. Tilson with a platter of ham, Caroline with roast potatoes in one hand and asparagus in the other. Together they kept making trips into the kitchen until the table was set. Henry sat to his father's left facing Caroline. Frank carved the ham. His hands shook, but he managed to get enough onto each plate. Everyone started to eat.

"Open the wine please, Henry," Mrs. Tilson said. She sat at the foot of the table facing Frank. "I must say I'm looking forward to a glass of that."

"The ham's done, anyway," Frank said.

"Everything's delicious," Caroline said.

Henry ate in silence. His father was eating in a particular order, as usual—first his meat, then his potatoes, followed by vegetables. He didn't appear to taste anything. It reminded Henry of life before

Caroline. He started to fidget in his chair. Across the table, Caroline seemed to be considering something—doubting, perhaps, the extent of her feelings. Sitting beside Frank, this older version of himself, who could blame her?

The silenced continued, since everyone had abandoned polite conversation. Henry's mood kept plunging. Only a fool would join his family. Even the term itself—family—didn't seem appropriate. He and Frank might have been a couple of aging strangers, sharing nothing but the occasional argument and a legacy of buried graves. The longer the meal lasted, the more Caroline seemed to drift. Henry wanted to reach across the table and bring her back. She might have been a figment of his imagination, even as she sat there eating ham. "Dad," Henry heard himself say, "I'm sorry for snapping at you earlier."

His father stopped eating. Caroline looked up from her plate. The only sound was Mrs. Tilson's cutlery against the china.

His father sighed heavily. His blue eyes dripped with the beginnings of tears. "I only want your happiness, Henry. You can't blame me for that."

Henry reached for his wine glass as if for protection. His father always shamed him in front of people. He wished he could take Caroline and leave.

"Henry doesn't blame you," Mrs. Tilson said, pouring more wine. "Don't be the martyr, Frank."

Frank put down his cutlery. "I'm the martyr? What about my son?"

"I'm right here," Henry said. "I can speak for myself, you know."

His father grunted. "You hear that? Henry couldn't speak for himself if his life depended on it. If he doesn't act soon, Caroline will find someone else."

"Leave me be," Henry said. "Why don't you just admit the truth? You don't want me to be happy. You'd rather me miserable, like you."

Frank clasped his hands and addressed the wall. "Will you listen to that? He thinks I want him to be unhappy. A fine thing for a boy to say. What about all those years I worked?"

"We know, Dad, we know. Spare us the stories of how you're so bloody tough."

"I'm old now," Frank said, his eyes still on the wall. "But I do have my memory. I worked every day to put food on his plate."

"You sat in your armchair like a stone. You taught me how to be miserable."

"Henry," Caroline said. "Stop it."

"I did my best to raise a son," Frank said.

"And you did a wonderful job," Caroline said. She put her hand on Frank's shoulder.

"It wasn't easy," Frank said, to the wall. "Why am I to blame for wanting to look at grandchildren? I don't have long to live. Neither does he!"

"Shut your mouth!" Henry shouted. "Shut your goddamn mouth!"

The walls seemed to shake, along with the china. Caroline stared at her plate.

"Henry and Frank," Mrs. Tilson said. "Behave, now. We're celebrating."

"Mark my words," Frank said to her. "Women like Caroline don't wait around."

"I've been waiting, haven't I?" Mrs. Tilson said.

Frank picked up his cutlery and tore apart his asparagus. "Nonsense," he said.

"It's a little soon for marriage announcements," Caroline said. "Henry and I only met six months ago. You needn't worry, Frank."

Henry sank into his chair. He wanted to propose right now—in front of Mrs. Tilson and his father, in front of all the people of Chalk. He wanted to tell everyone about the café and the stiff chair and that jewellery shop in Brighton.

"I needn't worry?" Frank said, turning to Caroline with bits of asparagus in his teeth. "What's keeping you here, then? Brighton's a hell of a lot better than Chalk. Even that stinking pensioners' home."

"Chalk isn't so bad," Caroline said. She sounded almost offended. "Anyway, I'm not going anywhere. I signed a contract for another year this morning."

Henry sat up. In an instant, the room brightened. "You did?"

"This calls for a toast," Mrs. Tilson said, raising her glass.

"I'm never certain about much," Frank said. He put his hand on Caroline's and patted it. "But the last time I met someone like you, she turned out to be my wife."

Mrs. Tilson cleared her throat. "I'll get the pie out of the cooker. We can have it at the coffee table."

Frank sat forward, reaching for his dessert fork. "What kind is it?"

"You know very well what kind. You asked for rhubarb."

"Frank," Caroline said, as she cleared their plates, "tell us about you and Evelyn."

*   *   *

Everyone switched to tea but Frank. He filled his wine glass and took the armchair by the window while Henry, Caroline, and Mrs. Tilson sat across from him on the sofa, like children listening to a bedtime story.

"Most people didn't know we were together," Frank began. The trace of a smile crossed his face. "In a way, I wasn't sure myself—which is why I proposed."

"How do you mean?" Caroline asked.

"Evelyn was a rare find."

"Evelyn loved you," Mrs. Tilson said. She poured the tea. "Long before you noticed."

"Anyway," Frank went on, smiling openly now, "I took it into my head to propose. We hadn't even slept together." With one swallow, he finished all his wine.

Henry stared at the ceiling. Mrs. Tilson tried to pour more tea, but all the cups were full. Getting up, she went to the kitchen and returned with a second bottle of wine. "I don't know why I indulge you, Frank," she said. Henry uncorked the bottle and filled his father's glass.

"Go back a little," Caroline said. "How did you start seeing each other in the first place?"

"Chalk's a small village. I had an idea Evelyn liked me. She came to all my burials."

"You never told me that," Henry said.

"She said it was for academic purposes."

"Evelyn was always interested in archaeology," Mrs. Tilson explained.

Frank snorted. "A thin excuse. I told her as much. To prove me wrong she started showing up two or three times a week, bringing along a notepad. She watched me dig for hours. I quite liked it."

Caroline sipped her tea. "And then?"

"I took her to dinner a few times. We went to the beach in Brighton, Springmer for some shopping. Dating, I suppose. I had mum's engagement ring because she'd left it me when she died. I started carrying the damn thing around, even to work. Then one day, before I began the filling in, I got up the nerve."

Henry bolted forward. "You proposed during a burial?"

"Right over an open grave! Shocked the hell out of her. She didn't say yes. I think she wanted a more formal setting."

"I can't imagine why," Mrs. Tilson said.

"So one night, up at The Black Ram, we were alone in the snuggery. She knew what was coming. Up at the bar a woman was singing, and I'll never forget that song—"

Henry put down his cup. "Wait. A woman singing in the pub?"

"Yes. So I got on one knee. When I brought out the ring, Evelyn—"

"Someone was singing the other night as well," Henry said.

Frank frowned. "Pardon me?"

Henry stood up and sat back down. He seized Caroline's hands. "Do you remember?"

Caroline laughed. "What are you talking about?"

"The night after the newspaper ran that story on me. You pulled me up out of the chair, and we danced to that woman singing." Caroline just stared. "I thought maybe it was fate," he said.

Mrs. Tilson stood up. "A lovely story, Frank. Would anyone like more tea?"

"I wasn't finished!" Frank said.

Henry opened his collar. He couldn't get enough air.

"Henry," Caroline said, putting her hand to his cheek. "You've gone white!"

"He's gone batty," Frank said. "One photo in the paper, and suddenly the world revolves around him."

The room became a blur. Henry tried to count the seconds—anything to stop his heart from racing—but the numbers slipped away as soon as he could grasp them. Across the room his father faded into the armchair, and everything went dark.

* * *

"I've never seen anyone faint before," Caroline said. They'd taken Frank next door and up to the guest room, then walked to Bates Farm for the night. She tucked Henry into bed. "Sleep," she said. "Don't think." Turning out the light, she closed the door.

Henry stared at the ceiling and forced himself to stay awake. He needed to think. Why had he heard a woman singing, and how had his parents had the same experience? He wanted to believe it was a signal from God, blessing their love, and their futures together.

When Henry finally fell asleep, he dreamed he was at The Black Ram, surrounded by the regulars—Reverend Pierce, William Harvey, Dick Miles, Roger Lowry, Trevor and Vickie, Chris Crawley. Nobody once looked at him. Sid didn't pour him a pint of Cuckoo. When he spoke nobody heard.

Only Oliver noticed him. The pocks on his face were red and inflamed. "You're waiting for the truth," he said.

Henry was glad to be recognised, even by Oliver. "Yes, I suppose I am."

"Poor thing." Taking Henry's hand, Oliver led him outside. "I have the key to the cellar," he said. They walked along the road in the dark, all the way to the church gate. Henry hung back, afraid. "Come on," Oliver said, pulling him up the path and around to the back.

All the gravestones were missing. In their place, empty holes covered the mounds. "Please," Henry said, "Let me go." Oliver wasn't holding his hand any longer, and still he couldn't break free. He shouted across the churchyard, and nobody answered.

At the cellar door Oliver produced a key. "Now you're going to know the truth," he said, unlocking the door. Together they went down the stairs into the shadows.

When Henry's eyes adjusted he saw that Chalk's cellar held a secret worse than Burgess Green's. Instead of gravestones, there were hundreds of skeletons on their backs, stacked neatly from one wall to the next. Oliver led Henry right up to them. They were streaked with mud.

"I took them out of the churchyard," Oliver said. "It's better than letting them sink into the earth. Feel this. It's amazing how dead bones feel just like our own," he said, placing Henry's hand on the shoulder of one of the skeletons. "Go on, feel this shoulder. This is Malcolm, the man your father replaced." Oliver brought Henry's hand along the dirty ribs, and down the curve of the hip. He made Henry touch the legs, the feet, the toes.

"Frank will go up here, Henry. Right on top of Malcolm, at the top of this pile. When you die, your skeleton will fit on top of your dad's."

The cellar went black. At the top of the stairs, the door slammed shut. Henry cried out, but Oliver had gone.

A skeleton tumbled from the stack. The skull hit the floor and its jaw opened. There was a cracking sound, and the whole pile of skeletons gave way. All at once the bones were everywhere—legs, arms, skulls. Henry scrambled for the stairs and climbed toward the light.

He woke screaming with his arms at his sides. He thought he was still in the cellar until Caroline opened the door.

FIFTEEN

The village wall passed right by Oliver's front garden. Crouching beside the wall, Henry peered over at the cotton grass, the bog-rush, the assortment of weeds from other countries, other ages. It was time to face facts. He had a responsibility to the people he buried. He had obligations to the church itself. How could he dig Mrs. Tilson's grave, or even his father's, without knowing they'd be safe? Could he get married in St. Margaret's if someone like Oliver held the keys to its cellar?

Oliver stood inside a hole with a spade in his hands. A tee shirt revealed long, bone-white arms. The wind blew the pollen around in the afternoon. As if smelling something unusual, Oliver stopped digging and looked up. Henry ducked. He stayed beneath the wall, his heart thumping, until Oliver spoke.

"I saw you, Henry. You might as well stand up."

Henry did. There was no point in hiding. Oliver came out of the hole, the spade still in his hands. He moved behind a thicket of tall grass and stayed there.

"Come out of there, Oliver. I stood up when you asked me to. Now you're hiding from me! You're digging a grave, aren't you?"

"Reverend Pierce already paid me a visit. I won't bother you any more."

"I didn't come about your damn notes."

Oliver came out of the grass and stood in a clearing with his spade. "Do you know," he said, "that you're my first visitor?"

"Whose grave is that you're digging?"

"Technically it's just a hole, Henry. Until there's a deceased, that is. Are you going to stand in the road or come into the garden?"

Henry found wooden steps on the other side of the wall. He climbed over and onto a landscaped path. From the roads, the garden looked covered with weeds, but in fact there was plenty of cleared space—plots, to be exact—behind the house, around the perimeter, and near the front door where Oliver had been digging. The grass over each plot was cut short, like turf.

Oliver led Henry to the hole he'd been working on. The walls were smooth and symmetrical, the site meticulously clean, even around the mound. "An impressive bit of digging. And these?" Henry waved his hand across the garden, indicating the plots.

"We've always buried our own."

Oliver pointed. "I put granny there. Beside my dad. Mum dug that one—her little brother, it was. That one there's her sister. Granny dug mum's grave over there, beside that lime grass."

Henry had seen house burials, but nothing of this magnitude. "Nobody from your family went in the churchyard?"

"We've all been atheists." He nodded at the empty hole. "I'm not going in the churchyard either."

"Christ, Oliver. Why don't you just leave your burial instructions in a will?"

"And how would I know it's done right?"

"But…how do you plan on burying yourself?"

"I'm not going to become a vegetable and a burden to others. When I'm ready, I'll get in there with a gun. I'll cover myself with topsoil, then…bang!"

Taking his spade, Oliver lowered himself into the grave. He moved carefully, as if occupying a sacred tomb. "My grandfather started this," he said. "He wanted to keep the family together, not among a bunch of hypocrites who find God at the last minute."

Henry let the comment go. "If you're dead, what does it matter?"

"Burying your own gives you control. It's the same with suicide—it doesn't make death so random. Anyway, I like this grave. I like digging it." Oliver went back to digging, as if to prove it.

Henry stood over the edge of the hole. Above his head, along the branches of an oak, an orange cat inched forward. It sat and watched, licking its paws. "You spend so much energy railing against the church," Henry said. "And you're like a pharaoh, designing your burial chamber."

Oliver unearthed a root. He tugged on it with both hands. "People should plan for what they want, not pray for it." He hacked at the root with the end of his spade. "The church is dying out, anyway. Eventually nobody will go to services."

"Nobody except you." Henry sat beside the grave. It had been a long time since he'd watched another man dig. Oliver was good at it. "You'll be there tomorrow, I'm assuming."

"It's something to do on Sundays," Oliver said. "And Reverend Pierce has been good to me. He visited Granny after my parents died. He pushed me through school. For all the good that did."

Henry stretched his legs out on the grass. Up in the tree, the cat looked about to pounce. "What about our church cellar, Oliver?"

"I've never seen it."

The cat jumped to a neighbouring branch, just missing a bluebird. "The vicar's got the only key?"

"I didn't say that." Oliver went to the foot of the grave and shaved it down. "I don't want to appear in any newspaper articles."

"This is just my own curiosity."

"You keep looking for scraps—signs of something—but there aren't any to be found. A cellar is just a room."

"This one isn't!" Henry said, standing up. "It's inside a church, Oliver. The church across from my home. Where I dig, where I pray. A place where I might get married."

"But you're not even a believer!"

Henry shrugged. "I'm trying. Maybe you are, too. Nobody goes to church every Sunday just for something to do."

"It's not healthy, this curiosity of yours," Oliver said, digging faster. "What are you trying to accomplish, being everyone's moral watchdog? If Reverend Pierce found out—"

"He wouldn't. Not if we did it late. Say midnight—tonight?"

Oliver threw down his spade and climbed out. They stood facing each other beside the hole. "I'm not saying there aren't headstones in that cellar. I'm saying I don't know." He wiped his hands on his jeans. "You'll probably find a box of old Bibles and think the Devil is to blame."

* * *

Henry waited on the bench while the shapes moved among the gravestones—the shadows of owls, cats prowling for mice. It wasn't yet midnight when a man darted into the churchyard. He was quick on his feet. He kept coming in a criss-cross pattern, growing taller as he neared the bench.

Henry trembled. "Evening, Lord," he said, getting to his feet.

Sammy Wembles had on a black jumper and a felt hunter's cap. A moustache slouched across his upper lip like a lapdog. "Call me Sammy," he said. There was alcohol on his breath.

It was the first time Henry had spoken to Lord Wembles. He couldn't address him Sammy. He looked round the churchyard with his hands in his pockets, as if searching for something he'd lost. Then, realising it was impolite to have his hands in his pockets, he took them out again. "A quiet night," he said. "Out for a walk?"

"No, I'm not."

Henry inched away. "I certainly won't be any trouble. I'm just enjoying the fresh air."

"Wait," Lord Wembles said. "You can't open a tomb, can you?"

"You mean—here?"

"Not right this minute, of course. It's George and Lady Anne, over in our family chapel. I want to make sure they're inside. I have the certificate of burial, but you never know these days, do you?"

Henry glanced at the church. He thought he saw someone coming toward them along the boundary hedge. "That tomb doesn't appear to be damaged," he said.

"Could you open it if you had to?"

"It's alabaster. I'd have to use a hammer and chisel."

Lord Wembles smiled. "Good. We don't know for certain they're in that thing, you see. Nobody in the family can show me proof. It wouldn't make much sense for me to pray in there—pray for their souls I mean, if they weren't buried in there to begin with."

"I understand," Henry said.

"That was a damn fine thing you did in Burgess Green, Henry. A damn fine thing. If we can't protect our deceased—well, where does that leave us?" Lord Wembles shook Henry's hand and returned along the path. Henry sat on the bench and listened to the crickets. It was half twelve by his wristwatch, and he didn't know if Oliver had changed his mind. He'd hang on for five more minutes, he decided. The evening was thrown into chaos. The five minutes had nearly passed when Oliver appeared. He seemed to step straight out of the hedge. "Sammy's on a bender," Oliver said. "He's been kneeling beside that effigy to confess all sorts of shameful rubbish. He's lost too much of the ancestral land."

"You could be a bit more forgiving."

Oliver rolled his eyes. "Nobody hears God in Chalk."

"Maybe not," Henry said. "But some of us are trying."

"What does the cellar have to do with that?"

"A church shouldn't be a place of horror. I have to find out what's inside."

They walked over the mounds to the cellar door. Oliver took a key from his pocket. There was no creak as he opened the door, not even a gust of wind. Oliver switched on the torch he'd brought, and they started down the steps.

They found a cold and empty room. Henry took the torch out of Oliver's hand and searched every corner. There was a floor and four walls, and that was all. The room didn't look like it had ever been used, either for evil or for good. There weren't even any cobwebs.

As they came back up the stairs, Henry was grateful for Oliver's silence. He realised he had no reason to be overly hopeful or senselessly afraid. He could propose to Caroline and get on with his life. Chalk appeared not to need any more investigating. People lived quietly, the dead left underground.

*   *   *

The next morning Henry rose a little later than normal. When he looked in the mirror he noticed something missing in his eyes. It was his hunger.

He dressed and went across the road to St. Margaret's. It was a Sunday, and long before any congregants would be arriving. He ducked into the third stall on the left and pulled back the kneeler. He placed the felt box holding Caroline's fitted engagement ring on the seat with its lid open. The diamond, he hoped, might have summoning powers.

"Heavenly Father," he said, his voice barely above a whisper, "I'm here again."

Week after week, the vicar stood at the altar, conducting evening services. If God existed, why did He make the vicar do this alone? Then the reverse struck him: if God didn't exist, why would people continue to pray?

But these were just questions. Inside the church, Henry heard only silence. He sought God's blessing for the future of his marriage. "Please answer," Henry said. He opened his eyes hoping to see something—a glow around the altar, a flash of light.

The stained glass window to his left showed Jesus on a hill, preaching to a crowd. One man stood out, and it wasn't Jesus. It was a farmer holding a pitchfork. He was standing at the back of the crowd and smirking as if he didn't believe a word, as if he'd come a long distance to fight for doubt. The church didn't hold signs of God. It held people like this farmer. It held worried prayer cushions and tear-stained hymnals. Even the altar had been made by human hands. Maybe St. Margaret's would always be a church in which people struggled against the worst parts of themselves. Five hundred years of congregants there had been, kneeling and waiting for something to appear. If God existed not a second of this time was wasted. "Will you bless my marriage?" Henry asked. "The love I feel?"

Other congregants had endured more difficult times. Even now there were people suffering in ways he couldn't imagine. And he'd come for a blessing? Henry closed his eyes and concentrated. He chose an affliction—starvation—and prayed for it to end. He prayed for what seemed a long time. "What am I supposed to do?" he cried, opening his eyes to will the hunger back. "Devote my life…" Hadn't he worked extra hours in the churchyards? Hadn't he been a decent man? The doubtful farmer kept smirking, and Henry looked away.

Psychological anxiety—that's what Caroline would call it. He had a fear of death, she said, a need for meaning, or at least a better father figure. Everyone used excuses. Nobody cared for God any longer—not the real thing, not what he wanted. "I promise," he said, "to live a more devoted life." If God only sent a sign, he'd work even harder at being useful.

Henry waited. He decided to take anything as proof—even a tiny click in his mind. There was only silence. He didn't know how to supplicate himself further. Two people, it seemed, were kneeling on the stool—someone who hoped, and someone who would never believe.

"No use," Henry muttered, glaring at the altar. "I don't need you for my happiness." He kicked over the prayer stool and bashed open the stall door, leaving it cracked at the hinges.

* * *

"What have I done?"

In front of his mirror, Henry shook with fear. Giving up on God made him feel no better than an animal. He'd wanted to propose tonight, but his reflection scared him. His mouth hung open, twisted into a shape he didn't recognise. It was as if God, knowing he had something important to say, made him look menacing.

Didn't Caroline love him, regardless of his expression? She was his redemption, not God. Henry headed downstairs and stopped. Caroline would get the truth out of him. She would make him discuss his troubles, just as she always did. Even if he made it to the proposal, his voice would betray him.

The staircase seemed to shake. Reaching for the banister, Henry took deep breaths. Pain crept into the base of his spine and worked its way up, clutching at his muscles. His neck burned hot— then as quickly as it came, the attack disappeared. Slowly, Henry straightened his back. He let go of the rail and stared at the bottom of the stairs.

One, two, three, four. Each second was a shovelful of dirt, splattering a casket. Five, six, seven, eight. The landing darkened. Nine shovels of dirt, then ten. When would he ever find the strength to propose? Would the fear leave his face long enough for the words to come? Henry reached for the ring in his pocket and it wasn't there.

Then he could see himself, as if from above, taking the stairs two at a time. He didn't care any longer if his back seized. He couldn't have said when the counting stopped for good—when he leaped his gate, when he ran across the road and into the church, or when he found Caroline standing in his stall, the ring in her hand.

"You found it," he said.

"It's beautiful. It was just sitting here." She came out of the stall and searched his eyes.

He took the ring from her. This moment would be the sign he needed. "What are you doing here, Caroline?"

"I come to the church now and then."

He nodded. "To pray in my stall?"

"I don't recall seeing your name on it—my God!" She put her hand to her mouth.

"Caroline," he said, kneeling. He took her hand. The words still wouldn't come.

"I love you," she whispered.

"Will you marry me?"

Caroline smiled through her tears, and when she said yes, he slid the ring on her finger. She dropped to her knees and threw her arms around his neck. They stayed there for a while without moving. When the vicar arrived, he discovered the two of them kneeling like statues someone had delivered to the nave.

* * *

The bats swooped from all directions and flapped their wings. Trevor rang Chris Crawley again, but after being awoken three times already, his best friend had disconnected the phone.

It had been promising, Trevor's self-imposed rehabilitation. He'd kept away from the out-of-town pubs. He'd stayed as faithful as a spaniel. Every week, he searched the job listings. Vickie had started to believe that he'd changed. Then, last night, he'd driven to The Red Lion in Kington. He'd had a couple of pints, exchanged glances with a woman down the bar. A few pints later they were having a frenzied romp in the back seat of his Citroen. After it was over he couldn't even remember her face.

Early this morning he began sinking into despair. He didn't want anything to get in the way of it. There was a beauty to despair, especially on Sundays. Trevor knew he would make a full confession to Vickie. The truth freed his conscience, allowed him to sin.

The house phone rang. A relic from the `50s, it hung on the kitchen wall. "Poor Vickie," Trevor said, reaching across the table for his gin. They'd had plans to meet at her house last night for supper. A little later, the phone rang again. She'd simply come over soon, he knew. She thought she was upset now—she had no idea what was in store.

Without the gin he didn't know where he'd be. He had another swig. Then he had some more.

"Trevor?"

Trevor bolted upright at the table. Vickie stood inside his kitchen. Grabbing the bottle, Trevor stood up and sat down. She had her handbag on her shoulder. Her hair was brushed, her mouth pinched tight. "What's going on?" she asked.

"I'm having a drink," he said.

"It's eight in the morning. We had plans."

"I know it." The confession was coming soon, he could feel it. He wouldn't blame her for the anger that would follow. "My fault," he said, "forgetting."

She didn't want to know the truth just yet. Shifting her handbag, she delayed coming to the point. "How much of that gin have you had?"

"Too much. No—not enough, quite yet."

"Was that bottle full?"

"Yes. What the fuck do you think? I was out last night."

She backed toward the door, her face pale. "You've done it, haven't you? That's why you're being so rude to me."

"I'm an evil man. Now we know, once and for all. No use pretending."

Vickie shook her head. "I never want to see you again," she said. And yet she still stood there in his kitchen, looking at him.

"It was a mistake, Vick," he said. He had a swig of gin. "No excuse." He couldn't help finding an excuse anyway, like a parting gift. "I get so hemmed in, I suppose. I tried, Vickie, I really did."

She came across the table and slapped him hard across the face. The pain of it made him lonely. Then she left, and he didn't try to stop her.

✳ ✳ ✳

Henry woke a few hours later in Caroline's bed, rested and strangely calm. Her clock said it was just before noon. He couldn't recall the last time he'd taken a nap in the morning. Caroline stirred a little as he sat up, her bare arm across his lap. The arm was round and smooth, and he took advantage of his opportunity to study it. Then he saw the ring—his ring, on her hand.

Perhaps, as she'd told him this morning, they'd been searching for each other all their lives. Perhaps if you opened yourself to change, love became possible. He wanted to wake her, to tell her how this commitment made him liberated, how after all his fears of growing older, he now felt pleasantly mature.

After the church, they'd walked to Bates Farm, and she'd pressed him for details. He described the jewellery shop above the florist's, and she'd known it because it had always been her favourite. He could only imagine what such a coincidence might prove—luck, at the very least—not to mention finding her in his stall, just when he'd run back for the ring. She wanted to drive to Brighton and surprise his father with the news.

In her bungalow they'd had a late breakfast and gone over tentative wedding plans. Henry let himself become swept up in the details— the people they'd invite, the music they'd have at the reception, where they might go on honeymoon. Everything sounded too fanciful to be true. Funerals he'd seen, not weddings. They decided to marry late that autumn, with Reverend Pierce presiding.

Never before could he have imagined being married. But he began to see their future boldly unfolding. There were houses for sale in Chalk, she said. Why not buy one? With their combined income, they could consider it. She wanted to know what names he liked for children. With Caroline it was hard not to talk about every little thing, to go over the possibilities. Instead of Brighton they'd fallen into bed.

Now, looking at her arm in his lap, her shoulder, her hair sprawled across the pillow, he couldn't help saying her name. It came out louder than he wanted, and she opened her eyes.

"Do you dig tomorrow?"

"No. Nothing."

"Why don't we go into Brighton for a late lunch? I can see the café where you had your first coffee. We can visit your dad, maybe get a hotel for the night."

"All right."

She stared at him until he blushed. "You've never had lunch in Brighton, have you?"

"You know I haven't."

As they dressed, she kept looking at her ring. "I'll go home," he said. "I'll bring the van round."

He kissed her goodbye and ran all the way. He didn't run to save time. He ran because he was happy.

* * *

"I have a confession to make," Caroline said, as Henry turned onto the Estate Road. She slipped her hand down the back of his neck. "I had a premonition we'd end up together the first day I saw you digging in the churchyard."

Henry banged the dashboard to get it to stop rattling. They had their windows rolled down, but the van felt stuffy. The sun was hot and bright on the windscreen. An hour it was to Brighton, barring traffic. "A premonition—about us?"

"I didn't want to tell you until you proposed."

"I'm glad you didn't. Here I was, thinking it was my idea."

They neared the turn toward Glynde. Henry thought he saw a man running toward them. "Is that Trevor?"

Caroline leaned over and banged the dashboard. "Can't you get that thing to stop? Henry, watch out!"

The man jumped into the middle of the road, and Henry barely had time to swerve. The van headed straight for an oak. A branch came through the windscreen like a giant arm, crushing everything in its way. The glove box flew open. Receipts and sandwich wrappers and loose pages of maps fluttered inside the van amidst the circling oak leaves.

Something fell off the front bumper. Then the papers and leaves settled, and everything went quiet. Caroline's life had gone. Her head hung at a right angle, and the rest of her lay somewhere behind the seat. Henry willed himself to move, to try and save what had already been lost, but his hands remained on the steering wheel. Only his eyes responded to his commands.

A fine sun hung above the fields. Henry saw the beauty in it well enough. How could a man ignore the sun? Along the oak branch, ants swarmed. In the road, Trevor crept toward the van, sniffing the air like a fearful dog.

Henry counted a minute in his head. When it passed, his hands still hadn't left the wheel. He was afraid to look at Caroline again. Instead he passed his eyes over the freshly ploughed fields until he couldn't see through his tears.

A car slowed behind the van. Henry could hear the driver having no luck with Trevor. Then he heard footsteps. "Are you okay?" a man said, bending into the window. "Oh, dear God," he said. He noticed Caroline. "Just sit right there and I'll ring for an ambulance."

Henry blinked. There it stood, the sun in the cloudless sky. On the horizon something flashed and disappeared. Every line was distinct, all the colours sharp. He could hear the man shouting into his mobile, roughly describing the location of Chalk. The ants kept swarming along the branch. A bluebird fluttered onto the hood of the van. It looked through the shattered windscreen and chirped, as if just waking up.

SIXTEEN

His inability to move, the doctor said, was due to shock. In minutes, as if the information itself were a cure, Henry began to have feeling in his body. Mrs. Tilson drove into Brighton to collect him, and he was home by five in the afternoon. Soon afterward a constable arrived to take Henry's statement. He deemed an inquest unnecessary, and Caroline's body was sent to Hetherington's freezer.

Funeral arrangements proceeded. After speaking by telephone to Reverend Pierce, Caroline's parents decided it was best to bury their daughter in St. Margaret's churchyard. Henry asked to be the gravedigger, and Hetherington agreed.

The burial service was set for Wednesday. On Monday afternoon Reverend Pierce visited. He brought a Bible with a bookmark at Job and placed it on the coffee table. Many of Chalk's congregants came along with him—William Harvey, Karen Bates, Mr. and Mrs. Yapton, Penny Pierce. Kevin Yapton left a basket of groceries in the kitchen. Mrs. Bates told Henry that he was welcome to take whatever he wanted from the bungalow before Caroline's parents arrived. Henry sat in his armchair without speaking. Over in the cot, Jackie lay growling at all the company with her head between her paws.

Frank rang. He was feeling poorly, he said, or otherwise would have asked Mrs. Tilson to fetch him. He warned Henry that sleeping would be difficult and told him he'd make it to Chalk for the funeral.

By two in the afternoon everyone had left except Reverend Pierce and Mrs. Tilson. Henry wanted them to leave. He knew that pointed words were coming, words meant to heal. He stared at the wall and barely listened, willing himself not to break down.

"There are limits to human reason," Reverend Pierce said. He sat on the sofa and kept shaking his head at the carpet.

"Thank you for coming," Henry said, in an effort to be polite. He was surprised to see the vicar's eyes filled with tears.

"It's a terrible thing, Henry. She changed this village. I don't understand why…"

Reverend Pierce stood up and came to the armchair, his nose dripping. He put his hand on Henry's shoulder. "The Lord's ways are impossible to fathom. We're here for you, Henry. The people of Chalk are your family. Every one of us is praying for you."

The vicar left. Mrs. Tilson remained on the sofa, eyeing Henry suspiciously. She told him she wasn't about to leave him alone for a second. She rang the undertakers of the parish and cancelled the other graves he had scheduled for the week. Now and then, she leaned against the telephone table and wept quietly into her sleeve.

Henry stared straight ahead, his feet planted. If he showed any signs of instability, he knew, he might not be allowed to dig Caroline's grave. He'd never be left alone. Then, when the time came, it would be that much harder to kill himself. He'd made the decision right after the accident, well before the ambulance arrived.

Vickie Eckleton rang. She sobbed as she told Henry what happened, Sunday morning before the accident. If only she'd stayed, she said, to keep Trevor from such drunken destruction. She said that Chris Crawley blamed himself for ignoring all of Trevor's calls. Henry didn't reply. To anchor himself to his decision, he went over the accident again and again in his mind's eye. Each time, he was left with awe.

The timing had to have been perfect—predetermined, as the vicar implied—to have rounded the corner just as Trevor jumped into the road. Maybe if he and Caroline hadn't taken that nap. If they hadn't decided to rush off to Brighton, or maybe if the dashboard hadn't distracted him with its rattle, Caroline would be alive. How had he swerved into the only tree on the road? It didn't seem an accident at all.

Mrs. Tilson stayed up with Henry well into the evening. She brought him tea, urged him to eat. He forced down one of the egg sandwiches she prepared, even though it kept sticking in his throat.

A little after nine, Mrs. Tilson finally fell asleep. She'd been sitting on the sofa blinking at the television when her chin sank to her neck.

Henry watched angrily as the old woman's shoulders rose, and her chest expanded with air.

* * *

The next morning brought pain. He lay curled in a ball, sweating under his sheet, too stricken to move. His stomach was a knot that reached all the way to his bowels. The sun shone hot against the bedroom window. Outside were sounds of summer—a child's voice, a song on a radio, the rumble of car engines. His father had been wrong. Being awake was harder than sleeping.

Any doubts about taking his life disappeared. Henry wanted to get through one more day and die. Getting dressed would have been impossible otherwise. Downstairs, Mrs. Tilson lay stretched out on the sofa. She jerked awake as he reached the bottom step, her arms flying forward as if warding off an attacker. "What? Who's there?"

Henry stayed at the staircase, his hand on the banister. "Don't worry about me any more, Mrs. Tilson. Please go home."

"I'm not going anywhere, and that's final." She sat up and straightened her clothes. "You're still in shock." Before he could stop her, Mrs. Tilson had come over to him. She pressed her face against his chest and started to cry.

Henry took the old woman's shoulders in his hands. She was grieving too openly for his comfort. His heart pounded, his emotions getting the better of him. He decided not to go through Caroline's bungalow. He'd want to touch her clothes, put his lips to her wine glasses, crawl into her bed. "There now," he said, as much to Mrs. Tilson as to himself. He wouldn't press her to go home. It would be easier, anyway, to pass his final day with some company.

Mrs. Tilson went upstairs to wash. When she came down she went straight into the kitchen. She fed Jackie and cooked breakfast. Henry ate in the armchair, facing Mrs. Tilson on the sofa. He had difficulty with the bacon, but he finished.

"Kevin Yapton brought you some good cuts," Mrs. Tilson said.

Henry nodded. He hadn't tasted anything. A knock came at the door. His eyes swollen, Chris Crawley poked his head inside. "Sorry to bother you," he said, crouching to pet Jackie as she ran at his feet. "May I come in?"

Henry hesitated. "Of course you can," Mrs. Tilson said.

Chris ducked under the low roof and came carefully inside in his overalls and work boots, as if afraid of breaking something. The sitting room seemed to shrink. In the armchair, Henry could feel his anger building. Chris slumped on the sofa, wringing his hands. Mrs. Tilson cleared the breakfast plates and went upstairs to the guest room. Henry listened for the door but didn't hear it close.

"At least you're able to eat," Chris said, sniffing the air. It sounded like an accusation. "Henry, Trevor kept ringing me yesterday morning."

"The constable told me he was drunk."

"He wouldn't stop pestering me—you know how could get. Don't look at me like that."

Henry turned his face to the wall. "Like what?"

"I just couldn't take it, Henry. I wanted to sleep in, so I switched off my mobile. If I'd just talked to him, he might not have—"

"I know, damn you! I've thought about this already." Upstairs, the floorboards creaked. "You can't blame yourself any more than Vickie can. I was the one behind the wheel."

Chris shook his head. "He likes to jump in front of traffic when he's drunk and feeling guilty. Trevor wishes you'd hit him, you know. He just sits in front of the telly in a daze."

"What would you have me do, ring him up? Beg him not to feel guilty?" Henry looked down at his knuckles, turning white.

"I'm sorry," Chris said, standing up. "I'm sorry, all right? Will you at least look at me, Henry? I thought if we could talk a little…"

"I don't feel like talking."

Chris picked up the Bible on the coffee table and put it back. "Is there anything I can do, Henry? Anything at all?"

"Come to the service," Henry said. He waited until he heard the door close, and he unclenched his fists.

* * *

"Do you remember, Henry, after you and Caroline separated, how you moped around the house, feeling sorry for yourself? You didn't shave or take Jackie on walks. Your mail went unopened. Once you get in one of your moods, there's no telling with you. Henry? Are you listening?"

Henry nodded. It was torture putting up with this, but he'd be damned if someone else dug Caroline's grave. "I'm listening," he said.

"Well. It's the first time you've spoken in an hour." Mrs. Tilson leaned forward, her elbows on her knees. "You're frightening me, Henry, do you know that? I don't want to have to ring the doctor."

"I'm fine."

"Are you sure you won't have some tea? Do you want me to collect your father early? He says he's not feeling well, but I think he's just taking this very hard. When your mother died it was the most painful sight. He loved her so much. For a while, he—well, he didn't think he could continue."

Henry put up his hand. "Please, Mrs. Tilson. I'd like to be left alone now, if that's all right."

She started to cry. "If you let yourself drift again, Henry, I'm afraid of what might happen. You can't forget what Caroline stood for. You said yourself that she made you come alive."

"She did. She always said…" He turned to the wall.

Mrs. Tilson came over to his chair, tugging at her sleeves. "The life Caroline brought you doesn't disappear when she's gone! When my husband died, I thought I was meant to be alone. It wasn't true, Henry. It wasn't true."

"All right," Henry said. "I've heard you."

Mrs. Tilson collected her purse. "I'll leave you alone for one hour, and no longer. I'll fix us a nice meal. And I'll take Jackie next door so she won't be a bother to you." She reached for his hand, and he flinched. "Henry," she said.

"What?"

She kissed him on the cheek. Her lips were cracked. "I'm going now. Are you listening?" The door opened and closed, and she was gone.

He had to make it until tomorrow, but the clock ticked too slowly. It was only three in the afternoon. The photo of his parents on their wedding day stared down from the mantle.

Henry stood up and turned the frame to the wall. He wanted to destroy all that he saw, to smash everything he could touch. He watched the second hand of the clock for a minute, then closed his eyes to count. With one motion he swept the clock off the mantle. The walnut casing smashed on the hearth. The clock had been his father's. It probably hadn't moved from the mantle in sixty years. Henry held the broken pieces in his hands—silly as it was to care—

and his grief surfaced in wave after wave. It came up through his stomach and into his shoulders, making him kneel and sob. The pain was unbearable, and yet he had to stand up.

He went into his garden for air. The sun was still bright. He didn't want to live—not a year, not a day. Why should he? He could go across the road right now. Before anyone could stop him, he could load one of the vicar's hunting rifles. What did it matter who had to clean up the mess?

But the plan he had required patience. He didn't want a further scene for Caroline's parents. He would dig the grave late tonight, while everyone slept. Then, if he didn't make any mistakes, people would just think he'd disappeared.

*　*　*

After supper, the minutes dragged on. Henry sat beside Mrs. Tilson on the sofa and watched TV. Then he paced the sitting room and thought of Caroline's shoulder. It had been round and soft, a perfect companion for his hand. The strength of the memory was horrible. He returned to the sofa with his face to the wall, but Caroline's shoulder, exposed above the bedsheets, wouldn't leave his mind.

He picked up the Bible. He didn't do it for solace, or even guidance. He did it for Reverend Pierce. He'd known the vicar all his life. As he'd felt obliged to listen to Mrs. Tilson, he would read what the vicar suggested.

Job had done nothing to deserve the trials he suffered. God destroyed his property, afflicted his body with painful sores. God killed his children. But Job never lost faith, and ultimately God rewarded him with more children, more property, and more happiness than he'd known before. It was clear why the vicar had marked the chapter. It didn't matter—Henry still wanted to die.

Don't forget what Caroline stood for, Mrs. Tilson said. If anything, she had believed life should be a series of tests. Caroline had urged him to find meaning, to search, to hope. But what had hope delivered? The more Henry thought about it, the more he came to believe the worst possibility of all: the accident, like life itself, held no greater purpose. He couldn't blame anyone—not Trevor, not himself, not even God.

When he asked to be left alone, Mrs. Tilson studied him and nodded with exhaustion. "You listened to me this afternoon," she said. "You've got a big day tomorrow, and I know you're going to get through this."

She went next door to her own bed. Henry brought his wheelbarrow and tools outside and placed them by the door. Then he sat in the armchair and waited for the village to turn black.

*　*　*

Reverend Pierce's grave marker pointed to the next plot in the row. There weren't any nearby trees or shrubs. The neighbouring graves, tilting in the clumpy grass, were all Henry's.

The moon was nearly full and provided plenty of light. Henry cut the turf into sections and stacked them to the side of the plot. He stared down at the topsoil, hardly able to believe Caroline would lie under a pile of dirt tomorrow. Just yesterday, they'd discussed possible names for children.

The tin sheet felt heavy as he placed it lengthwise beside the plot. Someone else would have to do the filling-in. People would say he'd been irresponsible for leaving the job unfinished. The gravedigger had disappeared, they'd say, started over somewhere else. Others would suspect the truth. They wouldn't know how he'd done it, but they'd think him the lesser for it. Only a coward took his own life.

"A coward?" Henry muttered as he dug. "Couldn't I have killed myself years ago? Or this afternoon?"

His knotted stomach tormented him, and he hunched his back. There was a comfort in the pain, in locating a physical place for grief. His hunched back would become permanent if he kept on plodding forward, like an ox. Why did people keep on existing for the sake of it? To end up like his father, an angry old man?

His father would be the first to call him a coward. As he moved to the foot to dig, Henry could practically hear Frank say it. Henry hunched his back further, shifting the pain to his hips. He was tired of counting the seconds. They could call him a coward all they wanted. He wasn't going to be around to hear them anyway—he'd be inside the grave. He stood up a moment and caught his breath.

The night and the stars made him tremble. He went to the head, started a new spit.

It was Oliver who'd given him the idea. He would dig Caroline's grave an extra foot deep. He'd place the mats and putlogs, take away his tools. The gravesite would look as though he'd finished and left. Then he'd take one of the vicar's rifles down into the grave, cover his body with topsoil, and end it. The next morning they'd lower the casket on top of him. One of the wardens would do the filling-in— William Harvey, maybe Oliver. The mound would settle and he'd be with Caroline once more.

Henry dug faster. He was almost two feet down. Climbing out, he dragged the tin sheet across the churchyard to the boundary hedge. The heavy dirt made the going difficult, but work was a welcome distraction. After sitting idle all day, it was almost invigorating. How could it be that he still felt young? He sat on the ground to rest.

It was a little after one by his watch. The night had quickly turned cold. As he rubbed his legs to keep warm, he realised how absurd it was—why should he care about keeping warm? He was going to kill himself, wasn't he?

He didn't trust himself to stay awake. He didn't trust God. Jumping to his feet, Henry decided not to rest until he'd finished.

* * *

For two hours he worked without pause. Drained of energy, he started slowing down. When the top of his head reached ground level—his usual stopping point—he kept digging. This was the extra spit, the one for himself. He ran into some chalk and used the pickaxe. He shaved the walls carefully with the edge of his spade and tried not to think about what they would hold. Starting at the head, he worked his way slowly backward, flinging the dirt high over his shoulder. When he finished he leaned the spade against the wall and used it as a ledge to climb out. It was a quarter past three.

He paced the perimeter of the grave, breathing heavily in visible gusts. He looked up at the stars, and again he trembled. What if he changed his mind? As he placed the sideboards around the hole, his hands shook. Fear didn't change the meaninglessness of life. A man couldn't live only for his next meal, and for a good night's sleep.

Lying flat on his stomach, he reached into the grave for the spade. He shovelled a loose layer of soil from the mound to cover himself with. How foolish it had seemed, counting her smiles, calculating the days they had left. All along he'd been right to be worried. He swept in the stray dirt and placed the putlogs across the centre. It looked as if he'd dug the grave and gone home.

When he returned home to put away his tools, Jackie sat up in her cot. She studied him from across the room, confused, almost suspicious. Mrs. Tilson would take care of her. Henry hesitated as he switched off the house lights. Seeing the back of his armchair, he fought an impulse to sit and rest, to think it through.

✳   ✳   ✳

Henry moved quickly down the nave, taking care not to glance at the third stall on the left. If he went in there again, he might never come out. He could imagine being discovered in the morning, sobbing, covered with grave dirt. He crossed the chancel rail, passed the altar, and pulled open the curtain of the Wembles Chapel.

He opened the wardrobe. Behind the choir robes he felt for the rifles. They were there, all three of them, the barrels cold in his hands. He pulled them out one by one. The light was better under the altar, so he carried them out and laid them flat on the carpet. The longest rifle looked the newest. Only the stock was broken— splintered in two, straight down the middle. Aiming wouldn't be an issue. He wiped the nose of the barrel with his shirtsleeve and stuck it in his mouth. It tasted like rust. With his other hand he reached for the trigger. It seemed as if it would work.

He put the other rifles back and loaded the one he'd chosen from the box of bullets. He thought of testing it, but couldn't risk the noise. He stared at the rifle in his hands as he stood beside the altar. Near the door, something moved in the shadows.

"Who's there?"

Henry stepped over the chancel rail. He came a few steps down the nave. A shape was lurking by the hymnals. It looked like Oliver. "Get out of here." Henry pointed the gun. "Go on, get out."

"You cancelled your graves for the week," Oliver said.

"Others can dig." Henry bit his lip. He bit too hard, and it bled. "I can do what I please. You said as much."

"At least hear what I have to say." Oliver came out of the shadows and stood in front of the door. "Most people age badly. You got better."

"So what?"

"People count on you. They don't want to remember you as the gravedigger who took his own life. It was Caroline who made you wake up. Now bear the responsibility of it."

Henry raised the rifle. He was done listening. He wanted to be numb, to be dead. "Don't you say her name, Oliver."

"Why can't I? Was Caroline your personal possession? Look at you shaking. You know what you're doing is wrong."

"You don't know right from wrong. Now get out of here before I—"

Oliver came toward him. Henry wanted to get away from him and out into the open air. "Stop, Oliver. I'm warning you."

Oliver stopped at the last stall, his chin lowered. "The graveyards are full of bad suicides. Don't you see why I'm digging now, while I'm still fit? Digging will let me die properly. It lets me live."

"Live, then! Nobody's stopping you. Me—I'm ready now." Henry wiped his tears with his shoulder.

"That's right," Oliver said. "From here on it gets difficult. You either give up, or be brave."

"Get out of here! Go home, or I swear I'll fire."

Oliver turned and walked to the door. Cold wind shot down the length of the nave. Then the door banged shut like a lid.

*　*　*

Anyone watching wouldn't have said Henry stood very long beside the willow. He said goodbye to his mother and continued across the mounds to the gravesite.

He sat on the mats, held the rifle to his chest, and lowered his legs into the hole. He ducked under the putlogs and slid into the bottom of the grave. It was colder than he thought it would be.

He swept the loose dirt over his feet and legs, and piled it on top of his waist. Everything seemed to be happening too quickly. He wanted to think things over one last time, but he was afraid of losing his nerve. Even as he glanced at the stars it seemed Caroline was up there already, urging him to live, to let the dead rest in peace.

This was only something he wanted to believe, nothing more. He secured the butt of the rifle against the grave wall and angled it toward the place his head would be.

He leaned back for the last time. He covered his head entirely. Under the soil he found the barrel with his mouth. Then he felt for the trigger.

* * *

Reverend Pierce spoke at the altar with a hoarse voice, as if recovering from a sleepless night.

"Caroline Ford brought change to Chalk. We know in our hearts that it's true. We are reminded that faith and reason are like fated lovers. They quarrel, but are lost without each other. Faith alone makes impulsive decisions. Reason doubts the higher truths, even when these truths are most needed. In fact, the two are in us always. We must work throughout our lives to draw them together in our hearts and minds, and in our souls."

Mopping his forehead, the vicar left the church, followed by Hetherington, and the bearers with Caroline's casket. The stalls emptied. Outside, the mourners arranged themselves around the gravesite amidst the headstones of their ancestors. The schoolchildren wore uniforms for the occasion. For the second time this year they formed a straight line behind the burial mound, with Darren Roberts and Robert Briggs holding up opposite ends.

Caroline's father stood at the bench glaring at nobody in particular. He maintained the posture of a field marshal. Mrs. Ford had her daughter's green, reckless eyes. Throughout the service she scanned the churchyard from one end to the other, as if to find an explanation in it.

Trevor Nelson swayed on his feet, possibly medicated. Vickie Eckleton stood at his side, dabbing at his mouth with a handkerchief. The Yaptons closed the shop to join the service. From the Wembles Estate, Dick Miles the gatekeeper attended, in addition to the butler Roger Lowry and his wife. Penny Pierce stood beside Mr. and Mrs. Bates. Chris Crawley, wearing a suit, accompanied Sid Book, his wife, and their baby daughter. Lord and Lady Wembles never stopped holding hands.

At the foot of the grave, Frank stared into the soil. Beside him Mrs.

Tilson blinked at the sky, her hand in the crook of his arm. Reverend Pierce led everyone in a hymn, then bowed his head for the Lord's Prayer. Everyone joined in, regardless of faith. Oliver Marsh, standing at the vicar's shoulder, surprised the entire village with his voice.

Henry stood with his back to the boundary hedge. His wheelbarrow waited at his side. He felt simultaneously cowardly and brave. He'd combed his hair, put on his suit, and shaved. His stomach had knotted further, but he didn't allow his back to buckle, for fear that a hunchback might appear hideous.

A warm breeze blew across the churchyard. The mourners lifted their heads to it. Henry caught stray phrases of the vicar's committal. His tongue felt enormous and dry. It seemed that black shapes swooped over his head like crows.

"God placed us in the world not to withdraw from it…"

The bearers had no trouble with the end boards. They stepped carefully over the burial mats and hoisted the casket. Hetherington removed the putlogs, and Caroline slipped into the ground.

Henry's shoulders shook. He didn't know if he'd make it through the filling-in. But Chalk's mourners turned to him, as if for guidance, so he lifted his wheelbarrow and pushed it to the grave.

Also Available from UNO Press:

William Christenberry: Art & Family by J. Richard Gruber (2000)

The El Cholo Feeling Passes by Fredrick Barton (2003)

A House Divided by Fredrick Barton (2003)

Coming Out the Door for the Ninth Ward edited by Rachel Breunlin
    from The Neighborhood Story Project series (2006)

The Change Cycle Handbook by Will Lannes (2008)

Cornerstones: Celebrating the Everyday Monuments & Gathering Places of New Orleans
    edited by Rachel Breunlin, from The Neighborhood Story Project series (2008)

A Gallery of Ghosts by John Gery (2008)

Hearing Your Story: Songs of History and Life for Sand Roses by Nabile Farès
    translated by Peter Thompson, from The Engaged Writers Series (2008)

The Imagist Poem: Modern Poetry in Miniature edited by William Pratt
    from The Ezra Pound Center for Literature series (2008)

The Katrina Papers: A Journal of Trauma and Recovery by Jerry W. Ward, Jr.
    from The Engaged Writers Series (2008)

On Higher Ground: The University of New Orleans at Fifty by Dr. Robert Dupont
    (2008)

Us Four Plus Four: Eight Russian Poets Conversing translated by Don Mager (2008)

Voices Rising: Stories from the Katrina Narrative Project edited by Rebeca Antoine
    (2008)

Gravestones (Lápidas) by Antonio Gamoneda, translated by Donald Wellman
    from The Engaged Writers Series (2009)

The House of Dance and Feathers: A Museum by Ronald W. Lewis by Rachel Breunlin
    & Ronald W. Lewis, from The Neighborhood Story Project series (2009)

I hope it's not over, and good-by: Selected Poems of Everette Maddox by Everette Maddox
    (2009)

Portraits: Photographs in New Orleans 1998-2009 by Jonathan Traviesa (2009)

Theoretical Killings: Essays & Accidents by Steven Church (2009)

Voices Rising II: More Stories from the Katrina Narrative Project edited by Rebeca
    Antoine (2010)

Rowing to Sweden: Essays on Faith, Love, Politics, and Movies by Fredrick Barton
    (2010)

Dogs in My Life: The New Orleans Photographs of John Tibule Mendes (2010)

Understanding the Music Business: A Comprehensive View edited by Harmon Greenblatt
& Irwin Steinberg (2010)

The Fox's Window by Naoko Awa, translated by Toshiya Kamei (2010)

A Passenger from the West by Nabile Farès, translated by Peter Thompson
from The Engaged Writers Series (2010)

The Schüssel Era in Austria: Contemporary Austrian Studies, Volume 18
edited by Günter Bischof & Fritz Plasser (2010)

The Gravedigger by Rob Magnuson Smith (2010)

Everybody Knows What Time It Is by Reginald Martin (2010)

When the Water Came: Evacuees of Hurricane Katrina by Cynthia Hogue & Rebecca
Ross
from The Engaged Writers Series (2010)

Aunt Alice Vs. Bob Marley by Kareem Kennedy, from The Neighborhood Story Project
series (2010)

Houses of Beauty: From Englishtown to the Seventh Ward by Susan Henry
from The Neighborhood Story Project series (2010)

Signed, The President by Kenneth Phillips, from The Neighborhood Story Project
series (2010)

Beyond the Bricks by Daron Crawford & Pernell Russell
from The Neighborhood Story Project series (2010)

unopress.org

About the Author

Rob Magnuson Smith was raised in England and the United States. He has won numerous prizes for his fiction, including The David Higham Award at the University of East Anglia's Program in Creative Writing. This is his first novel.